THE MOST WANTED WITCH

TALES OF XEST #3

DONNA AUGUSTINE

1

A cold nose pressed against my cheek, the body it belonged to invisible. Dusty, the Elusive Rare Dust Bunny that had somehow become a pet of sorts, was spending more time invisible these days. It was an ability I was becoming more and more envious of.

"We'll get used to it," I said, making no move to get out of bed, in spite of the constant steps and people yelling to each other outside my door.

"Musso! Dinner is getting cold!" Bertha, Musso's wife, boomed through the stairwell from the landing of the first floor.

"I'm coming!" Musso yelled from above, before his steps thudded overhead like his feet were boulders. Musso and his wife had moved in a couple of months ago, along with others. Gone were the good ol' days when there hadn't been a third floor.

Another set of steps sounded from down the hall. I was still on the second floor, but it was much larger these days.

"Tippi, you coming down?" Oscar asked from the other side of my closed door.

Oscar had moved in a few days before Musso and his wife, which had been right before—

More steps thudded. It was hard to think at this point with all the noise. The steps were soon followed by pounding on my door.

"Tippi, come on! Get out of bed," Zab yelled. "Bibbi thinks you're sick again."

Yeah, so Zab had moved in right after Musso, but right before Bibbi. I still wasn't sure why everyone had decided this was the place to hole up, but now I was surrounded, everyone so close. Too close, some might say. Uncomfortably close, a sane person might suggest.

I liked living alone. I enjoyed putting things down in a spot and having them be there when I went back, and having quiet to think my thoughts. Now I was surrounded from the moment I woke up to the second I fell asleep. Every waking moment, someone was there, talking, yelling—*being*.

"Tell her I'm coming," I yelled back.

I'd locked myself up here for a couple hours, just to get my head together. It wasn't as if I'd become a full-on hermit. If anyone disappeared for too long, though, you could count on Bibbi to gather the troops. She'd fuss that they must be sick, dead, or lying in an alley somewhere, with a horde of grouslies eating their flesh to the bone. Considering the current darkness shrouding Xest, it wasn't that outlandish a fear—except that everyone knew where I was.

I got up and pulled my hair back into a tight ponytail, ignoring all the streaks of colors that were startlingly bright in contrast to the half of my hair that had remained a normal black. My boots with the heavy tread were excellent for a good, swift kick, and went well with my soft leather pants. I was ready for dinner.

The No Evil monkeys were up to their normal antics in the office. They'd transitioned from music to stand-up comedy.

I walked in, and Speak No Evil said, "A girl walked into a building..."

My glare cut his words short. For some reason, all their jokes started with this *mysterious* girl.

"I know who the girl is," I said. "Find some different jokes."

Speak No Evil glared back at me as his two cohorts watched on. Finally, his face softened and he shrugged. "Fine. But this is censorship."

I rolled my eyes and continued on to the back room. It was nearly triple the size it had been a few months ago. A full kitchen and cupboards were where the tea and cocoa station had once been. The fireplace had been enlarged and now had a metal rod to swing a pot over, which Bertha manned diligently from sunup to sundown, acting like a loving but pushy drill sergeant most of the day. I'd found out that she'd owned a meal delivery company, Hearty Brews on Brooms, before she retired. She ran this kitchen like it was her business and we were all her sous-chefs.

"Tippi, good job on the dicing," she said, nodding.

"Thanks." I'd done a good bit of prepping and chopping before I'd gone to hide, afraid to skip out on my food chores.

She handed me a plate and pushed me toward the table. "Make sure you eat well. You're too skinny."

I smiled and nodded. Any will to resist Bertha had

withered after the first week. The war against the darkness taking over Xest might be possible to defeat, but no one and nothing would beat her.

I took a seat at the table beside Musso, who was eating cold eggs.

"And people wondered why I didn't bring her to the office," Musso mumbled, but his stare was what said it all. I'd never seen such love packed into a glance in my life. For all their yelling and bickering, and there was a lot, the looks between them showed the truth of their relationship.

"That's enough out of you, old man," Bertha teased as she dumped another piece of meat on his plate.

Bibbi didn't appear her normally perky self, with her lavender hair sticking out this way and that. Her eyes were red as she took a seat on the other side of me.

"Yellow bellies again?" I kept my voice low.

"Yep," she whispered, afraid Bertha would hear her complaining.

Yellow bellies were a type of onion in Xest that had to be shredded. Bibbi had made the unfortunate error of saying something needed more flavor a couple weeks ago. Now it seemed she was getting stuck on yellow bellies every time a recipe called for them.

"You want me to try to talk to her?"

"No." She jerked back as if I'd said something shocking. "What if she stops cooking? I know I complained that one time, but her food is amazing. We can't risk it."

Zab, who'd sat down on the other side, laughed as he listened in. "Good," he said, and leaned forward so he could see me. "I would've had to tackle you if you tried."

Oscar strolled in the back door, letting in a brutal gust of fifth wind as he took his time.

"Shut the door," I yelled, my voice drowned out by the other four voices yelling the same.

Oscar strolled over, smiling at the plates of food on the table. He reached to fill a plate, and Bertha whacked his hand.

"Um, *ooow*?" Oscar said, looking at his attacker.

"You were supposed to trim fat today. Where were you?" she asked, pointing her spoon at him.

"I had an errand for Hawk. Had to be handled."

Bertha scowled but lowered her spoon. Oscar slowly reached out to the food, waiting to get his knuckles rapped again.

I took one last bite before I got up. "Thanks, Bertha. Dinner was amazing as usual."

I edged over toward the door to the office, hoping no one was watching me grab my jacket.

"Going for your walk?" Oscar asked, smirking, as he alerted the entire room to my departure.

Bibbi swung around, glaring at me.

"I'll be back in a little while." I shrugged on my jacket. Not even my mother had hovered the way she did. Although that might not mean much.

"Shouldn't you have someone with you? I don't like how you head out alone every night. We're not supposed to go out without a buddy."

Oscar laughed. "Don't worry, Bibbi, she'll have a buddy."

"I'll be okay." I made a fast exit before I decided to steal Bertha's spoon and whack Oscar over the head.

2

The warm glow from the homemade dinner with people I loved was immediately wiped away the second I stepped out of the broker building. The fifth wind was worse than ever, burning my skin where it touched. The streets were quiet tonight, but they were always quiet these days. That didn't mean safe.

No one left their homes unless they had to, all for differing reasons. Some didn't want to get involved in the conflict. Others had some strange belief that the roaming hordes of grouslies couldn't get them if they hid indoors, which showed how little they knew. They didn't get it. Walls meant nothing. No one was truly safe in Xest anymore.

The feeling of Dread, which was what we called the evil that had slowly been growing, was all around. The only place I could escape it completely anymore was in the broker building. Others had put up wards against it, but as a testimony to its strength, very few were able to keep the feeling at bay completely. Hawk was helping people shore up their defenses while he could before the shit hit the fan. I wasn't sure exactly what was coming, but I could sense it gathering strength.

We just didn't know what it really wanted. Was it looking to drive half of Xest out? Or for complete dominance in this place? Or was it going to sweep through and wreck Xest before moving on to bigger and badder things?

Some were speculating that it wanted to move on to Rest after here. The thing was that everyone was guessing, and even the people who were on its side didn't know what was going to happen, from what intelligence we'd managed to gather. I spent more nights hunting for something to pin it down than actually finding anything.

I walked past Raydam's house on the square, which had been taken over by Jarro, the new leader of the opposition. Cut the head off a snake and a new one will slither to the front. Jarro didn't have anywhere near the power or pull of his dead predecessor, so we'd see how long he lasted before he was cannibalized by his own. He wasn't even worth a passing glance.

I stopped walking, hearing something that snared my interest. Low growls came from the alley on the west side of his house. Stepping closer, I saw there was a herd of grouslies gathered, all looking my way. I took another slow step, hoping they wouldn't run, even though history told me they would. They'd attack others, and had many times in the last several months, but not me anymore.

I took another step, staring at their beady little eyes, and like usual, I'd gotten a step too close and they ran off.

"Dammit."

I turned toward the sound of steps, knowing already they'd be Hawk's. I'd witnessed him move without a whisper, but it seemed sometimes when he walked the streets at night, he liked to dare someone to come for him.

The fifth wind carried his scent of spice, forest, and magic as he neared. His dark hair ruffled slightly in the air as his steely eyes met mine. I turned, glad I could blame the wind, not that I'd gotten caught staring, for the burn in my cheeks. Sometimes it seemed my heart would thud faster before his presence even hit my consciousness.

Hawk always seemed to catch up to me while I was in this spot. That wasn't why I'd stopped. It had just become a habit.

He stopped beside me, staring into the alley as well.

"Amusing yourself with some grouslies tonight?" he asked.

I didn't ask how he knew what had been in the alley. Maybe he'd seen or heard them somehow from a distance that should've made that impossible. Maybe his magic had picked up on theirs. Either way, I wouldn't ask. He had his secrets, I had mine, and right now I liked them all tucked away neatly. I wouldn't try to pry open his Pandora's box as long as he didn't try to force mine open, especially since mine might have more monsters lurking inside.

After all, what was wrong with me that one of the things people feared the most ran when I got near? I couldn't even egg on an attack, as others ran screaming from them. They'd gotten a taste of me and didn't want another. What did that say?

Hawk turned slightly, his arm brushing mine as he moved closer. His heat seeped my way, adding another shot of adrenaline to my blood.

"Why do you always stop here, in the middle of the square—every...single...night? Don't you think you got your point across the first few times?" Hawk asked, as if he didn't have the same motives.

I let my eyes move past Raydam's, and now Jarro's house, to down the way, where the wish factory was, and across the street to its barracks, and then to all the other shops and buildings.

The first time I'd stopped here on my walk, it had been to take in the scene, really absorb what my situation had become, what was at stake and who the threats were. A place of orientation at first. Then it had become something else entirely.

After months of the same routine, all of Xest knew I'd be here at some point in the night, including Dread. This had become my guns drawn at noon. My place of duels. My open invitation to anyone and anything that wanted me enough to take me on. It was the moment I reminded myself that if they did, I'd handle it one way or another. This was the time and place that told the world I could handle anything they threw at me.

"I keep thinking maybe one of these times..."

Knowing enough time had passed to have made my point clear, having checked off one more night of delivering the message, I continued on my route.

Hawk fell into step beside me.

"You don't have to walk with me." I'd lost count of how many times I'd said that to him in the past several months. I might've felt compelled to do my tour of duty, but I was okay doing it alone. I resented his presence as much as I sometimes craved it. The more I craved it, the more I resented it. Seemed I was bound to be unhappy with either scenario, and I didn't think even a good shrink would be able to fix this one.

"I was heading this way."

It was impossible to recall how many times he'd replied that as well, but it was the same count.

"Did you go by the east side tonight? I haven't gotten over there in a bit," I said, knowing he'd done a sweep of the other side of Xest before he joined me, as he always did.

"Slight increase of its presence in certain pockets, but not enough for most to notice."

He would, though. Hawk could clear a sidewalk like no one else I'd ever seen, but Dread did something to him that rattled me. I'd never forget seeing him weak the way he'd been in the dome, right before I'd shattered us out of it.

I'd spent months avoiding a question that needed an answer. I could stare down a dragon, but damned if this one thing didn't make me feel weak in the knees.

It *had* to be asked.

"How much more do you think you can handle before it's a problem for you?" I asked, feeling good about getting the question out in spite of the pure panic over the possible answer. Could Hawk die in Xest if it got too bad? Would he be willing to go to Rest, the way Rabbit did? What if he wouldn't?

I kept waiting for an answer that wasn't coming until I forced myself to look at him, afraid of the bad news he didn't want to deliver.

I stopped walking, and for the first time in months of my tour, I concentrated all my attention on him. This was the exact reason I was better off alone. He was a distraction. And he might end up a dead distraction. If I couldn't handle even the thought of him dying when he was healthy, how would I handle the reality?

Why was he smiling?

"I might've exaggerated the effect it had on me."

"Exaggerated?" And I might've been ready to kill him. "You're kidding, right?"

"I did what the moment called for. I didn't say I was going to die at any second, but that I wasn't going to make it out, which is true. We didn't have water or food. We both would have eventually died in there."

He was rubbing his shadowed jaw, trying to distract me from why I should be angry. Except he didn't know I liked his jaw and maybe he just felt like rubbing his face.

"You flopped out on the ground," I said.

"I was preserving my strength." He shrugged.

"You just lay there and let me do all the heavy lifting?"

"I wasn't going to be able to get us out. It was hard enough to get in, and I had a hunch you could, but you needed motivating."

I shook my head and started walking again. "And I believed you."

"Why do you always pretend to be mad at me? What is that about?" he asked as he walked along with me.

"I'm pretending nothing. I *am* mad at you."

He laughed.

"Next dome we get stuck in, you won't find it so funny, because I'll be the one sitting it out." See how he liked that. He wouldn't.

"What's funny is how much effort you put into trying to pretend you're mad when I can tell by your voice when you actually are. Which you'll probably be shortly."

And here it came. One of these times, he was going to skip this talk. Every week, I hoped he'd give up. Guess it wouldn't be this time.

"There's a meeting tomorrow," he said.

"I'm always there," I said shortly, and there was no faking this time.

"That's not my point, and you know it." His laughter was gone.

My sigh was just short of morphing into a groan. I was going to have to find a different path to walk on the eve of the weekly meetings. Without fail, it always came to this, and I wasn't ready. Everyone else might want it, but I didn't, and he wouldn't let it go.

"You need to step up," he said.

"I *have* stepped up. I've done as much stepping as I'm capable of without something to get close enough to attack."

"That's bullshit."

Now we were both angry.

"Fine. You're right. How about I've done as much stepping as I'm willing to? Does that work for you?" I walked faster, knowing it was futile, but it served as an outlet so I didn't try to punch him.

"You're the one that wanted to stay here, fought tooth and nail to do it," he said, keeping pace.

"Staying, living, and working is different than leading the war." As any moron would see if he wasn't a stubborn ass. I wasn't quite ready to devolve our fight to that level, but it was coming—maybe next week, in fact.

"When you patrol the streets at night, what exactly is it that you think you're doing?"

He was like a dog with a bone.

"See? This is the problem. I'm not patrolling the streets. I'm taking a walk as I check up on things like a concerned citizen, who will do her fair share. Can you just back off?"

We'd nearly double-timed it back to the office, and I grabbed for the door.

"No, I can't." He planted a hand on it, keeping it closed.

"Why?" I asked, ready to devolve into kicking and screaming in a minute. That was not the look of a leader, and maybe he needed to see that.

"Because people look to you, and you need to step up for them. So are you going to step up tomorrow, or are you going to blend into the wall again?" He moved his hand out of the way, as if expecting me to be a mature adult and do what was needed. He didn't realize that I'd come about as far as I was capable of in the time allotted, and it was quite a bit. But I was not going to be anyone's leader. No way.

I made a fast grab for the door and swung it open. I stood at the threshold and said, "I'm going to blend like a damned chameleon."

Leader my ass. Wars were a messy thing. I was a soldier and that was it. If someone died, there wouldn't be any blood on my hands. Let someone else lead them to their deaths. It wouldn't be me.

3

Bautere paced around me, walking on his hind legs and looking more man than bear today. He scanned me as I turned with him, making sure he couldn't find an opening.

He made a noise that was part huff, part growl. I nodded at his sign of approval but didn't drop my guard.

He stopped circling. "You've come a long way since you first came. I've done all I can for you. The rest you must learn on your own."

I relaxed my fighting stance and grabbed a heavier jacket that was thrown over a branch. "Why does that sound like you're kicking me to the curb?"

He angled his head to the side. "What does that mean?"

"That you're dumping me." I pulled the end of my ponytail out of my jacket, then put my attention into buttoning up while I waited to hear his verdict.

"I would never *dump* you, as you say."

I finished buttoning and glanced up. "So we'll still practice sometimes?"

"Whenever you desire. Now come. There's something you need to see." He dropped down to all fours and began to walk, looking more the bear now.

This wasn't what we did. We'd meet in the field. We'd practice. We'd both leave, going our separate ways. We never walked anywhere. I didn't hesitate to follow him, and fast. His white coat blended into the snow, and I'd lose him if I didn't.

Bautere might practice a little rough, but he would never kill me. In some ways, I trusted him more than anyone. After all, he'd pulled his punches more times than either of us could count. He could've easily slipped a couple blows that would've laid me up and left me vulnerable. His control was remarkable, come to think of it.

His pace was fast, as I was nearly jogging after him.

"A little farther," he said.

I'd never been this far from town, or into this corner of Xest. Looking at the hulking figure of Bautere, I thought that maybe no one had, and for a good reason.

But it wasn't just Bautere that lent a certain ruggedness to this place. There was something different about this area, with its white expanses and fewer trees. The air felt crisper and somehow more unforgiving.

There was something alive in this place, an ancient knowing of sorts, and I could feel the tingle of power. The more we walked, the more it nearly pulsed.

Finally he stopped at the foot of a small hill, not saying anything for several moments.

"Where are we going?" I asked after a few moments. I didn't typically like to rush Bautere. I'd learned that he took the time he was going to, no matter what you did.

Bautere was staring at the small mound and didn't answer for another few minutes.

"I dreamt of bringing you here. My kind take dreams very seriously."

Okay, so he'd had a dream. That was interesting...I guessed. More important, how many of his kind were there? I'd never seen another, nor heard of any mentioned. Were they friendly? Would I spot them coming if they snuck up in the snow?

He began to walk again. "Come. There is someone else who wants to meet you."

I would've followed him into hell right now to not be left alone with an unknown number of his kind around.

We hadn't gone much farther before we were descending a slope and ducking into a small opening in the rocks. Torches were lit as we entered what became more of an expansive cavern. Ten feet or so farther, there was a large wooden door.

Bautere let us into a room sparsely furnished with a table and pelts scattered about the place. There was a fire burning in a pit in the center, with a hole above in the ceiling that smoke billowed up to.

"Sit," he said, pointing to the pelts as he went through another interior door.

I settled down, waiting, wondering why someone wanted to meet me. Was it another one of his kind? I fidgeted with the fur I was sitting on, taking in the place. It was rustic but comfortable. There were iron pans sitting on a shelf and a well in the corner that must've been tapped into some sort of spring, as the water seemed to constantly move.

The sound of someone approaching drew my eye to the doorway. Bautere stepped out first but was followed by a smaller version of himself. There was something more diminutive about his companion, and feminine as well.

Her gait was slower, as if old bones ground with each movement, but there was still a strength and dignity about her.

"This is Zuda. She is the leader of our kind."

Leader? I hadn't known there were others until today, and now there were enough to need a leader? Bautere wasn't one for words, but maybe he could've given me a few details after hours and hours together.

She approached me, and continued to get closer until her muzzle was uncomfortably close. Young teeth or old, those choppers were going to hurt if she decided to take a bite.

I tried not to fidget or move fast. Or to even breathe. I trusted Bautere, but this was a fully grown polar bear sniffing me. Would it be like a dog that could decide it didn't like something about my scent? Forget a bite—one swipe of her paw might kill me.

She continued to sniff me for another moment, and then pulled back a few feet, taking me in from every angle. An eternity later, she sat.

"I believe you are good. That is not the issue. Your magic is very strong. That I'd already gathered. What I don't know is, are *you* strong enough for whatever is to come?"

It was a little hard to answer an open-ended question when I wasn't quite sure what was to come. That didn't stop her from staring at me as she waited for an answer.

Would I be strong enough? A year ago I was happy hiding away for the rest of my life. Even now, there would still be a knee-jerk reaction to run and hide. I was stronger than I'd thought, but to manage what was to come? How could I ever make that sort of presumption?

"I'll try to be. I hope I will be. I don't *want* to fail."

She nodded, as if I'd passed one test. "You're humble. That's good. No one knows what they can handle until they have to. *I* believe you are strong enough, because you'll have to be. There are many counting upon you to fix this world. If this place perishes, so do we. There is no other place for us. If it is destroyed, so are my people. So are many. You don't have the luxury of failure. Do you understand?"

I nodded. I understood too well, and I didn't want to. She was right. Where would her people go if Xest was ever destroyed? Certainly not to Rest. There was no way to pass as normal for them. They were tied to this land like no other. I might hold these people's lives in my hands, and I didn't want to let them down.

"Yes," I replied. Could I do anything to save them? That was an unknown. "I can make something that might ease your pain," I said, feeling wholly inadequate. She was asking me to save Xest and I was offering her a tonic for age?

"The magic that Bautere tried to give me? I appreciate the offer, but no. I don't know how much more time I have left in this world, but I've already received much. When the spirit comes for me, I'll be ready. I can leave knowing Bautere will lead. I've done what I was put here to do." She leaned closer. "Now *you* must fulfill your duties."

I nodded again, afraid to commit to something that might be impossible.

4

I yawned as I leaned my head on the back of the couch, looking at the lists. There were three columns: *With Us*, *Against Us*, and *Unknown*. The first two were fairly even. The third seemed a mile long.

Hawk was standing beside the list in the crowded room. He liked standing, and even more so when he was ready to fight. Unfortunately, we were having a problem nailing down our enemy to one spot, or one form, or pretty much nailing down anything at all. We still didn't know what it was, where it came from, or where to find it. Had it always been here and just revealed itself? Had it come from somewhere else? Who knew? Certainly not us.

It was tough when it felt like treading water all the time. It didn't want to show itself. This had turned into a war with an invisible enemy. There would be grouslie attacks weekly, but Dread wouldn't show its face. Every week, we talked about what to do and how to pin it down. The meetings never lasted very long.

I glanced around at the people filing in and got sloppy,

catching Hawk's gaze. The silent message was not flattering.

Okay, maybe he was right. I'd been reclining my way through months of them, perfecting my ability to ignore Hawk's gaze as I did. On meeting nights, I'd don my comfiest pants, grab a throw blanket off the back of the couch before they all got nabbed, and settle in with a hot tea before all the good seats were taken. These meetings weren't much to begin with. Try sitting through one on a hard stool with no back. Near torture, if you asked me, which nobody did, thankfully.

He kept glaring.

I got it. He wanted me to step up. Now Zuda wanted me to step up. This stepping-up thing was becoming a contagion, and I wasn't ready to catch it. I'd stepped up enough, and now I was supposed to be up in front? No, and definitely not today.

Considering the monkeys had woken me up five times last night as they laughed at their own jokes, and then I had to meet Zuda as she dumped the fate of their race on me, I'd recline my way through this weekly ordeal.

Musso walked to the list as the crowd finished settling in. Hawk was too busy glaring my way.

"Any updates on the Unknown? Anything suspicious noticed?" Musso knocked on the board with his knuckles.

The Unknown name didn't make it to a different list unless someone was willing to bet their lives on the person's allegiance. No one spoke, and a few shook their heads. It was hard to see something out of sorts when people were hunkered down all the time.

Hawk was so intent on me stepping up, but what would it change? As we went through the normal roll calls and usual questions that went unanswered, week after week? People would slowly fade out of the room, as they always did. No one could blame them. They probably had things in their life they could do instead of sitting here and trying to pretend we were being productive. Even Hawk was leaning against a table as if all the drive had leached out of him and his mind was somewhere else.

By the time Bibbi raised her hand, no one was left in the room but the people who lived here. The only reason I was on the couch still was that I was too tired to go upstairs.

Musso squinted, as if he didn't understand what was going on.

"Bibbi, you don't have to raise your hand," Hawk said.

Bibbi smiled as she slowly lowered it. "How are we supposed to fight something when we don't know what it is? We don't know what to target. We can't even locate it to try to burn it and find out if it likes fire, or try to drown it to discover if it breathes in water. I mean, we can't even see it. We need to change up our game plan before no one even shows up for meetings anymore and we're a scattered group essentially fighting on our own." She scanned the room, looking at the few of us left.

And I'd thought Bibbi was going to be useless other than moral support, which was good in its own way. Who knew she'd be so brilliant at bringing our failures to the forefront?

"We all know that, Bibbi," Hawk said, crossing his arms. "Was there something else?"

"Well, yes. I have an idea." She was beginning to wring her hands, and then she got to her feet, as if she couldn't stay seated any longer.

"What is it, Bibbi? We all want to hear," I said. What a bald-faced lie that was. The mental groans that were surely echoing throughout the room were nearly deafening my senses. Still, if Hawk was going to make us do this weekly, when I could've already been doing my rounds, then why should I be the only tortured soul?

Bibbi shot me a co-conspirator smile. We'd come a long way since I'd first seen her stealing my job. Now I viewed her as a helpful replacement, when we had work, anyway. That had dropped off significantly with contractors not wanting to leave their house or declare a side, which working with us was viewed as doing.

Bibbi kept her attention on me. "Hawk has one of those stones, right? A testing stone? The kind that flashes colors and such?"

Hawk's glare spiked a few degrees hotter as he stared in my direction. There was the slightest shake of his head. Clearly, he wanted me to say no. But why in the world would I do that? He had one, and if she had a good idea, we should hear her out.

"He does," I said, pretending I'd missed the message. If he wanted help, he had to take everyone's ideas seriously. He couldn't rule every move of the group, no matter how much he wanted.

"Is there any correlation between colors and magic?" she asked.

I turned to Hawk. His glare looked no friendlier than it had a second ago. "Is there?"

His jaw shifted. "It's not an exact science, but there's a correlation between brightness and strength. Sometimes colors indicate certain things as well."

"Why don't we see if we can bring the stone closer to where it's present and see what happens?" Bibbi said, near bouncing.

Hawk cleared his throat. "Because we can't pin it down, remember?"

Bibbi didn't lose any of her bounce. "We know it's connected to the grouslies somehow, and we also know how they like to attack lone people. If they're connected to it, they might show something. We could lay a trap and use them."

I nodded in Bibbi's direction. "It's more than we know now. I think it's worth a try. If we can lure it in, we might be able to find out something." Hawk wanted a contribution. I was contributing. He couldn't dictate how I contributed.

"How do we lay a trap for them?" Oscar asked, someone else finally speaking. It was as if the rest of the room sensed the war brewing between Hawk and me and hadn't wanted to declare themselves on our personal lists of *For* and *Against*.

"I'd do it, but they won't come near me." I wasn't sure how many of us were aware of that, but it had started to feel like I was lugging around a sled of boulders behind me. Now that I'd put it out there, I'd finally be able to park the sled. It wasn't like people didn't suspect I was different. It shouldn't come as a surprise.

From the swivel of heads, maybe more surprising than I'd guessed? I'd imagined Hawk had told some of them. Did the man confide in no one? Stupid question.

Even in this weird world, I was top of the heap. But there was only a two-second glitch before the awkwardness was broken by Bibbi. "And I thought I just envied your clothes. That's *so* cool."

"What happened since the last time they attacked you?" Zab asked.

"I don't know. Maybe they decided they didn't like how

I tasted." The grouslies definitely remembered me, but it wasn't my taste that bothered them. That wouldn't make them take off if I got too close, but I'd shared enough awkward truths for now. "Point is, I can't be bait."

"I'll do it," Bibbi said without a second of hesitation. "I'll be the bait."

The room went silent.

"Um, oh," Bertha said. "That would be..."

Nice? Clearly it wouldn't be. Not at all.

I sat up. Fun and games had officially ended. "Maybe someone else—"

"Why someone else? You don't think I can handle it? I can handle it." All her bounce was instantly gone, as if I'd popped a smiley balloon and it was just a sad, saggy piece of yellow flop.

I looked over at Hawk, wondering why he wasn't stepping up. Why didn't he offer to do it? He couldn't let Bibbi be the bait when he was so much more equipped to handle that kind of situation.

Oh shit. Maybe he couldn't. He went out by himself all the time, and nothing ever went near him either. Were the grouslies afraid of him as well? I wanted to groan into my hands. This was why I shouldn't be contributing. Now maybe he'd learn.

Hawk was giving me a look like I'd stepped in it. Bibbi was staring as if I'd stabbed her repeatedly in the chest. No one else was stepping up either.

"I just worry, but I know you're capable," I said to her.

"Good. It's settled, then. We should do it soon. Maybe tomorrow?"

Hawk shrugged, as if he'd given up this fight. He never gave up a fight. What was wrong with him?

The rest of us seemed shell-shocked.

"I'm going to go pick out an outfit," Bibbi said, near skipping from the room. The rest of them disappeared in pairs afterward, Zab and Oscar, and then Bertha and Musso, all probably heading out to gossip about how badly I'd messed that up.

As soon as the room cleared, I headed straight to where Hawk was fixing himself a drink.

"Why didn't you intervene? We can't let Bibbi do this. She could get hurt."

"We'll be there." He sipped his tea, as if it was another day in the office.

"I'd rather it be someone else," I said, not budging.

"No one else volunteered, and I can't do it. You're the one who backed her play. You should've considered some of this beforehand."

"You didn't even want this to happen, and now you're going to let her do it?"

"Are you admitting that you purposefully ignored me?" Hawk asked.

"Obviously." Did that even have to be said? He knew it. I knew it. Now he was going to make a thing of it? "You can't let this happen just because you're mad at me."

"That's not the case. But if you want to stop her, you should do that." He leaned against the counter, saying nothing else.

I walked out.

5

There was a soft rap at my door before Bibbi whispered, "Tippi, you awake?"

"Yeah, come in." I sat up, putting Dusty, who'd just gone invisible, to the side.

She walked in, glancing both ways down the hall before she shut the door softly.

"What's wrong? Everything okay?" I asked.

She pulled a grey piece of paper out of her pocket and held it out to me. "A stealth flash came for you."

I took the folded slip that was the color of mist and seemed to almost disappear if you held it a certain way. "What's a stealth flash?"

"It's like a newsflash but secret. Whoever sent it messed up, because it kept banging on my window." She pointed to my name. "It's clearly addressed to you."

I flipped it open.

I have important information. Meet me at the tree in the square at quarter past moonrise. Come alone.

.   .   .

Mertie

I closed the note. "Bibbi, how soon is quarter past moonrise?"

She walked over to the window and looked up. "Just a little bit from now. Why? What's that?" She lifted her head, trying to peek at the note.

"I've got to go meet someone I knew from the factory."

"Now?"

"Yeah, but it's fine. Totally safe." I stood and picked up an invisible Dusty with me. "Can you keep Dusty company while I'm gone? He hates being alone."

Dusty bit my finger, and I held in the pain. Bibbi liked to put bows on Dusty's little head and sometimes dress him up. He'd have to take one for the team so I could get out of here in peace. It was going to cost me a lot of cocoas tomorrow, or there might be a massive dust explosion in my room.

"Oh! I'd love to." She was all over him, leaving to kidnap him to her room seconds later.

I slipped on my boots, grabbed my jacket, and made it to the office before anyone else intercepted me.

"Where are you going?" Oscar said from where he was sitting at Zab's desk, flipping through slips casually.

"Nowhere special. Just stretching my legs," I said, walking a little faster toward the door.

"Where are you going?" Hawk asked from the back door.

"Nowhere," Oscar answered.

"I was going to stretch my legs," I said, turning to leave.

Hawk walked in my direction. "I'll come with you. I wouldn't mind a little exercise."

I stopped at the door. "I really wanted a little quiet."

"I won't talk." He smiled as he shrugged on his jacket.

My shoulders slumped. Why was nothing ever easy in this place? Why was nothing ever easy with him?

"Fine. I have an appointment and need to go alone."

"Well, that was surprisingly easy," Oscar said, laughing as he kicked his heels up onto the desk.

"With who?" Hawk asked with no humor whatsoever.

I turned back to Hawk, to the stare that wouldn't quit and the stance that said he could go all night. "Is it possible for something to not be any of your business?"

"We're at war. Everything is my business, especially covert meetings in the middle of the night."

In other words, I could come clean now or he'd follow me and find out anyway.

"Let me ask you something: is this a wartime thing or a Hawk thing?"

"Hmm. Interesting question. My choice would be that the two are one and the same," Oscar said from the other side of the room.

Hawk didn't bother answering.

Well, that gave me nothing.

I glanced at the door, knowing I was running out of time to make my meeting and there was no way I was getting there in peace now.

Would it really be that bad if I did tell him? What if it was a setup? Hawk would be my best option for backup. Mertie had specifically instructed me not to bring anyone.

I was curious enough to follow her to the letter of the note, which hadn't said anything about not telling anyone.

"Fine, I'll tell you, but you need to know I'm sharing this information because it's a wartime decision, not because I feel you deserve to know everywhere I go."

He rolled his hand, as if he didn't particularly care what my reasoning was. "Who's the meeting with?"

"Mertie, and you can't come." I'd fight that battle to the end. If he thought he was going to rule every move I made, the ugliest battle I'd be fighting was with him.

"Go."

I put my hands on my hips as I eyed him. "You're not going to try to come?"

"No." He turned and walked back to Oscar. "Come on. Let's get going. We'll go out the back."

Hawk was already out of the room as Oscar unfolded himself from the chair and followed.

"Where are you two going?" I asked. What was more important than harassing me?

"Nowhere," Oscar said, laughing.

My crew, the gang I was stuck with and would probably die with, were a bunch of assholes.

I zipped my coat up until it swallowed the bottom half of my face and pulled my hat out of my pocket. That ate up everything north of my eyeballs, so there was only enough space to breathe and see. It was as covert as I could get.

It was a great meeting place because it obscured its inhabitants completely. It was a horrible meeting place if someone else happened to schedule a clandestine meeting at the same time or happened to be watching.

"You're late." Mertie was leaning on the trunk, smoking a cigarette.

"You said a quarter past moonrise. That's not a precise time."

"And what's with the weird getup?" Her cigarette made rings of smoke as she motioned to my apparel.

"I was trying to be discreet, per request."

"That's not discreet. You look like a weirdo about to rob something."

I quickly remembered how she'd never seemed to have any friends at the wish factory.

"What did you want? You've been avoiding me for months, and now I have to sneak around in the middle of the night."

"You do realize you're the most wanted witch in Xest? Of course I'm not going to talk to you in public. It could ruin my entire setup."

The most wanted witch. She made it sound like my face was plastered on the side of buildings with the most unflattering picture they could find, and a reward posted below it. The situation wasn't *that* bad. It wasn't like I didn't see the list of people on the other side of our crusade, but they weren't against *me*. They didn't like our side as a whole. There was also a long list of undecideds. Mertie didn't know if maybe they secretly agreed with us, and therefore me.

"There are people that like me too." There was no reason to make it sound quite so negative. The term "most wanted" might've gotten a bad rap from the police, but it could've been most wanted in a positive light, like most wanted gift of the year.

"Fine. You're *so* loved." She took another drag and exhaled on a groan. She blew out a cloud of smoke that would've made a city's smog jealous, flinging ashes all about as she did.

The way she said it made it hard to argue the point without sounding like a narcissist. Must she always be so unpleasant? I used to think it was a demon thing, but I was beginning to believe it was a Mertie thing.

"Look, I'm here. What did you want to talk about?" I asked in the most civil tone I could muster, which was pretty decent, because I wanted this conversation done and over with.

"Just so you know, the people who *don't* love you are having dreams of killing you."

That was what I got for being civil. Her personality was allergic to polite discourse.

"Thank you for beating that to death. I appreciate it. Now, what did you want? It's freezing out, and I've got a warm bed waiting."

"Considering a lot of important people think you're the key to saving this world, you're not being very impressive right now. I just *told* you why I called you here. They're all having dreams of killing you. Like synced-up dreams of murder, almost like they're being brainwashed or goaded by something dark and evil. That's a problem for you."

She gave me jazz hands, as if I needed the ta-da moment emphasized for my feeble mind to grasp the problem.

She could save the flourishes. It was sinking in just fine, like an iron tack hammered into my skull. They were having dreams of killing me, all together, a horde of them.

"How do you know? Are you having them too?" I took a harder look at the messenger, retreating a step. I was still underneath the canopy of the tree, but barely.

The proximity was suddenly a bit suffocating. Why had I insisted Hawk not come? Oh yeah, because I was tough and could handle my own business, and, most of all, I was pissed at him for thinking he knew best all the time.

She tsked. "*No.* You think I'd be clustered in with them? Never, but I can't get away from them. I hear them talking while they work. Most of them don't shut the hell up. All I'm hearing lately is insistent chatter of how they dream of your blood." She finished one cigarette and then used the last embers to light the next. She took an unnaturally long drag before she started back up. "At first I thought it was random daydreams, you know, the typical sort you have of stabbing someone to death when they piss you off."

If I took another step back, I'd be outside the canopy. As appealing as that was, it was a better plan to get all the details, no matter how much I didn't want to hear them.

She took another drag and then continued to speak, the words smoke-laden. "Then I saw a trend: it was happening between groups that didn't socialize. The dreams all sounded a little too similar, too. You know, not how they killed you exactly, but how they all had this uneasy feeling and agitation that was replaced by this feeling of elation as you lay dead at their feet.

"They all had slightly different twists to their endings. Some talked of carrying your dead body through the streets and others putting your head on a spike, but that's not really important." She took another drag and glanced my way, as if remembering I was listening to her. "Yeah, so I figured you might want to know how Dread is trying to come for you. That's what you call it, right? Dread? Not the most original, but fitting, I guess."

I nodded, taking in deep breaths and then letting them out slowly to calm the racing of my heart.

"You look a little paler than your normal ghostly self." Mertie straightened off the tree and waved a hand to the spot she'd been leaning. "You need to relax or something? You're not gonna throw up, right?" She took a step away from me, as if she were afraid I'd get sick and splatter her hooves.

"I'm fine."

"You don't look it. That little strip of flesh still visible looks near ghostly, and I've seen my fair share."

"No, I'm good. Just cold." I jumped around in my spot a bit, as if warming up as I tried to get some blood pumping.

Mertie went back to leaning in her spot while I tried to stay on my feet as the reality hit. A retired demon was warning me that there was a mass hypnosis going on, plotting my death. Dread couldn't kill me. Its creatures couldn't kill me. A few of his top people hadn't been able to kill me. So was it going to come at me with an army of brainwashed minions? What was I supposed to do with that kind of information? It wasn't like I could kill half of Xest.

It was dreams and I was well known. It might mean absolutely nothing.

"I don't have anything else, by the way." Mertie was looking at me, as if wondering why I was still standing there.

She didn't have to encourage me to get going. I was ready before I'd gotten there. "Thanks for the heads-up."

She lifted her chin a hair.

I went to leave, but couldn't stop myself from asking one last question. "Why'd you warn me? I've always gotten the impression you didn't like me."

She shrugged again. "I don't know. I haven't picked a

side yet, and I like having options. If you're dead, there aren't as many options left. Don't think you're special because I gave you a warning. It doesn't mean I like you."

So happy she'd cleared that up.

"Yeah, well, thanks." I walked out from the tree, my tolerance for Mertie hitting its capacity for the night.

I'd made it halfway home before Hawk was walking beside me.

"What did she want?"

If I didn't tell him, he'd hound me. It wasn't really a big deal, was it? People dreamt all the time. They didn't usually turn into homicidal maniacs. Maybe they'd like me a little less, but it wouldn't make them a bloodthirsty horde. He'd surely agree that it was nothing. Maybe using him as a sounding board wasn't a bad idea.

"People are having dreams."

"What kind of dreams?" he asked, with no levity at all.

"Ones where they kill me and have a parade afterward. It's a little mass hysteria. Nothing to get all up in arms about." He might need a hint so he realized this wasn't a big deal.

I could feel his energy shifting, ratcheting up until it nearly sizzled in the air around us. This wasn't helping matters. At. All.

"It's just dreams," I said. "It's not like anything happened or there's some mass organizing to come kill me tomorrow. I'm fine. You haven't lost any of your advantages. It's all good."

I saw him nod out of the corner of my eye, but he wasn't talking. He wouldn't take my bait to fight. He just let me zig without zagging back. The energy kept building up around him.

By the time we got back to the building, all I wanted

was to get away from him too. It was dreams. People dreamt horrible things all the time. I wasn't going to blow it up into something catastrophic. Dreams meant nothing. I'd dreamt I went to dinner with no pants. I didn't turn around and go out with no clothes the next day.

This wasn't getting blown up into something it wasn't, not when I had too many issues that *were* something.

6

Hawk was on the other side of the room talking with Oscar, Zab, Musso, and Bertha.

Bibbi was zipping up her jacket, getting ready. I'd tried to broach the subject of how being bait wasn't a good idea all day. She'd shut me down every time until I'd given up. She was going to do this, and I was going to kill anything that got near her. Just the way it was going to go.

"I'm going to be close by," I said, not that she seemed to care. I was the one who couldn't stand still, who had to shove her hands in her pockets to hide the fidgeting.

She smiled. "I know."

"Very close. You'll never actually be alone." See? It would be fine. They wouldn't get anywhere close to her.

She nodded. "I know."

"You tucked those pants into the boots all the way down so they can't lift?" I stared at her ankles.

She tugged up a pants leg, displaying the metal underneath that would protect her if they got a nip. It had been Musso's brilliant idea. It was some weird material the grouslies would have trouble chewing through. Musso had gotten them from an ancestor who'd been a dragon trainer in a past life. Apparently it wasn't a very good job. Dragons didn't train well and usually killed their trainer eventually, like Musso's great-uncle. Musso had inherited the pants but had passed on the occupation.

"And don't lean down to pluck them off. They'll get your hands."

"Hawk went over all of this. And Oscar, and Musso too, but at that point I was sort of drifting, so I'm not sure. I'm ready, so don't worry. I've got this." She didn't stop smiling.

Just the fact that she said she had this under control made me feel like we were all standing on quicksand. She was Bibbi. She had nothing under control. She was my age and yet so much younger. She had zero idea of what she was doing.

"I know you do, but don't be overconfident. That's when people screw up." She was heading into battle. I couldn't have her going in shaking, but damned if I'd have her walk in like she was indestructible.

"Even if I do mess up, it's not like I'll be alone for long."

I tried to smile back. If it had been anyone but her doing this...

I looked about the room at the familiar faces, people who'd become more a family to me than my mother had been. They annoyed the hell out of me sometimes, and when they did, there was no escape. I worked with them, I ate with them, and sometimes I fought with them. And then something would happen like this and I'd be fighting beside them. I'd fight to the death for any of them. It didn't really matter which one of them was going; it would be horrible.

Hawk walked over with the box that held the gem and opened the lid. "You get them close and drop it. That's all you need to do," he said.

His hands were steady and his voice was calm. What was wrong with him? Why was I the only person that saw the potential disaster?

Bibbi plucked the gem out of the box, and it glowed a soft lavender, like a night-light of sorts. It was warm and soothing. If I'd been a Whimsy, was that what my magic would've looked like? Probably.

She tucked it into her pocket. "Thanks," she said, as if he were doing her a favor.

"You ready? It's almost dusk, and that's their most active time," Oscar said, coming over.

"I was born ready." She laughed, almost gleeful.

Kill me now, because she was going to take me out with a heart attack before the night was over.

Zab handed her a bag of bloody meat. It had been explained that it was similar to throwing chum in the water for a shark.

I stepped in front of her, blocking everyone else. "You follow the plan. You walk the path. We'll be right behind you. You don't deviate."

"I got it," she said, acting as if I were being a mother hen. "See you on the other side with hopefully a couple more answers." She waved to us as if she were leaving to go on a holiday then walked out of the front door of the office alone.

Oscar and Zab would follow her through the front a few minutes later. Musso and Bertha would leave and take a different route. Hawk and I headed toward the back door, going yet another way.

Hawk grabbed my arm as I rushed. "You have to give

her a minute. If we're going to do this, we might as well get it done the first time. The grouslies won't get close if they sense you anywhere around."

"There's not going to be a second time." I opened the door.

I walked fast, my feet refusing to listen to logic and keeping time with my heart, the one that would break if anything happened to Bibbi. My breathing was heavier, and not from the strain of the pace but from the weight of what I'd helped set in motion.

Bibbi was a kid. I shouldn't have gone along with this. For what? To catch a glimpse of a stone's color? Who cared? Would it really help much?

Slow down.

This was her choice. If she wanted to do this, I had to let her. I slowed my pace for all of two minutes before I double-timed it, making up for the loss and then some. Of course I didn't have to let her. She was being an idiot.

"It will be okay," Hawk said, following at my pace.

"She doesn't know what she's doing."

The alley split off and I couldn't remember which way to go as my nerves wiped away my memory. "Left or right? Which way?" I turned around. "Hurry up."

"Left."

By the next turn, he was pointing the directions before I got there. My head had been clearer when I was fighting a giant bat for my life. *That* was the key to the problem. *I'd* been fighting for my life, not lying in wait as Bibbi fought for hers. This was the stupidest thing I'd ever done, even if it hadn't been my idea.

Oscar and Zab had taken the direct route behind her because they'd be less likely to scare off the Grouslies.

Another dumb idea. What if they couldn't scare off the grouslies at all?

"Even if they get a bite in, I've got the treatment on me to stop it. It'll be okay," Hawk said, still calm.

"Have they ever almost eaten you to death? No. Nothing about this is fine."

How was it that the person who hadn't wanted this to happen was now telling me it wasn't that bad?

The sound of a whistle broke the air. It was Oscar's signal that they were moving in on her.

We both took off at a run.

I turned the corner just as the herd surrounded Bibbi about fifty feet away.

"Come on, I know you want this." She was drawing them close in, holding the bag of meat out, her other hand in her pocket. "Just a little closer," she said, as calm as if she didn't have a single nerve in her body.

I watched as they circled her, as was their way.

Hawk grabbed my arm, trying to hold me back so she could do what she needed to do.

He didn't have to bother. I'd been running here to save her, but she didn't need me, not yet. She had this under control.

The grouslies moved in slowly, as if they sensed a trap.

"What's she waiting for?" How close was she going to let them get before she used the stone? It would hit at least one of them, and we'd get some sense. She didn't have to take a bite in the process.

"She's drawing them in tighter to make sure. She's pretty good at this," he said, as if he hadn't expected it.

We were both asses, then, because I hadn't either. She might be a Whimsy witch, but what she lacked in magic, she definitely made up for in balls. The grouslies drew in so slowly. She shook the bag, and a few more pieces of meat dropped to the ground in front of her. They snapped, the bloody meat driving them into a frenzy. She followed it immediately with the stone, dropping it right on top of where they made a blanket covering the meat.

The stone fell in between the bodies, but that didn't stop the light from blasting into the alley. A rainbow of light. The only time I'd seen anything like it was when I held the stone myself. It had shone brightly for me, but still, I was the only one I knew of with a rainbow.

One creature moved from the meat, turning its attention to Bibbi, and it snapped me out of my daze. I ran forward just as it moved to sink its teeth into her ankle.

They scattered, dragging some of the meat off with them, leaving a trail of blood.

Another sound drew my attention to the opposite end of the alley, the one we'd just come from, and I saw a group of kids running off.

How long had they been there? Had they seen the light? Would they put it together the way I had? How could they not? All they had to do was see the grouslies flashing the same colors and glance at my hair. It was impossible not to add those two things up. Even if they needed a little help, the next fifty people or so they told, someone would figure it out.

I shut that out of my mind for now.

"Did it get you?" I asked Bibbi, motioning to her ankle as Oscar and Zab approached from the other side.

"It tried, but I don't think it broke the skin," she said, even as her attention was on my hair as she tried to figure out why the grouslies, and maybe Dread, would have the same colors.

I didn't go for the hat I had tucked in my pocket. It was too late anyway.

There was an awkward silence as Oscar and Zab didn't say much. They didn't have to. I saw the wheels turning. Musso cleared his throat, but didn't say anything. Bertha was the only one with enough restraint to not look at my hair, even though they'd arrived in time to see the flash of color.

"Let's check your leg, just in case," Hawk said, stepping in and breaking the silence.

"Huh?" Bibbi asked.

"Your leg, where it tried to bite you? I want to make sure it didn't break the skin." He stepped in front of me, disrupting her concentration on my hair.

"Oh. Yeah." She nodded and then tugged up the pants, as if the wheels in her brain had finally found something else to spin on than the muddy rut of my current dilemma.

She knelt down and tugged up her pants, letting everyone check out her skin for any possible penetration as I took a few steps back.

I'd always known something was off, that I'd been connected to it in some way. But flashing the same magic? I took another step back before catching myself and locking my legs down so my feet couldn't take me anywhere else.

Frozen in place, I felt like a human slushy machine, spinning but too cold and numb to think straight.

What did that mean? Why did that light look like mine?

Musso edged toward me while they continued to examine Bibbi. "Don't worry about it, kid. There are worse things in life than flashing the same color magic. Doesn't mean anything."

I shrugged. "No, yeah, not a big deal. I'm sure it's happened before."

His lips parted and his eyes closed up a bit as I waited to hear his words of wisdom. "Well, that I can't say. But nothing to do about it. If there's a similarity, then there's a similarity. Like I said, doesn't mean anything."

When I looked at him, his eyes shot away from my hands. "Not sure I'll ever get used to the fifth wind of Xest." I shoved them inside my jacket pockets so he couldn't see the tremble.

Hawk pointed to the gem on the ground. "Someone grab that and let's head back." Hawk began walking, pausing for a second once he got to where I was standing.

I started walking, falling into step with him the way we usually did, out of habit.

"But what did that mean?" Bibbi asked, trailing behind us as we all walked from the alley.

"It meant nothing," Hawk said. "Absolutely nothing."

7

When we got back to the broker building, everyone went their separate ways while I lingered by my desk, flipping through some cards.

Hawk was on the other side, by Zab's desk, not pretending to do anything but wait for the room to empty out.

He was the only one who didn't seem rattled by the revelation, almost as if it hadn't been a surprise. It was hitting me all wrong. Something was off. He wasn't bringing it up in front of anyone, not showing any curiosity at all.

The room downstairs emptied with unusual quiet. No one stayed to talk about what had been revealed. No one was talking about anything. They left with a few curious looks backward.

As soon as they were gone, Hawk straightened from where he was leaning and walked into the empty back room.

I followed him.

The absence of all other sound meant he'd muted the

back room. As soon as he did, my suspicions turned into a landslide of murky truth.

"You knew something was going to be weird, that I was linked to Dread somehow. That's why you didn't want Bibbi to go through with her plan. That's why Jasper thought I was evil. He knew too."

He settled on one of the couches. "I didn't know but thought it might be a possibility."

"Why?"

"Because I've never seen magic like yours, the way it threw off that kind of intensity and that array, not with any other witch or warlock in Xest."

"You suspected and didn't think you should tell me, of all people?"

"No. I didn't." He kept staring at me as he shrugged.

"How could you not?"

He let out a sigh, as if this was the last conversation he wanted to have right now. "Because you can't defend yourself without twisting your motivations into some story of why it's good for your opponent if you win. If it turned out I was right, I didn't think this would help matters. From the look of you right now, the waves of agitation you're throwing off, I was right. You took ten steps back the minute you realized."

I'd give him one thing: he'd never been more correct. I was rattled so badly that if I crumbled into a thousand pieces right now, it wouldn't be a surprise. The only thing keeping me standing was pure resolve, backed by nothing other than the knowledge that I had to keep going.

But that didn't make it any better. I was somehow connected to something that was pure evil. What did that make me? How could I be good if I was linked to evil? All the fears I'd barely buried felt like they were being washed ashore by the storm of tonight's revelation.

This wouldn't do. I couldn't afford to have a crisis of self on top of all the other problems happening. I needed to be on top of my game, not clinging to stay in the arena.

His eyes tracked me around the room, making me realize I'd been pacing. I stopped moving, gripping the back of the couch in front of me with both hands to anchor myself. I'd use whatever I had to get through this, even a stupid piece of furniture.

He wasn't talking, but his gaze didn't leave me, as if he were waiting to see if I was going to implode.

"It was a shock, but I'm fine. You don't need to worry about me. I can take care of myself."

He nodded, not fighting. It had an altogether placating feel that I wasn't fond of. The fight I could handle. This was new territory.

"You didn't want to run this little experiment because of me, did you?" I asked.

"No. If there was a connection, I did not want an audience to observe it. Just as you're rattled, I was afraid of others being rattled and the possible ramifications. If word gets out that it throws off a rainbow, all they need to do is look at your hair to know there's some link."

"*If* word gets out..." I scoffed. There was no way it wouldn't, but we both knew that. As soon as two people know a secret, it's not a secret, and a lot more than two knew. Besides our group, we'd had an audience at the end of the alley.

I didn't need to ask if this was going to become a bigger issue. It would. Impossible for it not to.

"Will our alliance hold?" Half of Xest hated me

enough to dream of murder. I couldn't afford to lose the other half, not even a fraction of it.

"It will hold even if I have to make it hold." The placating tone was replaced by steel. This was a Hawk that was much more familiar.

"If you had told me..." The woulda/couldas were piling up in my head so high that I'd be scaling a mountain before I slept tonight.

"We already covered this. I wasn't getting in your head over a guess. No one knew what was going to happen."

But some of us had guessed better than others.

"There's one good thing that came out of this," he said.

I waited for him to continue, hoping he had something good. I needed a silver lining in this cloud like a person getting pounded by a category five hurricane on the slippery rocks of the coast.

"We don't know what Dread is, but if we follow the connection back, figure out where your magic originated, we might be able to find Dread's origin. If you know what a thing is, you can destroy it. Tonight did serve a purpose. Bibbi was right. This was our first step toward getting Dread."

"Yeah, it proved I'm connected to this monster somehow." I waited for shock, condemnation, revulsion, something that mirrored the dredged-up feelings shifting inside me.

He continued to sit there, staring at me, no change in his expression.

"Well? You've got nothing to say about that?" I asked, daring him to speak the truth, that I might be a monster as well.

"No. I thought that a possible connection was an obvious problem."

I took a step closer, still waiting for the disgust I was feeling to show on his face. What was wrong with this man? Couldn't he put two and two together? Had he failed math completely?

"I'm connected to a monster." Did he not understand what that meant? The worst evil Xest might've ever known, and I was linked to it.

"I know." Still as calm as ever.

Screw it. I was going to have to spell it out. "What if I'm not just casually connected but *from* it somehow?"

"You mean you think your mother slept with the invisible evil?" He cocked a brow, not looking sold on my theory. Then, to top it off, he scoffed and shook his head.

Really? Did he think it was impossible?

"It could've happened," I said, waiting for him to finally wake up. My own mother had called me evil. Maybe this was why.

"I'm not arguing about this. There is nothing you can say that will make that believable."

That was what he thought. Telling me not to argue only meant he wasn't taking this seriously enough. He might as well have waved the flag for me to start my engine.

I leaned toward him, bringing my fist to my chest. "You saw the colors. I could very well be half monster, and you can't say otherwise. I might be genetically programmed to be half evil." Why couldn't he admit that it was possible? That I could be?

"Even if somehow you were part of that monster, I've told you before and I'm telling you again, you're not evil. I've stood toe to toe with evil. I know it when I see it. The positive is that at least this gives us a lead."

If my connection was a silver lining, it was the most pathetic sliver of tarnished metal I'd ever seen.

It was hours later when I put my ear to my door and listened. Nothing, finally. With this place constantly crawling with people, there wasn't a minute left to get Helen alone. I made my way downstairs, forgoing shoes or anything that might add noise. I closed the door as softly as I could and then sighed as it shut.

Her gears hummed as I walked over to the wall she covered.

"Helen, we need to talk."

Her gears sped up for a second before slowing down again.

"Glad you agree. I'm guessing you know what happened tonight."

She made a clicking sound.

Of course she knew. Helen knew everything that happened.

"This thing out there, it doesn't like me. I already knew that." I hopped up and sat on Zab's desk, knowing this next part was going to be the big one. "It looks like me and Dread, well, we might be linked somehow. Is there anything you can say about that?"

Her gears didn't move—nothing hummed, no clicks or ticks. I gave her another few moments, in case she needed some time to think, but it was becoming clear quickly that she wasn't going to reply.

"I know we're not exactly friends, but I'm lost. I was just hoping..." I shrugged before dropping my gaze to the floor.

A slip flew out. This one landed on the desk beside me, face up.

I'm sorry, but I can't speak of it.

"I'm on my own with this? Nothing at all to add?"

No slips. No grinding. My stomach clenched. All I got was silence.

8

Bertha put out a plate of buttered rolls and another platter of brownies on the table. We were like a barely restrained pack of wolves as we all grabbed for our favorite. If the others were freaked out by the color display last night, no one had shown it so far. No one had even brought it up, which was a little strange, but I hadn't seen a reason to complain.

"Do you have anything booked tomorrow?" I asked Zab right before I ate half my brownie in one bite.

"Not too much. I think I've got one client still willing to come in. Word of our lists are spreading, and everyone is afraid to end up on one side or another if they're in the middle."

"Not the worst thing ever. I could use some vacation time. Haven't taken some time off in decades," Musso said, leaning back with his brownie.

Bibbi reached past me for a roll and then took the seat next to me, and proceeded to not eat the roll. I could feel her attention on me as she broke a tiny piece off and still didn't eat.

"I wanted to talk to you if you had a second."

Pre-glowing alley revelation, Bibbi would've just spoken. Now she stared at the roll, waiting for an invite.

"We live together," I said. "You can't start walking on eggshells around me or it's going to be hard to coexist. Whatever it is, spit it out."

That was all it took. She dropped her roll to the table and turned to face me directly. "I'm sorry if I looked at you like you were a freak last night, but that was just sort of surprising. I mean, you, it." She lifted a finger toward my hair. "You understand, right?"

Everyone else in the room froze. Seemed there was a lot of interest in my reaction.

"It threw me for a bit too," I said. "Don't worry. You weren't thinking anything different than I was."

There were some definite quiet sighs going on around the room.

"Look, even if you are connected or maybe a little freakish in the magic department, we're still tight, right?" Bibbi asked, as if I'd be the one kicking her to the curb.

"I'm the weirdo, remember? You'd have to get rid of me. That's how these things work," I said.

"I don't care if you're a weirdo. Weirdos are much more interesting, in my opinion," Zab said.

"I already knew she was a freak. You people are a little slow on the uptake," Oscar added, laughing.

I joined him, never feeling so good to be called a freak. Maybe I was a freak, but no one seemed to care, and that felt better than trying to pretend.

The monkeys walked in, little bags in their hands, and cleared their throats.

"We wanted to let you all know we will be leaving," Speak No Evil said.

No one spoke.

"If anyone cares, we will be going to Zark's, where we won't be artistically censored any longer." His little chin went up, and the other two followed suit.

No one said anything, and they were clearly waiting for something.

"Good luck to you," Bibbi said.

"Yes, I'm sorry that we didn't appreciate your talents," I added. I would've said anything to get them out of here.

"Yes, us too," Zab said.

"Thank you. Perhaps next time you won't make the same error." Speak No Evil nodded, and then the three of them walked out.

Hawk walked in from the office a few minutes later.

"Did you see the monkeys leaving?" Zab asked.

"I paid Zark a lot of coins to take them. They better be leaving."

"Now it makes sense," Oscar said as the rest of us nodded.

Hawk tensed where he was standing on the other side of the room. He turned in the direction of the office, and I could nearly feel his hackles rise. Without saying a word, he walked back into the office.

I glanced at Oscar, who was also staring in the direction of the door. He took one look at me, and I could read his expression clearly. No way we were *both* wrong.

We shot to our feet at the same time.

"And here I thought I'd have a relaxing morning," Musso said.

"What's going on?" Zab asked.

Neither Oscar nor I replied. We didn't have answers or time as we rushed into the office. Chairs skidded and clanged behind us.

Hawk wasn't alone in the office. A few feet from him stood a...a man? The suit he was wearing was the only normal thing about him. His skin was a deep red and unnaturally smooth. He had horns on his head and hoofed feet. There was only one person I'd seen that looked like him. Mertie.

I groaned softly, my mind shooting to a weird memory of a man, a bucket of black goop from hell, and a warning about keeping the situation under control. The goop hadn't worked so well, and we certainly hadn't kept things under control. It might *not* be what I feared, but it very well could be.

"You know what this is about?" Oscar whispered to me as we hung back a bit from this stranger. I shook my head, not wanting to give the newcomer any ideas if that wasn't why he was here.

The demon's eyes shot past Hawk, to me, lingering there.

"What's your purpose here?" Hawk asked, not looking anywhere but at the demon in front of him. He moved, so that he broke the direct line of vision between the demon and myself.

My heart thudded as I waited to hear what the demon said. There wasn't a whisper behind me, even though there was a full audience.

"You were warned that if you didn't get this situation under control, we'd step in. The situation is most certainly not under control."

"You have no authority here, Xazier."

"The territory of Xest is experiencing unrest that threatens to spill into other realms. We have full authority to come in according to the pact, written and agreed to between the realms." Xazier held up his hand, and a parchment dropped down. "If happenings in any other realm threaten the peace of a different and separate realm, the threatened realm has full authority to intervene as they see fit."

"There's no threat to your realm. This is a power grab, and you know it."

Hawk continued to argue his point, but I was distracted from him by the low churning of Helen's gears. A slip shot out of her slot and dropped to the ground. It moved along the floor until it was by my toes.

According to the pact, in order for one realm to assert authority over another realm, a formal warning shall be given first and a full moon cycle shall be allowed to rectify such grievances.

I shoved the note in my pocket and stepped up to the demon, standing shoulder to shoulder with Hawk.

Hawk was giving me the stare that he still thought worked. I wasn't sure why he hadn't figured out that it didn't, but he kept trying. Maybe he'd had such a high success rate with it in the past that he couldn't wrap his head around it failing. He'd figure it out eventually.

The demon looked intrigued. That wasn't good either. Didn't matter. I was all in now. I'd inserted myself. Time to act.

"By the rule of pact, you have to give us a full moon cycle after a formal complaint to rectify that problem before you can assume any authority."

Hawk looked at me, clearly wondering where this

knowledge was coming from. Didn't matter. Helen knew, and I'd bet my last coin she was right.

"You *were* warned," Xazier said.

"By a passing comment? I highly doubt that would hold up," I scoffed.

The demon went silent. He wasn't leaving, though. He stood there, staring at me with an intensity that made the hair on the back of my neck stand up.

"I'm correct, am I not?" I asked, trying anything to break the strange moment that was dragging out.

He squinted and tilted his head, continuing to look at me. And he kept on looking.

"I might be able to work something out. I'll need a moment," he said, and then walked out of the office. Once outside, he began talking to the air.

Hawk dropped his gaze to me, his stare deepening. "I don't want you involved in this."

"If I hadn't gotten involved, you'd still be arguing that they couldn't take over Xest right now."

"I'm handling it."

"I'm helping you handle it."

"I'm asking you not—"

The door opened, and Xazier walked back into the office and stopped a few feet from us. He took in a deep breath, and steam literally came out of his mouth as he sighed.

He turned to me. "Fine. You can have your month. But if you want to hold us to the letter of the law, it works both ways. We'll be expecting collateral during this extension."

"No," Hawk replied.

I didn't know what Xazier wanted, but clearly it was going to be a disadvantage for us.

"It's not up to you, is it?" Xazier asked. "You know the

rules. She brought up the clause. She'll be the one to offer the collateral."

"What's the collateral?" I asked.

Xazier smiled. "You. If you fail to get the situation under control in the month given, we get Xest *and* you."

Helen was lucky that I didn't have a hammer right now. I'd be taking a swing at her gears for leading me down this road. What had she been thinking?

"Do you agree?" Xazier asked me.

"Don't," Hawk said.

"If I don't?" I asked, avoiding Hawk's gaze.

"If you don't agree, we take Xest tomorrow as planned."

"I agree."

I expected a flash of magic but didn't get one. Wasn't that what normally happened when you made a deal in Xest? Xazier didn't seem to notice, so I certainly wasn't going to bring it up.

"You have one cycle to rectify the problem," Xazier said.

"One cycle. Not a minute sooner," Hawk said, his anger clear.

Looked like we'd be brawling again tonight.

"You'll need to provide updates in the interim. Once a week should be sufficient. If you need to reach me in the meantime, just call my name into the fifth wind. I'll put you on my contact list." Xazier walked out. The second he went through the door, he disappeared into thin air.

No one in the room spoke. Hawk didn't need to say anything. The expression in his eyes said it all before he turned and walked away from me.

That I hadn't expected. Yelling and fighting? Oh yes.

"I was trying to help," I yelled at his back.

"You didn't. You walked into a setup." He disappeared into the back room, and then the outer door slammed a second later.

Oscar was shaking his head at me. "What the hell is wrong with you? You can barely defend yourself half the time, and now you think you've got it all covered? You're letting that freak stuff go to your head. You're human like the rest of us, not invincible. You need to think before you talk. Maybe you *don't* have all the answers."

"I didn't think I did, and what the hell is your issue?"

"You act like it, that's my issue." Oscar walked away.

Bertha was trying to smile. It was warm but not encouraging. She clearly thought I'd stepped in it as well.

"I don't know why they're giving you such a problem, kid," Musso said, lifting his stocky shoulders.

The tension began to ease.

Then he continued, "I mean, how are you going to learn if you don't screw shit up sometimes? You might take a couple of lumps, but you'll be okay."

"I'll fix you a nice dinner and a big breakfast in the morning," Bertha said, encouraging Musso to head toward the stairs.

What did that mean? Was she trying to feed me my last meals? Did she think I was going to die or something?

Zab and Bibbi walked over, standing on either side of me. I ran my hands over my face and then through my hair, so they probably thought I didn't see the look they shot each other. I had. Oh yes, I wasn't just going to die. I'd do it in hell. What was that old saying? The road to hell is paved with good intentions. I'd always thought that was just a saying. No one warned me it was literal.

"I'm sure it'll work out," Bibbi said.

She was officially the worst liar in Xest.

"Yeah, I'm sure this will work out," Zab said. "Just because we haven't been able to fix anything for months doesn't mean a miracle can't happen."

They all thought I was a goner.

No one banged on my door for dinner. How was that possible? I could hear the chattering in the back room, but it died quickly as I walked in and everyone made a point of not looking at me, but not *not* looking at me either.

"So like I was saying, it should be a slow day tomorrow," Zab said, as if *that* had been the conversation going on before I walked in.

"The tea tastes a little funny today, right?" Bibbi said.

"It does taste odd," Musso agreed. "Did you notice the clouds today? I think we're going to have a few more inches of snow by morning."

Bertha agreed and then chimed in about a new spell for knitting she'd read about. The conversation went in circles like this, while everyone tried to avoid talking about my issue. The space between sentences lengthened and they couldn't think up one more mundane thing to discuss. Then the topping on the cake finally arrived with Hawk, who wasn't acknowledging me at all. He walked into the room as if I wasn't there, not a glance, a nod, nothing.

The tension was suffocating to all in the room, and one by one, they found an excuse to leave. I wasn't leaving. I still didn't think I'd done anything wrong.

I curled up on the couch, the idea of sleep so far away that I might not see it for days.

It's not that bad. What else was I supposed to do? Did I

*really have a choice? No. I didn't, and of course now he's all
bent out of shape because whenever there is no choice he seems
to get mad.*

I jumped as Oscar dropped onto the couch beside me.

"You know, you have a really strange way of getting
messed up in every possible predicament there is." He
smiled right before he sipped his tea.

He wasn't screaming at me, but clearly Hawk wasn't
the only angry one here. I'd done the right thing to help
save Xest and now everyone either thought I was insane
or a dead woman walking.

"Um, thanks?"

"Sure, let's pretend that was a compliment." He
continued to sip on his tea.

"What is your problem?" I gave him all of two seconds
before I continued. "The way I see it, I was doing the right
thing. I was saving your asses for a month. I can't imagine
what Hawk's issue is with it, or yours. It makes no sense.
You people should be happy."

"Yeah, can't imagine why we'd be pissed off," Oscar
said. "Not like I didn't have to work at getting your ass a
job and making sure no one killed you or threw you out of
Xest. I did a lot of work so you could just toss it all away."

I sat up straighter. "I'm not tossing it away. I'm trying to
repay the favor."

"It's not repaying the favor when you might be the
only way we can get rid of what's ruining Xest." He put his
drink down and turned so he was sitting sideways on the
couch, facing me. He didn't speak for a few seconds.
"Don't you get it? You're the only thing it's afraid of, and
there's got to be a reason. If you're gone, we're sunk. How
is that a favor?"

I knew some people might've viewed me as the key to

the solution, but Oscar? "I'm not the key. I'm a stopgap. I know me, and I don't have what it takes to stop whatever that thing is."

"Then you better figure out how to get whatever it takes, because you're all we've got."

9

My back slammed into the snow.

Bautere hovered over me. "Why did you want to practice if this is what you're going to do?"

"I thought it would be a good idea."

"Go home. It's getting late, and I'm tired of knocking you on your ass." Bautere walked away, leaving me in the field alone.

I'd left a note that I would be gone. After, I'd walked Xest several times, hunting for grouslies. I'd come here, thinking I could work out the aggravation. The only thing I'd accomplished was being cold, tired, and now bruised as I got up and headed home—but I had one stop left.

I took the long way to the rusty mailbox and dug out the letter that was bent and wrinkled from being in my pocket all day.

I didn't have an address, only a name: Xest Immigration.

I'd have to deal with those three unpleasant hags again, but they'd have answers. Hawk had made one very good point: we knew I was linked to Dread. If we traced back my origins, we might find Dread's as well. There was only one place to start—my mother. She'd come from Xest, and they were the best source of information.

Zab was going to have to lend me his cauldron again. If I brewed them up something nice, things would go easier.

The sky was dark when I returned to the broker building. Getting back after dinner hadn't been an accident. I swung by the back room, hoping there might be some leftovers, and found a plate waiting for me.

It was still hot, as Bertha's food always was. She had a spell to keep everything at the perfect temperature. It had been handed down from generations in her family, and no one else knew how to do it. She said she'd only give it out on her deathbed. Yes, there might be other spells that would heat food, but not keep it just as moist as if it had just left the oven. The woman was a near genius with anything culinary.

I carried my plate up to my room to find a note stuck on my door.

Meeting in the back room at moonrise, Hawk, you, and me.

Oscar

I shoved the note in my back pocket, debating whether it was wise to go. Was there really a choice? It was hard to avoid. If I wanted a cup of coffee or tea, boom, I was at the meeting. Plus, he'd just stalk me until I met with him anyway. That was the trouble with living with the people you wanted to avoid.

I changed into something that didn't scream I'd been out hunting grouslies while I choked down my stew. Then I slowed my pace. Choking down anything Bertha made was a crime.

By the time I made my way downstairs again, Oscar and Hawk were already sitting in the back room. The fact Hawk was willing to attend was probably an improvement, even if it was only because Oscar asked him to. *Or they were combining forces to tell me how stupid I was.*

Oscar waved his hand toward the other side of the couch. "I know you two are out of sorts, but we've got bigger issues. I'm not overly confident in our ability to take care of Dread in a month." He turned to Hawk. "If we lose her, the only thing Dread seems to avoid, I'm even less confident we have a chance in hell of fixing this situation. Those idiots over from hell don't know their asses from their heads. They'll definitely blow it. And I know she got us into this situation, but we need to come together and fix it."

Was this him trying to bridge the gap and mend fences or another way to spend the night calling me stupid?

"I was trying to do the right thing," I said, for what seemed like the fiftieth time in days. You would've thought they'd all be grateful that I was willing to put my life on the line. No. Every single one of them was annoyed by it.

"It wasn't, though, was it? We had this talk. Let's not drag out the ugly details," Oscar said.

"You talked. I didn't agree."

Hawk leaned forward, resting his forearms on his legs, and we both fell silent. Oscar might've been in a state of shock over Hawk's appearance of possible participation.

He wasn't the only one. I'd thought he was going to sit and glare all night.

Hawk looked at me, and I could see the anger still swirling, like I'd betrayed him somehow, before he turned to Oscar.

"It doesn't matter if they want to take her," Hawk said.

He might as well have packed my bags and tossed them in the alley. We'd had our problems, but I'd thought this was just a tiff. Could he really turn his back on me so easily? Would there never be any loyalty between us? Would he be willing to toss me away continually like I was nothing?

I didn't say a word. I was too busy swallowing the big, fat boulder in my throat and pretending my eyes weren't burning. I didn't cry, ever, and I wasn't breaking that streak for this man. He didn't deserve to hurt me.

Oscar, who looked like he'd taken the same sucker punch I had, said, "How can you say that? Even if she did screw up, she's not only our only hope, but she's our friend. Say you don't mean that."

"You're missing my point. It doesn't matter if they *want* to. They can't." Hawk's voice was ice cold and calculating. This was the Hawk I'd met when I first came here. The one always looking at every angle.

"What do you mean? She put herself up as collateral," Oscar said.

At least I wasn't the only one confused. Nice of Hawk to fill us in. He'd let me sweat it out for days and he'd already worked something out.

"She offered up collateral that isn't hers to give," Hawk said.

"She put herself up. You're not making any sense." Oscar was still frowning, trying to wrap his head around what Hawk was saying. I was already getting a bad sense that I knew where this was going.

"Hawk, what did you do?" I asked.

"I safeguarded for this very situation." It was the longest sentence he'd said to me in days, and I immediately wished he'd gone back to not speaking to me.

"How?"

He leaned back in his chair, calm and emotionless. "That spell, way back when you agreed to work for me. It wasn't quite as cut and dried as you might've thought. You agreed to work for me until a time of my choosing. I couldn't fire you, but you can't quit either, so you aren't actually able to offer yourself as collateral, since you've already been promised to this place."

Oscar gasped. "I knew something seemed off about her right around the time she started working here as a broker. *That's* what it was."

While Oscar was relishing in his ah-ha moment, I was having one of my own. "For how long? How long am I actually stuck here?"

"Until we do a joint release. It was an insurance policy against immigration being able to evict you from Xest."

All the nerves, wondering if I'd done the wrong thing, went up in smoke from the fire he'd just lit. "How could you do that without telling me?"

"Don't act as if you had no idea. You were aware I did something. It was very obvious you didn't want to know the details. After the immigration trial, you asked me what I did that swayed the hags. I told you the timing wasn't right to answer that question. You dropped it then, and in the months since, you haven't once mentioned it. That's not someone who wants to know." He was still being that calm, ice-cold Hawk of old.

"I never thought you'd do something like this, or I would've asked."

"Then you should've. You know me well enough to realize I'll do whatever it takes."

Oh, he was right there. I never should've underestimated that at all.

"You might've mentioned this earlier," Oscar said.

I sprang to my feet. "You need to undo it."

"You sure about that?" Hawk asked. "Do you want to risk them being able to take you? If that's what you want, say the word."

I was stuck, hanging out in owned limbo. But what bothered me more than anything was that I didn't think he'd really do it anyway, even if I truly did want him to.

I moved closer until my toes were nearly brushing his. "You know what? I'll take my chances. Undo it."

This might've been the stupidest thing I'd ever asked for. What if he did undo it?

He stood. "You'd cut off your nose to spite your face?"

"No, she wouldn't. She doesn't want you to really do it. Right, Tippi?" Oscar got to his feet as well, trying to angle into the small space between us. "Tell him you don't want that, Tippi, because it would be *incredibly* stupid." Oscar was looking at me like I'd lost my mind and he was sure hoping I'd find it fast.

He was right. I might've lost my mind. No, I'd *definitely* lost it, and I wasn't finding it anytime soon. I was going down with this ship.

"Oscar, I know what I'm doing. Step out of the way."

Oscar closed his eyes for a second, groaned softly, and then stepped back.

No buffer left. It was just me and Hawk now. "Undo it."

His eyes didn't flinch from my gaze. "Do you realize what you're asking for?"

"Yes. I'm saying the words. And I'm asking you to undo it." Probably too clearly. That didn't bode well for my sanity, but no one was controlling my life. Not anymore.

He looked down at me. "No."

"You won't undo it?"

"No, I won't. Even if you care so little about your well-being that you'd risk everything, as demonstrated by the actions you've taken in the last few days, I'm not going to compound your mistakes." The lines of his face were hard, but there was something calling to me in his eyes, a warmth that might undo me if I let it.

I wouldn't. I wasn't falling for the little glimmers and hints of what Hawk could be when the man before me was being an ass, again.

"That's the thing. They're my mistakes to make."

Oscar had dropped onto the couch, groaning after my last comment.

"And if you die?" Hawk said. "Where does that leave everyone else? Or do you not care what that would mean to other people?" The rage was building in him, wiping out all traces of softness.

"And you do? This is about everyone else now? I think this is about you and keeping your situation afloat." That was all he ever cared about. Him, his place, what he needed. "This is getting undone whether you want it to or not."

He crossed his arms, making a point of looking down at me. "We've faced off before. Doesn't tend to work out well for you."

"Really? If I remember correctly, you didn't want me in

Xest, and I'm here." I pointed to the floor I was standing on.

"Because I helped you by doing the exact thing you're telling me to undo now. Thankfully, I'm not following your game plan."

I took a few steps away from him, afraid I'd start swinging if I didn't. "I knew I was better off hating you."

"Another reason why you don't really want me to undo it. You have another reason to add to your list of why you're angry at me. This is good news for you."

"Don't try to turn this. Everything has to be your way."

"When the other options are pure stupidity? Yes. I guess they do."

I gave him my back, leaving the room before I tried to kill him.

"Well, *I guess* the meeting is over. At least that takes care of that. No one will be taking her anywhere, it seems," Oscar said as I left.

10

I was sipping tea, organizing some requests, and tossing ones that were already too old to fulfill, giving myself busywork and pretending Hawk wasn't on the other side of the room, doing his own busywork. We hadn't said one word in greeting, not that he was chatty anyway. But typically, there'd be a nod, a glance, some acknowledgment of another life form. Today? Nothing, and it was mutual.

I was doing my damnedest to pretend he wasn't in the office, and that I didn't hear everything he said, and that I didn't know when he told Musso he was leaving, or that he nodded toward Bibbi and Zab as he left.

I was glad he'd left. It was much easier to concentrate on my busywork without him constantly moving about the place.

Hawk had been gone for twenty minutes when the door opened. A man in a white polo shirt and equally bright pants, a crisp pleat down the center of each leg, walked into the office. Nothing about him looked local. He might've been strolling in from a barbecue, instead of a snowfield that would give Antarctica a good run for its money.

Musso and Zab didn't appear to recognize him either.

He took off his sunglasses, tucking them into his shirt pocket. His hat came off next as he looked around the place.

"Can I help you?" Musso asked, standing.

The man in white looked at Musso, as if he were startled he'd been addressed, even though he'd walked into our office.

"Yes, sir, you may. I was wondering if a friend of mine might've stopped by?" He raised his hand about level with his own height. "About this tall, dark hair, loves to wear all black. Horns just so." He held his index fingers up near his head.

Friend? I doubted that. Oh yes, the man he was looking for had been here.

I leaned back in my chair so hard that I almost rocked myself right onto the floor. This had to be some sort of sick joke. We barely got one strange man out the door and now we had another?

Bibbi was at her table, leaning forward, her lips parted. Her eyes continued to take in this new guest from head to toe. Zab and Musso were speechless.

Musso cleared his throat, but didn't say anything. I got it. You didn't shoot the shit with angels every day. Or demons, for that matter. Must have been my lucky week.

"What was this friend's name?" I asked, stalling as we tried to figure out what to do.

"Xazier." He turned his full attention on me. "My name is Lou. Have you seen him?"

"I think someone fitting that description passed through here, but I haven't seen him in a bit."

Lou walked closer to my desk. "And you are?" His stare's intensity reminded me of how his "friend" had also looked at me.

There was a two-second glitch where old habits warred in my head, screaming that I should retreat. Then my new self's chest puffed out a bit, and I smiled like a person who had nothing in the world to fear.

I stood with more confidence than I'd thought I could muster and said, "I'm Tippi," in a way that dared him to do his worst, because he better not screw with me.

His perusal only intensified, as if I'd flipped the lights on and he could see all the better.

His eyes flickered over me again, taking in every detail but not hovering anywhere untoward, giving me the impression that his interest was anything but sexual. What he saw, I couldn't imagine, but it didn't seem to be my fashion he was admiring.

He rubbed his knuckles over his chin. "And you're a...witch?"

The way he asked that made me rethink my bravado. "Of course. What else would I be?" I asked, daring him to contradict me.

"Yes, what else indeed." He took a step back, looking around the place again before turning back to me. "Well, if my friend passes through again, let him know I'm aware of the situation. He'll understand." He put his hat back on and nodded. "I'll be off now. I don't want to take up too much of your time."

He headed to the door, stopping and giving me a last look that got stuck too long for comfort. It made me almost revert to my hiding ways. I stood my ground until he turned, but if he'd stayed any longer, I couldn't have guaranteed my feet would've stuck it out.

The door clanged shut, and I got up to get a better view of him leaving. I watched as he made a right, and then disappeared completely.

Bibbi got out of her chair and came to stand beside me. "What in the hell was that?"

Zab came and stood on the other side of her. Musso walked over as well, rubbing his jaw. "You might want to say *what in heaven* was that, would be my guess."

"*That* was not normal. I gotta call Hawk," Zab said, walking to where a fresh stack of newsflash papers were sitting on his desk.

"What happened?" Hawk said as he walked in from the back room. "I felt something unusual cross my ward. Who was here?"

Hawk's gaze met mine and our eyes locked. We hadn't said a word to each other since I'd discovered what he'd done. Didn't plan on doing it now, either, unless absolutely necessary. That wasn't the case when I had Zab.

Was this place rigged with some magic surveillance system? Did it send Hawk some fairy ding, telling him to get back here? Not to mention, someone needed to put a bell on that back door. When he came from upstairs, at least the stairs creaked. Although maybe not for him. He had a sneaky way of being really quiet that was definitely not human.

As I mused on how to set up my own traps around this place, Zab didn't hesitate to spell out all the details to Hawk, down to the extra attention Lou seemed to pay me.

Hawk walked to the front, as if tracing the man's steps. He placed his hand on the doorknob and paused.

"What the hell," he said softly before saying to Zab, "Send Mertie a newsflash. Tell her to get here immediately."

"Will Mertie come here?" I asked Musso in a soft voice. After the meeting the other night, it had seemed quite apparent that she was avoiding any appearances of taking sides.

"Everyone comes if Hawk calls," Musso said, not softly at all.

Had he not picked up on that fact I'd whispered? This was why I shouldn't have asked.

Zab sent the newsflash, a nice, tame-looking little bird of a thing. If Hawk really wanted to make a point, he should've asked me to do it, not that I would've.

I'd taken two steps toward the back room to get a fresh tea when the door slammed open. I guess Musso was right. She'd come, and fast.

Her hooves hit the floor with a thudding noise as her hands parked themselves on her hips. "What is it now? You know even setting a foot in here makes me look bad, right? I'm trying to steer clear of the mess you people are making, if you haven't figured that out."

Hawk had commandeered Zab's desk and kicked his feet up on it. "Why is Lou here?"

"You mean the butcher?" She began shaking her head. "You called me here to ask about the butcher?" She turned to leave. "These stupid humans think all I have is time to gossip or put in their meat order for them. It's absolutely ridiculous that—"

"Not Lou the butcher. Lou who doesn't live here or in Rest and likes to wear all white," Hawk said, raising his voice so he was loud and clear.

Mertie stopped and spun around so fast that her hooves nearly squealed. "Why would that Lou be here? What did he say?" All the steam was gone and she fumbled in her jacket, pulling out a cigarette.

"He was inquiring after another visitor we had a couple of days ago by the name of Xazier."

As much as I didn't want to talk to him, was he really doing the right thing here? We had no idea who she was aligned with. You'd think he was the new witch to Xest. Yeah, she'd given me a heads-up about some dreams, but that might've been a setup. Maybe it was mental warfare?

I cleared my throat and then shot him a glare.

Mertie let out a small laugh, drawing my attention back to her. "This is just brilliant. Disco girl lights up the alley and now she's worried about saying too much?"

"What are you talking about? I didn't light up the alley."

"Oh, this is just perfect. She doesn't even know."

I glanced around, hoping someone would explain.

"You were glowing a bit in the alley." Bibbi gave me a half shrug.

Now they told me? I'd thought it was my hair that had freaked everyone out.

"We still love you, kid," Musso said.

"It's all right to be a little different," Zab said.

Don't look at Hawk. Not him.

I looked anyway.

He was smiling. "You knew I thought it was a bad idea."

That was why I shouldn't have looked.

Mertie started stomping around the place. "I'm not sure you people realize it, but we're a hair away from an invasion if they're both showing up. What is wrong with you people? Are you trying to wreck a good thing? We don't want that kind here. Neither of them. One thinks they're too good for everyone, and the other thinks we're not good enough for anybody. Either way, they're trouble."

"So you know them both?" I asked, moving closer in case she tried to make a run for it. Most of the people I tried to question did. Hawk had already let it all out of the bag anyway. I might as well get the pertinent questions answered.

She stopped her pacing. "Of course I know them. What kind of demon loser do you think I am? One of the grubs who only did the dirty work? I might've quit, but I had some pull in my day."

"Any idea why they're both here?" Hawk asked.

"Yeah, because you guys really screwed this place up, obviously." She started shaking her head again, taking long drags from her cigarette. "I don't care what they say. I'll go to that hellhole Rest before I take orders from any of them again." She pointed at all of us, creating a stream of smoke as she did. "You people better fix this. I'm not paying for your sins."

Mertie's hands flew up. "No, no more questions. I don't want any part of whatever craziness you have going on. You guys made this mess, and you guys need to clean it up."

She nearly ran to the door before she stopped short. "And don't newsflash me again. I won't come." She slammed the door shut and took off.

Why they're both *here.* That was what Hawk had said. Didn't we already know why one of them was here? Or did we?

11

There was a stack of slips sitting on my desk but a lean list of clients willing to do the work. Considering the traffic coming in and out of here lately, I wouldn't come either. I dropped the slips back on my desk and walked past Musso, Bibbi, and Zab, who were playing a card game at Zab's desk.

"Tippi, you sure you don't want to play?" Zab asked.

"No, thanks. I'm good." There was no way I'd be able to learn anything new with the way my thoughts were scattered these days. The only thing that might get me through the day was lots of tea and cocoa.

I was making tea in the back when the sounds from the other room faded, signaling that someone had muted the room.

Hawk walked over and leaned on the counter beside me. "I know what you did."

Hawk didn't bluff. If he said he knew, he knew. Only problem I was having was which thing did he know? I was accumulating quite a pile of secrets lately. It was hardly a good idea to dump out my entire treasure chest of information at his feet. Odds were he was talking about immigration, but just in case...

"I didn't have a choice." I shrugged, hoping that the conversation to follow might lead me to a few breadcrumbs of what knowledge he possessed.

"You didn't?"

I made a show of stirring my tea. "No."

He crossed his arms, leaning back further. "What am I talking about?"

I took a step away, drinking my tea. "The thing. You know, the thing I did that you're upset about."

"You reached out to immigration."

Dammit. How'd he find out so fast? I didn't know if the mailbox trick would work, and he already knew about it?

"Are you going to talk?"

"You tell me how you know and I'll talk." I hadn't planned on letting him in, but if anyone would help keep me here, it was Hawk. More than anything else, Hawk was a survivor. Sometimes I was afraid to know what ends he might go to in the process of surviving. Right now, it worked to my benefit, because he thought I was a key to his and Xest's survival.

"I have an agreement with the mailman," he said nonchalantly, as if that were nothing.

"You know him?" In Xest, that was like saying you knew the Rolling Stones. How was that even possible?

"Yes. Now, why did you reach out and not fill me in?"

He was watching me intently. Every time he looked at me this way, it made me a little tingly inside where I shouldn't tingle. I walked over to the couch, a safer distance away.

"Did you stop my letter?" I asked, the thought suddenly occurring to me.

"Answer my question first. That was the deal. An answer for an answer." He closed the distance, sitting on the other couch, eroding my buffer.

"At my immigration appointment, you alluded to them having been around for thousands of years. They're *immigration*; they must have some record of my mother. I'm tracing back my origins, trying to find a thread back to Dread so we can figure out how to get rid of it, once and for all. And I didn't tell you because we're not speaking."

I sipped my tea, acting as cool as he did.

"Which is why I was reaching out to them as well. Now that we both did it, we look scattered," he said.

He had too? I should've guessed. "Why didn't you tell me? It's okay for you to do it and keep it to yourself but not me?"

"I was going to tell you, but as you mentioned, we're not speaking."

We both fell silent, the new problem obvious. Neither of us knew who would hear back first. What if they contacted him? I wanted to be told immediately. There was only one thing to do: broker a deal with the enemy.

"Speaking or not, whoever hears first tells the other."

He made me sweat it out for a couple of minutes before he finally said, "Deal."

12

I grabbed my jacket, heading to the door as Zab yelled from the table, "Hey! Where are you going?"

I stopped walking as I pulled my jacket on. "Was going to get some air."

"Want company?"

Zab was good at keeping things light when he needed to, and considering my brain was weighed down with two tons of worry, I was ready to bribe him to come along.

"Yeah, definitely. We can get a cocoa while we're out—my treat." If there was one thing that got Zab moving, it was Sweet Shop cocoa. Gilli had a way with chocolate that couldn't be touched. Even Bertha seemed to avoid making anything chocolate based, and I'd bet coin it was because she didn't want to tarnish her reputation, coming in second with anything edible involved.

"All you had to do was ask. You didn't need to bribe me." He grabbed his jacket, moving a little faster.

"Does that mean you don't want cocoa?" I asked. "I'll drink them both if you want."

He held the door open. "Oh no, you offered and I'm getting a cocoa."

The streets were quiet as we made our way over, as they always seemed to be these days, especially after nightfall.

Zab looked both ways before walking far from the building, just as I did. Couldn't even cross the street without getting ready to defend yourself.

"Can't wait until this place is back to normal," Zab said as he continued to look in every direction.

"I know," I said, looking both ways myself, but for a different reason. There was one predator that liked to come out at night, and that was me. One of these times, I was going to manage to catch some grouslies.

The shop was empty when we walked in, one of Gilli's workers wiping down the shelving for lack of anything else to do. They were close enough to the broker office that I saw a lot of the foot traffic that passed us by. This place used to always be packed. If they got a couple of people an hour now, that was a lot.

She handed us two cocoas, knowing our order by heart, plus a bag of fudge on the house.

"Why do I never order these?" Zab asked, popping fudge into his mouth as we walked out.

"I'm wondering the same," I said after my first bite. They were like little pieces of heaven in your mouth.

A muffled scream came from around the corner. I took off at a run in that direction, my cocoa splattering on the ground.

Gilli was standing behind the Sweet Shop with a herd of grouslies attacking her legs, her employee standing in the back door with a broom in her hand, looking for an opening she seemed too fearful to take even if she could.

"Stay close to me," I yelled to Zab, not wanting them to switch attacks and go for him after I scared them away from Gilli.

I didn't wait for him to agree as I ran toward her, the ground already covered in blood. The alley lit up, as if Zab had shined a spotlight on the grouslies.

They scattered well before I got within a few feet of them, running as if I were the devil himself and had come to collect them for hell.

Gilli was on the ground, her pants in shreds, her hands torn apart as she continued bleeding, a pitiful moaning coming from her. She turned on her side, balling up in a fetal position.

I dropped to the ground beside her, knowing we had to get her back to the broker building fast before the poison could spread.

"What should I do?" Her employee ran toward us but then stopped short, looking at me as if I were as scary as the grouslies.

"Go back in so you don't get attacked after we leave. We'll take care of her. Hawk knows how to treat this. She'll be fine." I turned my full attention back to Gilli. "I'm going to wrap your arm around my shoulders so we can get you help."

The only response I got was a moan.

Zab was already grabbing her other arm as we hoisted her up. "Should we bring Hawk here?"

"No. Quicker to get her there."

We stood, walking her back as fast as we could, leaving a trail of blood in our wake.

We walked into the office, each of us with one of Gilli's arms slung over our shoulders. She continued to moan, tears streaming down her face. I wasn't sure if she was even cognizant at this point.

"Get Hawk," I yelled to a frozen Bibbi.

Hawk was already there, walking in from the back room. He backed out of the door and pointed to the couch. "I've got to go get supplies. Keep her seated with her feet on the ground to limit circulation."

"What about the blood loss?" I yelled to him as he walked out.

"More concerned about the poison," he replied before he was gone.

Musso rushed over. "Damned grouslies again. Fifth attack in the last few weeks."

Bertha sat beside Gilli, draping a throw over her shoulders. "It'll be all right. Hawk will fix you up."

Hawk was back downstairs seconds later, covering her legs in the same tincture he'd used on me. I nodded to Zab, motioning over to the side of the room and out of earshot.

"Does she have family?" I asked as he joined me.

"No. Just her. I'll run over and tell her employees that she's okay. They'll figure out something to cover the shop tomorrow. They've been with her a while."

I put out my arm, blocking him from going. "I'll go. The grouslies won't bother me, and they might still be nearby."

"It's not a big deal. I'll shoot over—"

"Zab, let Tippi do it. We know they're close, and they won't touch her," Hawk said from where he was bent over working on Gilli.

I gave Zab an I-told-you-so look, knowing he wouldn't go against Hawk, not that he should. It was common sense.

"Before you go, what was that weird light-up thing you did when you were running at them?" he asked.

My stomach clenched and my mouth was suddenly dry. "What are you talking about? I thought that was you."

"That was definitely *not* me. Your skin was nearly glowing."

"I don't know. I guess I just got excited or something." And now I knew why Gilli's employee was looking at me weird, afraid to get close. I probably should've offered to escort Zab over there, but I couldn't walk it back now. The girl would have to get over it.

By the time I got back, Gilli and Hawk were no longer in the back room but everyone else was hanging around, having tea and basically sharing their nerves with each other. Oscar had gotten back and Bibbi was there too, petting something on her lap, which could only be Dusty, unless she'd developed a weird nervous tic.

"Where's Gilli? Is she okay?" I asked.

"Hawk put her in a room upstairs," Zab said, looking at the cocoa in my hand.

"She was rattled enough. I didn't even want her to give me this one. I couldn't very well ask her for another." She probably would've given me ten to get rid of me. The only reason the employee had made it was that she'd been looking for an excuse to keep her distance.

"Aren't you going to share?" Bibbi asked, as if she'd missed out as well.

"Sure. I guess. Who wants some?"

"Me," said everyone. I managed not to groan as my cocoa, the only bright spot of the evening, was decimated.

"What room is she in?" I asked.

"In his wing somewhere, I suppose," Bibbi said, in a slightly less cheerful way than normal. That was understandable, considering what Gilli had just gone through.

She was ripped up and attacked. Only a sicko would want to trade places with her, so what did that make me? Obviously a sicko.

I glanced down at the small drop of cocoa I had. This night was not going well.

13

"Did anyone see Gil yet?" Zab asked as I made my way into the back room for breakfast.

"I didn't," Bibbi answered, chewing on a pastry, the likes of which I'd never seen before.

When strange food started appearing, it meant only one thing: Bertha was on edge. Musso had admitted recently that as much as he hated when his wife was upset, there were a few perks to it. Looking at the spread on the table, he might be right. It looked like a wedding brunch spread.

"No, but I'm sure they'll be down soon." Bertha stopped moving for all of two seconds before turning to reach for another bowl. "We need more biscuits."

"Great idea, Bertha. Couldn't agree more." Oscar grabbed two more off a towering heap.

I followed Bertha over to the side, where she was cracking black eggs into a bowl. "Bertha, are you okay? I didn't know you were so close to Gilli."

She put the bowl down and began wringing her hands. "I'm not. I have to tell you something horrible. I used to get annoyed with her and her chocolate, always carrying on about how hers was the best and no one could make chocolate or fudge like her." She looked about the room, making sure no one was listening before she leaned in closer. "Sometimes I wished she wouldn't be able to make chocolate for a while just so she'd shut up."

"You didn't do this to her, though, and you have nothing to do with the grouslies."

"I don't know. Thoughts can be a tricky thing. You don't know how they might manifest. The least I can do is give her the best breakfast when she gets up, just in case my thoughts somehow contributed to this. It will make me feel better."

"Getting annoyed with her and grouslies attacking her are very different, but I understand. And I'm sure she's fine."

She nodded as Hawk walked in, Gilli cocooned in his arms, her one arm wrapped around his neck. Her fingers were getting very familiar with his shoulder, rubbing back and forth, as if she were petting him. Her cheeks were a healthy, glowing pink. Her smile nearly split her face in half as he carried her to the couch.

Bibbi came and stood beside me, nudging me with her boot. When I glanced her way, she wasn't looking at me but at Gilli's hand on Hawk's shoulder.

Bibbi had a point. Did Gilli really need to be carried?

Don't be petty. She'd been attacked, and even though I was able to get past the stiffness in a day without too much trouble, everyone was different. She might be struggling. He couldn't very well let her crawl downstairs.

Well...

No. He couldn't.

But...

No.

Bibbi kicked me again, as if once wasn't enough for the spectacle before us. She stood without a glance my way and a smile plastered on her face as she walked over and said, "Gilli, how are you feeling? Can I get you tea or cocoa? It won't be as good as yours, of course, but maybe you'd like something?"

Gilli glanced up from where she was sitting on the couch, the look on her face slightly off. "I prefer Gillian, if you don't mind? And a tea would be wonderful." She searched the area. "Is that okay, Hawk? Can I have tea?"

Hawk was already halfway across the room. "What?"

"Is it okay for me to have some tea?" Gillian asked, clutching the throw around her.

"Yeah, that's fine. You can eat and drink whatever you want," he said, before walking out.

"Then a tea, please, Bibbi."

"Here, I made you a nice plate of everything you might want." Bertha dragged a small table over in front of Gillian and piled up plates. Oscar managed to get a biscuit before everything was rearranged, but just barely.

"Thanks. This looks wonderful," Gillian said, as she lifted her hands so that Bertha could put a napkin on her lap.

It should. Bertha had made a smorgasbord like I'd never seen, and that meant a lot when you were talking about Bertha and cooking.

Gillian was already eating when I made my way over and sat on the other end of the couch. "I talked to your employee Verrey last night. She said she'd work the schedule out and they'd handle the shop for you for a few days."

"Oh, that's wonderful. Especially since after I get on

my feet I might need a day or two to get my stuff over here. Although I'm sure Hawk will help me and have his employees pitch in as well."

There were too many things wrong with that to swallow all at once. Over here? What was she talking about? There were too many people here already. And his employees would move her? I sat silently, afraid to speak until my thoughts were under control.

Gillian nibbled at a scone-like pastry. "Bertha, this is amazing. But you know what would really hit the spot? If we added some of my chocolate chips to it. What do you think?"

"Yes. I'm sure that would be good." Bertha looked like she could use a minute to sit silently beside me and get her words organized. She was white-knuckling the kitchen towel.

"Here's your tea," Bibbi said, and then squeezed onto the couch beside me. "So does that mean you're moving in?"

"Hawk insisted. Said we all needed to stick together during these times." Gillian took a sip of tea and then made a face.

"Is there a problem?" Bibbi asked.

"No, not at all. This will do." Gillian put the tea down, not drinking anymore.

I glanced around the room, but Hawk had already gone to the office. What was he thinking, moving her in?

She finished the scone that would've been better with her chocolate and moved on to some strips of meat. She picked up her tea and then held the cup out. "Bibbi, would you mind adding a touch more sugar? It's so hard for me to walk, and I'm used to tea that's not quite so bitter."

"Of course not." Bibbi's smile was near scary, not that Gillian seemed to notice.

Gillian focused on me next. "Tippi, would you mind checking over at my shop while I'm recuperating and seeing if they need anything?"

"Of course not." I would've paid for an excuse to get out of there. While I was at it, I'd get a cocoa too. Although I'd keep that to myself. Bertha already appeared to be beating her dough to death instead of gently kneading it.

"I'll help you," Bibbi said, splashing tea on Gillian as she hurried to my side.

We got out of the building before her yelling stopped.

Bibbi walked so close that she nearly ran me over. "She's trying to move in on our man. This is not happening."

"He's not technically our man." He wasn't Gillian's, either. She could pet his shoulder all day long and it wouldn't make it so. I didn't think. Either way, Bibbi didn't need to hear those thoughts. She was already at a ten on the riled-up scale.

"Yes, he is. He's yours first because he likes you better, and that's fine. I've accepted that. You were here first. But if that doesn't work out, I get him next. *That* one is not allowed to stroll in and jump the line." Her hands were balled into fists.

"Don't get worked up. You don't know that she wants him." Wow, how far I'd come in the lying department. That lie had flowed over my lips like water down a river.

"Did you see her face as he carried her to the couch? The way she asked, 'Hawk, is tea okay?'" she said in a mock falsetto. "She wants him, all right, and he's not hers to take. He's ours."

I took a step to the side before I got plastered into a nearby building as she raged. The denial route was not calming her down.

"Fine. But let's see what happens. I get the feeling that she isn't Hawk's type." It was the only thing safe to say, since sweet Bibbi was near growling and about to foam at the mouth like a Rottweiler defending its territory.

I didn't particularly like where Gilli's mind was going either, but I didn't own Hawk. We'd had a handful of kisses and more than twice that in fights. If you counted up both, the tally put him closer to enemy than ownership.

Plus, it was true what I'd said. He wasn't going to be interested in her. Gillian was a cute girl and all, with her big brown eyes and brown ringlets, but personality? Never. Even Belinda, for all her faults, had been made of tougher stuff than the *take care of me, I'm injured* Gillian. How could he possibly be attracted to her?

"Don't worry. He's not going to pay her attention. It's not going to be a problem. She'll get bored and go back home," I said as we got to the Sweet Shop.

"I hope so, because she's already irritating me. I don't know how long I'll last."

I held the door open for her. "You know, maybe we should get you a double today?"

"Good idea."

14

The front door blew open with a gust of wind. A stream of dark smoke twirled its way toward me until it formed glowing embers that hovered in the air, before turning into ash that piled up onto my desk. Everyone in the office watched as the ashes seemed to plump up and then bind themselves into a burned piece of paper that slowly turned cream.

There was only one person, or creature, this could be from. I leaned forward, reading the note without touching it.

I'll pick you up at the square tonight for our meeting.

Xazier

That was it. No "will you come?" or "does this time work for you?" Another man in my life who thought he could dictate to me. They were like a bag of chips. I couldn't stop plucking them out, and damned if I didn't feel salty about it. Unfortunately, this man was from hell, and he could dictate to me for the simple reason that his origin scared the living hell out of me and damned anyone who judged. If that didn't terrify a person, it would mean they'd lost all their marbles.

I grabbed a pencil, stabbing the note. It went up in a puff of smoke before it made it to the wastebasket.

"Well?" Zab asked. "Are you going to share, or are we going to have to beg for information?"

Musso's fuzzy brows rose.

"You gotta tell us. What did it say? The suspense is killing me." Bibbi leaned forward, wrapping her hands around the front edge of her table.

This discussion was as desirable as having my nails pulled out during a torture session, which might be on the table.

"It's Xazier. I have to meet with him tonight."

"What are you going to do? Are you going to go?" Zab asked.

"I have to go. Nothing else to do. I need to buy us time."

"Wow, you're really going to go," Bibbi said, sinking back into her chair.

"She'll be fine. She's tough. She can handle this," Musso added.

Dusty jumped onto my lap, making little whimpering noises.

Zab got out of his chair and reached for newsflash papers. "We should probably call—"

"We should call no one. This was my agreement, and there's nothing Hawk can do about it. I know. You don't like it. She doesn't like it," I said, pointing in Bibbi's direction. I looked at Musso. "I'm sure you didn't like it either."

He grunted.

"But it's done, and I'm going to uphold my end and buy us time. Now I'm going to go get ready before dinner, since I have no clients anyway."

All leather, the better for fighting? Or something a little softer so I didn't appear to be picking a fight? Maybe something in between? I settled on leather pants, along with boots that had a good grip and a hard sole, and a fuzzy sweater that clung to all the right spots.

Everyone was eating dinner when I went downstairs, but no one was talking. The room grew quiet as I took a seat. There wasn't any blame. It was hard to start a conversation that didn't involve the only thing we were all thinking: I had an evening engagement with a demon.

No matter how many times I said that in my head, it never lost its bite.

Hawk wasn't back, which wasn't altogether unusual. No one really knew what he did most of the day. Considering some of the secrets I did know, that might've been for the best. Plus, I didn't need anyone adding to my own chorus of doubts.

I took a scoop of stew and filled my bowl. I wasn't particularly hungry but ate like it was my last meal, just for the sake of it. If the leather pants and boots ended up being more appropriate for tonight, I'd need the sustenance.

"Cute outfit," Bibbi said in between bites of stew. "I don't remember seeing that sweater before."

She hadn't. It had been an impulse buy, a little too fuzzy and a little too deep a neckline for what I typically wore.

"If he's a warm-blooded—something or other—it should keep his attention," she said, as she dipped a roll into the broth.

"Can't hurt, I figure."

"You're not trying to date him, are you?" Gillian asked from across the table, looking like she'd been fed poison. "I mean, I heard you didn't get many dates, but don't you think this is a little bit much?"

"Of course she isn't," Bibbi snapped.

They continued to bicker as Oscar walked to the door and nodded for me to follow him. He was leaning on my desk when I joined him.

"You sure you know what you're doing?" He scanned my outfit with a look that was more like fatherly concern than the roguish looks he gave me when Hawk was about.

I walked over and leaned on the desk beside him. "Of course I don't. I barely know what I'm doing on a good day, but I'm going to figure this out the way I muddled my way through everything else."

"Stakes are pretty high."

"They weren't when I was hanging on to a giant bat's back?"

He half laughed, but he was still too somber for my liking. Or maybe it was the dimly lit room that was making things seem so bleak. I'd pretty much lay the blame on anything but what I'd gotten myself into at this point.

"As frightening as this sounds, yes, I think they were. We were there when you were on that bat, and whether or not you knew it, we would've stepped in if things turned.

This? Going off with him alone? I'm not comfortable with this. I don't know what this demon wants from you, but this isn't just about Xest."

"This is the first meeting. He's not going to cross the line that fast."

"I'm not sure why you're so confident, but I hope you're right."

"So do I." I straightened and grabbed my coat off the hook.

Hawk still wasn't here. Why I thought he'd somehow know and show up was beyond me. He wasn't psychic. Why it felt so weird to leave here and do this without a glance in his direction, a knowing look, something, was beyond me. I'd insisted Zab not tell him, and the guy might've actually listened for a change, as weird as that felt.

"Well, I'm going to head out," I said. "Don't want to be late, after all."

Oscar straightened. "Let me walk you over?" He moved to grab his jacket, but I waved him off.

"No. Arriving with backup isn't the look I'm going for. I've got this."

"You sure?"

"Positive." Not even close to confident. Closer to the realm of wishful thinking.

Oscar nodded, but his body seemed to be struggling not to follow me anyway. I hurried out the door to make it easier for him to stay behind.

I flipped up my collar and shoved my hands in my pockets, looking both ways before I got too far away from the safety of the building. Mertie's words from the other day still lingered in my psyche as I waited for a horde of delusional witches and warlocks to chase me down.

I sped up but then forced myself to slow down. There was no way I'd allow a crazy horde of witches to chase me off the streets of Xest. I'd spent too much time fighting for the right to be here.

I turned the corner, and Hawk stepped out in front of me. I stopped just shy of colliding with him.

"You don't have to go."

Of course he knew I was on my way. Had to have been Oscar. Or Zab. Zab would've ratted me out to Hawk if he thought it was the right thing. Musso might've given Hawk a heads-up. Bertha definitely would've. Bibbi might've been trying to protect me. There were too many options. It was impossible to figure out who it might have come from. It was like searching for a water leak in a colander.

"Yeah, except I kind of do," I said, walking again. I had enough jitters without having a second helping of the don't-do-this speech.

He grabbed my arm, forcing me to stop beside him.

I glanced at his hand and then met his gaze, making my feelings of being detained clear.

He didn't budge.

"I'm telling you if you don't want to go, you don't have to. We can ride out the consequences."

He dropped his hand, having said what he needed to say.

I should've walked away. Xazier would be waiting, but I was sort of stuck in place.

Hawk did have his upside. Problem was you were sometimes dragged up to that peak bound and gagged, whether you wanted to be or not.

I bit my lip, knowing I had to get going and having a hard time walking away. It was probably my destination. It had to be. It wasn't Hawk.

I forced myself to take a step before I stopped again.

"I'm not concerned about tonight. He's not going to do anything, at least not during this first meeting." As I said it, I believed it in my gut. It was too early in the game for Xazier to show his full hand.

Hawk reached into his pocket, grabbed my hand, and placed a small ball in it. "If you get into trouble, wrap your hand around this and call my name. I'll be able to find you wherever you are." His hand stayed wrapped around mine for a moment longer than needed.

"You think I'm not capable of handling this?"

"The things I think you're capable of would astound you."

I felt like my brain was melting, along with everything else inside of me.

"I've got to go. I've got a meeting." I spun, walking away before I did something crazy, like kiss him. I walked the rest of the way alone, refusing to check on Hawk's location even as I could feel his eyes still on me.

Xazier appeared the moment I reached the square. He held out his arm. "Are you ready?"

I smiled, reminding myself how I'd told everyone else this wouldn't be a problem. I believed that. I did. I definitely did.

"Where are we going?" I laid my hand on his arm, knowing it was that or make a scene. The strange feeling that Hawk was still watching wouldn't let me do that, no matter how panicked I was.

"Somewhere warmer. I detest the cold."

A second later, the sun was bright and the air was warm. We were no longer on the cold streets of Xest but standing on a terrace in the sun, overlooking the sea with a smattering of blue and white buildings scattered along the shoreline.

"Are we in..." I lost my words as I took in the human man, or human-looking man beside me. Gone was the red skin and horns, replaced by golden hair and blue eyes. His jacket and suit had been swapped out for a short-sleeved button-down and linen pants.

"We're in Greece. I keep a place here, among others. As for the other changes, it goes over easier with the human servants. May I?" He raised his hands to help me out of my jacket.

I turned, shrugging out of it but not before I palmed the stone from Hawk. Luckily I had, because Xazier didn't just help me with my jacket but my entire outfit. I was in a flouncy little white sundress that wasn't shy on the cleavage.

"Hope you don't mind, but I figured it would be more comfortable."

"It's perfect. Thank you."

I wouldn't have worn this in a million years. For all its cleavage, it had eyelets and a gathered hem. It was romantic and pure looking and everything I hadn't been since I was five, watching my mother get dragged away to the asylum the first time. I won't even get started on the strappy heels that wouldn't be worth the thread that held them on my feet if a fight broke out.

We took a seat at a bistro set that was on the terrace, overlooking the coast.

"Wine?" He raised his hand, summoning someone over before I could answer. "The new Cabernet that just came in."

As soon as the servant left, I said, "Are they human?"

"Yes. Demons make horrible servants. They really

aren't built to please. Whereas these humans can be controlled and paid off. Plus, if they complained, who would listen?"

"They don't get alarmed when you just appear?" I asked.

"They had some notice I'd be arriving with company. As far as my mode of arrival, it's not their business to ask questions or care either way." He spoke like someone who was above the law, the human race, all of it. As if nothing could touch him, and it probably couldn't.

The servant returned with a bottle and glasses that he filled.

"Try it. It's lovely. Won this at an auction last month." Xazier smiled, raising his glass to me.

I clinked glasses and took a sip for the same reason I pretended to like the dress. There weren't many other options right now.

"I'm not that familiar with wine, but it tastes wonderful," I said.

"Trust me, it is. Would you care for a snack or light meal?"

"No, I already ate. I wasn't sure where this meeting would take place. I didn't know if we'd have to go to your... place of business." This had never entered my imagination, not once. There had been days in Xest I'd missed the warmth of summer. Now the only thing I missed was the cold of Xest and the heat of the fireplace in the back room.

He threw back his head and laughed. "I certainly wouldn't bring you there. Oh no, not there. Right now, you're still an unknown to my colleagues. I think I'd like to keep it that way, until I get to know you a bit better myself." He continued to watch me, leaning forward and resting an arm on the table in between us. "There's something about you I find intriguing, and I can't quite put my finger on what it is. You present yourself like a common witch, but I'm not so sure you are what you appear."

"I am just a common witch. I have no delusions of grandeur. I couldn't even work a spell that well until a couple of months ago." How was it that my freak flag waved so brightly? Was it my hair? Was it something I did? How was I triggering people's radar? I need to figure it out and then shut that signal down.

"Maybe that's because you weren't meant to work a spell? No, I'm never wrong, and I can sense there's something different about you. I'm going to figure it out, too."

"Well, if you figure it out, you should share it with me." I took a big swig of wine then put my glass down before I repeated the mistake. Drinking myself out of this conversation wasn't a good plan considering my tolerance, or lack of. "A friend of yours, Lou, visited. Wanted me to tell you he was aware of the situation."

He leaned back, swirling his wine in his glass. "I figured he might come by. That's all right. He tends to be nosey that way."

He was staring at me over his glass, the same way he'd stared at me in the office the day we met. His human appearance didn't make it any more comfortable than the first time.

"So as to Xest, there's not much to tell you about at the moment. I appreciate the drink, but I don't want to take up too much of our time." I got up from my chair, hoping he'd follow suit.

He remained seated. "I thought maybe we could spend time getting to know each other a little better."

I nodded and then took a seat again.

"I heard about the immigration trials. Why don't you

tell me about those in your own words? Or what it was like when you first got to Xest? Your childhood in Salem. I want to hear everything."

We stood in front of the broker office several hours later, and I wanted nothing more than to collapse into bed. A marathon would've been easier than the mental chess I'd played, trying to dodge any answers or details that might come back to bite me. Not exactly a piece of cake, since I had no clue what to avoid. The questions had been nonstop until I'd begged exhaustion from the time difference. That hadn't been a lie.

"It was a lovely evening. I will see you very soon," Xazier said as we stood outside, looking into the darkness of the office.

I didn't completely relax until he disappeared.

I walked in, let the door shut, and then leaned against it, a long, slow sigh flowing out, carrying all the tension of the evening with it. The first meeting was over. In retrospect, it hadn't been that bad. It had gone more along the lines of a blind date than a meeting with a demon. It had been manageable, if a bit unpleasant.

I pushed off the door, making my way across the office. A shadowy figure sat at my desk. I would've been more surprised if Hawk hadn't been waiting.

"How did it go?" he asked, standing up and walking in my direction, his gaze taking in my bare legs. The only piece of clothing Xazier had returned to me was my jacket.

"Not horrible. Lots of useless questions about my childhood, but nothing meaningful."

His gaze continued running the length of me until it settled on my lips.

He didn't stop until he was a few inches from me.

"No information you give him is useless. Remember that. He'll store it all away for a purpose." His stare deepened. "I can smell him on you. Did he touch you?"

"He helped me with my jacket."

He nodded.

The office was dark, shadowing his expression, but I didn't need to see his face to feel the weight of his unhappiness.

"You're going to meet him again if he calls."

It wasn't a question, but I nodded anyway.

He turned to walk past me and then paused, his shoulder nearly brushing mine. He looked at me one last time before walking away.

15

I was on my third cocoa of the day, all from the Sweet Shop. I'd rather go down the street and pretend to check in than into the back room, where Gillian had set up a court on the couch. If you walked back there, you better be ready to pay homage. I'd seen Zab, Musso, Oscar, and Bibbi already make that mistake. Bertha had walked out mumbling curses minutes ago before she went upstairs, slamming the door behind her.

"I told her it wasn't a good idea to stay back there today, but she kept insisting," Musso said, shrugging his massive shoulders and raising puffy brows.

Bibbi looked over at me, shaking her head slowly, as if this matter needed to be handled. From the looks she gave, she thought I should be the one handling it. If someone didn't do something, Gilli might end up poisoned soon.

Hawk walked in, breaking Bibbi's gaze of death.

Instead of ignoring me, the way we'd silently decided to do most days since the latest fight, he walked over to me with a piece of yellow parchment in his hands.

"This was nailed to the door. We have a meeting at dusk." He dropped the parchment on the desk in front of me, the paper and form all too familiar. Immigration.

I skimmed the notice, which was short and to the point. I had a meeting. Not him.

As soon as Hawk walked out of the room, Bibbi and Zab both walked over, scanning the parchment together.

Bibbi sat on the corner of my desk. "Why do you want to meet immigration again? They don't like you much. Are you sure that's a good idea?"

I tapped a finger on the parchment, remembering exactly how much they did hate me. Maybe it wasn't the worst idea to have Hawk along. It wasn't like the meeting with Xazier, which had an altogether different vibe. With immigration, all the hate, distrust, and revulsion was out on the table.

"They might know something about my origins, and my origins might have something to do with Dread."

"That makes sense." Bibbi nodded, staring at my cocoa with a strange intensity while she drank her tea.

"Did you want me to go get you a cocoa?" I asked, then sipped my drink under the evil eye of Bibbi.

"No. I'm fine."

"What's the deal with the cocoa?" Zab asked.

"I don't think it tastes very good lately," Bibbi said, her tone suddenly snooty and her face matching.

"Really?" Zab nearly gave himself whiplash, he swung his head so fast toward Bibbi.

Musso laughed but then caught himself, looking at his papers and muttering, "Read something funny."

"Yes, it's bad cocoa," Bibbi said. "I'd rather have tea." She walked toward the back room. She paused at the threshold. Her shoulders rose with a deep inhale, and then she continued.

"Zab, did you bring your cauldron when you moved here?" I asked.

He squinted, looking toward the ceiling. "I think so. It might be in one of my boxes."

"Good. I need to borrow it."

I took a couple more steps toward where I thought their cottage would appear and then retreated again. It was a good twenty minutes past nightfall and still no sign. Every minute they took, the more my hackles rose. They'd been working against me since I'd met them. Thinking they could be bartered with might have been the stupidest move yet. It was one of the only moves we had, though. I had to trace back my origins to get to Dread, and this was the single best way, whether I liked it or not.

"They'll show. They wouldn't have bothered to reply if they weren't," Hawk said from beside me, in the same spot he'd been since we got here.

"What if it's a trap?"

"I don't think so. They want a steady supply of what's in your hand," he said, looking at the bottle I carried.

My attention was drawn away from where I thought the hags would show. "How did you know I'd even bring some?" I asked.

"I know what was in your letter." He smiled.

Damn mailman. Must be nice to have those kinds of connections. Maybe I should do some mailing and bring a net next time.

I was still staring at him when he said, "One of them is approaching."

I spun around. Where was the cottage? Where were the other two? Why was there a lone figure approaching in the distance?

The Lead Hag neared as a lone figure. She hadn't exactly been a favorite, but it was probably a tossup. None of them had liked me.

"Well, this is interesting. I think someone might be getting greedy," Hawk said, glancing at my hand and the bottle I held.

She walked slowly toward us, taking her time, her eyes fixated on the bottle.

"Is that it? Let me taste it," she said, looking nowhere else. She clenched her hands, as if she was struggling to not wrest the bottle from my hands.

"No," I said. "You've already gotten a taste of my potions, as your face can attest. This is going to go my way. You give the information. Then you get it."

Hawk let out a quick laugh. He might've approved of my handling, but Lead Hag wasn't thrilled. Her eyes turned to slits as her mouth flattened. She could stare me down all day. I was already a citizen of Xest and there was nothing she could do about that. She was done calling the shots. Although I should probably check into that matter before I pushed too hard.

"Do you have information for me?" I asked.

It took another few seconds for her to answer, and it was clear she was not used to taking orders. She glanced at Hawk, as if she'd rather deal with him.

"She's asking you a question," he said.

When he was good, he was really good. It was unfortunate that those times were so few and far between.

Lead Hag looked at me, her chest rising and falling a few times before she said, "She was on our rolls. She was a citizen here, born and bred until she was twenty-two or so. Occupation was listed as a Whimsy witch over at the wish factory."

"Is there anything else you can tell me? Any information on my father?"

"No and no. Now give me the potion." She shot a hand out, and I held the potion up and out of her grasp.

"Was I born here? Was I on the rolls at any point?" I asked.

"No. She disappeared and that was it. If you'd been born here, we wouldn't have been able to give you an immigration test. You would've been a born citizen."

She spat out that last bit as if I'd proven myself the idiot she thought I was. How was I supposed to have known? It wasn't like they had law books floating around. Actually, I should probably have checked into that. Maybe they did.

"I gave you your answers. Now give me the potion." She moved closer.

Hawk stepped in front of me. "I have a question first. Do you know anything about Dread?"

The anger faded from her expression as she glanced about. "No, but I wish I did," she said softly.

For once, it seemed we might be on the same side.

"Here. You can have it." I held out the potion. It seemed fair. "If you have any further information, I can supply more."

She gripped the potion in her hands tighter. "And I'll get it whenever I want?"

I nodded. "As long as you're offering me some information of value, so I'd hurry if I were you."

She hated me, but she'd be back if she found something else. That I was sure of.

She left, and I had more questions than before. Nothing was adding up.

I turned and headed back toward the shop with nothing but questions and a man I didn't want to ask anything of.

"You're going to eventually ask, so you might as well do it now," Hawk said.

For the record, he was ignoring me as well. I might have started it if you wanted to get technical about it, but he didn't deserve conversation. He was an active participant in the silence, and that counted for something.

He was also correct. I was going to break down and ask him anyway. It made it all so much worse to have to prove him right, but I'd dwell on that later.

"I thought that magic was typically inherited, like it was somewhat genetic and you fell in line with your parents to some degree. How would it be possible for a Whimsy witch to give birth to..." To what? A magical freak of nature? The only witch in Xest that Dread was afraid of? "How did she give birth to me?"

"You mean to a Maker? There's no reason to pretend you're anything less, and you might be more," Hawk said, watching me with those intense eyes that were impossible to hide from.

Maker. There it was. I'd learned enough to have suspected it was the case. I'd feared it was the truth. I wouldn't even think about the "more."

Why did that label scare me more than Whimsy had? I'd been so comfortable being seen as less than. Now that I was on the top of the magical heap, I couldn't get the word out, hated that he'd said it, as if speaking it made it true. It felt like a line of demarcation, that there'd be no going back from it.

I shouldn't have asked him. When would I ever learn?

"Why does that bother you so much?" he asked. "Why is being important and worthy so terrifying to you?"

"Am I supposed to pay you by the minute or by session?" I asked, and then turned and walked away, in case he somehow mistook that for an actual question.

"Getting a little testy. Must've struck a nerve."

"I'll strike a jaw if you don't shut up."

He laughed. "Message delivered. You aren't ready to delve into your inner demons quite yet."

"You care to share your demons? Like why I've never seen you hold the gem? What are you hiding?"

"I'll tell if you do."

I nearly tripped, missing a bump in the walk as my head whipped around to him. That was a mighty tempting carrot to dangle. Of all the stories to have laid out before me, Hawk's was the one I'd pick. I'd start with asking about that strange creature that he shifted into, then the avoidance of the stone, and I had a feeling that was only the tip of the iceberg. The ninety percent out of sight was probably a binge-worthy story.

Did that mean I'd have to unfold my story for him? He might already know most of it. His sources were deep, but I wasn't handing over the rest, and Hawk wouldn't take a one-sided deal.

We were back at the office before I cracked.

He opened the door for me and said, "To your question, it's extremely rare for a Whimsy witch to give birth to a Maker."

I glanced inside but didn't move. I needed one last answer. "Rare or impossible?"

His gaze locked on mine. "Before you? I would've said impossible."

16

Mertie walked out of the building, lit up a cigarette with her finger, turned right, and headed down the street. I waited for her to get a bit farther away before I ducked out of my alley, hot on her...hooves? It was what it was.

She walked to the great grey tree with black leaves, ducking under its canopy.

I edged up slowly, making sure I wasn't followed.

"You shouldn't be following people in times like these. It's a good way to get yourself killed," she said, right before she took an impossibly long drag on her cigarette until there was nothing but a stub.

That wasn't a threat. That was just Mertie, pleasant to the core, a regular bundle of joy.

"I need to talk to you."

"I assumed, since I've never seen you sneaking after anyone else." She reached into her back pocket, pulled out another cigarette, and lit it. "Well? Spit it out. I'm almost off break."

"Do you have records of all the witches who've worked in the factory?"

"You certainly can't imagine Marvin handling it? He can barely tie his shoes in the morning. No, I do it all. I've got access to every record involved with everything in that place. I have all the headaches and yet haven't gotten a raise in a decade."

"Could you look up someone's records for me?"

She rolled her eyes. "I can look up anything imaginable."

"What's the price?"

She didn't respond right away, looking toward the factory and taking another drag of her cigarette. She finally looked back at me.

"Is this completely confidential?"

"Did you see me waving a flag outside the factory?" I asked, using the only language she understood: sarcasm.

"If I need to get out of there, you're going to help me. That's my price."

"You want to leave Xest?" It was one thing to get a witch a job with Lorinda. There was no way I could pass off Mertie in Rest.

"Rest? I wouldn't set foot in that place. I mean out of the factory. I need somewhere else to go, and I don't have any friends. You people keep taking in everyone anyway. What's one more?"

"Why would you want to come to the broker building? Don't you realize what's going on? What's coming for us?"

"Yes, but I want to have options. Is it a deal or not?"

"Yeah, I mean, I guess." Hawk was going to kill me. Although he'd gotten us stuck with Gillian, so who was he to talk? Bibbi and Zab, they'd definitely kill me. Didn't matter. What were the odds she'd even come? Like she'd said, she just wanted options.

Even if she did come, would she last more than a day?

She'd hate it there. We laughed. We were pleasant. She'd be running back to the factory.

"Who's the witch you're looking for?"

I handed her a slip of paper with the name Jossi Tudor written on it. "I'm not sure if that's accurate, so if you could look up different last or first names…"

"You don't make anything easy, do you?" She took the slip and pocketed it, then looked down her nose at me. "Was there something else, or did you want to eat up my entire break?"

I turned and left. She could not move into the broker building or I'd be the most hated witch in my home.

I was halfway home when I stopped short.

Xazier popped up in front of me. "I'm sorry. Didn't mean to startle you."

"No, it's fine. I just wasn't expecting you—or I guess anyone, really—to pop up like that." I made my way around him, hoping it was an unfortunate coincidence.

"Mind if I walk with you for a spell?"

"Knock yourself out." Not the most diplomatic invite, but then again, I wasn't exactly feeling polite at the moment. First Mertie and now him. It was as if my night were cursed.

Xazier narrowed his eyes slightly, giving me the impression he wasn't pleased with my flippant reply, but he quickly regrouped and fell into step with me.

"I wanted to tell you I had a nice time getting to know you better the other day. It's clear you've had some hardships in your life and that they've molded you a certain way." He had a pleasantly condescending smile as he spoke.

This was starting off as wonderful as I'd imagined.

"It's remarkable how you've overcome everything you

have," he said. "And then when you got here, to have everyone try to push you out but to still stick to your guns in the face of all those who didn't want you, even allies. I did hear that right, didn't I? That Hawk had a hand in trying to force you out?"

He kept staring, waiting for me to acknowledge his question.

I could be naive, stubborn, and a long list of other faults, but Xazier's game was painfully obvious. He was trying to weaken me, poking around for my soft spot. It wouldn't work.

"We've come a long way since then. I don't hold that against him." A couple more minutes and I'd be at the broker building. Once a week was already too much time to spend with Xazier.

"Good for you. I'm not so sure I'd get over it as well, you know, having an ally publicly turn their back on you."

"You heard wrong. We weren't allies at the time it happened." He was laying out bait, but I was long past the days of being easy prey.

"Really? Because word is you were extremely close allies."

"We just had a parting of ways. Nothing that dramatic."

"Well, it's good to be so easygoing. I have colleagues that would rake me over the coals if I were so easy, and I mean that *literally*."

He said the word "easy" the way I used the word "schmuck." There wasn't a damned thing I was going to say to stop him, because you didn't pick a fight with a top demon for the underworld. Certain things I might need explained, or written out in a book of rules and regulations. This one was pure instinct, the way you knew by age five that you didn't stick your hand in a fire.

"I guess that's just me. Easygoing." I kept my tone light, ignoring the insults.

"Word is he gave your job away in a matter of days, stopped you from getting employment anywhere. He should realize that it's a miracle you speak to him at all. It stumps me why he thinks he could treat you that way, as if you're worthless and so easily replaced."

"Sounds like you've really gotten an earful lately. I guess people do like to gossip when they don't have anything else to do." My pulse was ratcheting up in spite of my effort to stay calm. It didn't help matters that he was using the truth against me. All of those things *did* happen.

"Oh, most definitely, and especially about situations like yours. They all get high and mighty about how they never would've tolerated what you did. Then again, they don't know your situation, right? Only you know the truth of the matter and why you decided to stay."

He pulled his jacket tighter and shuddered, as if the cold were getting to him. I believed it about as well as I believed that he didn't know how badly he was insulting me.

"Well, I'll be off. I look forward to our next chat."

I smiled as he left. I kept the smile partially in place as I continued on, not sure if he was watching, waiting for me to kick a stray cat or something.

He'd had one purpose tonight, to worm his way under my skin. He'd accomplished it. To the rest of Xest, I probably looked like the schmuck he'd called me, but they didn't know all the ins and outs, like the way working with Hawk had been the best thing at that moment. And I was working *with* him. I was not an employee, no matter how it appeared. I hadn't just rolled over. I'd put up a fight and demanded certain things.

When Hawk had locked me into a contract with no way out, I didn't speak to him—for the most part, unless it was really important.

I walked into the building, trying to not slam the door.

"Why do you look mad?" Zab asked.

"I'm fine." And the lies just kept coming.

I headed straight for my room before I screamed.

17

Bibbi looked up from her breakfast, her eyes big and round.

"I like your outfit," she said, eyeing up my new leggings and boots. Xazier had never returned my last pair of boots and left me with an unusable pair of sandals. "Did you get them at Bewitching?"

"Thanks. I did. You should go there." She was staring at my clothes with that longing look that made me want to go change. I wasn't used to being on the other side of this kind of reaction. I was the giver of those looks. I'd never been the one with an enviable wardrobe.

"They don't like my kind in that store," Bibbi said, going back to her breakfast.

"What do you mean?"

There was something definitely wrong about that statement. Zab and Musso kept going about their business, as if this were commonplace.

"The owners of the nicer places don't like Whimsys. It's too high-end for us."

"Why don't we go shopping?" I didn't wait for Bibbi to

agree before I looked at Musso and Zab. "You can handle things without us, right?"

"You mean the two people that might come in? Yeah. I think we can manage," Musso said, in his gruff way.

"You two go. We'll hold back the horde," Zab said, laughing.

"Bibbi, get your jacket." I could've told her to drop and give me twenty in the same tone.

"I almost want to go shopping with you. Not quite, but close," Zab said, laughing some more.

I waited at the door, watching Bibbi move around the room, grabbing her jacket in slow motion as if trying to figure out a way around going with me.

"You know, I'm not sure today is a good day. I've got an awful big stack of—"

"We're going."

The pretext of cooperation died and the jacket in her hand drooped.

"What if I don't want to?" She glanced around the room, weighing possible support if she tried to avoid me.

Zab and Musso were feigning interest in their paperwork. Good move on their part, because I was dragging her with me if she put up a fight. Bibbi was too high up on my list of people I cared for, and my tolerance for the caste system in Xest was zilch. I'd fix this place single-handedly if that was what it took. And this was something I *could* fix, at least in this one instance.

"You're going if I have to drag you there."

Bibbi shot me a dirty look but put on her jacket. Even a block away, she kept looking back over her shoulder, toward the office.

"I had your job and know it pays well," I said. "Maybe the Whimsy witches at the factory can't afford this place, but you can, and we are going to shop there. And if you don't want to spend the coin, I'll do it, but no one is telling you that you can't."

"That's not the only problem," she said, looking back again. "I don't like leaving Gillian alone without someone supervising what she's up to. Why do you think I keep going in for teas, even though she's in that back room? Someone has to try to keep her on the straight and narrow, even if you've given up the ship to her."

"That's your problem?"

"Mostly, yes. I hate leaving her alone there. She's sneaky. But if you're that set on me going broke on clothes, who am I to say no? It's not like I don't want to get away from her for a little while."

We stopped in front of the store.

"What happens if they say I can't?" she asked.

"They won't. People are a little afraid of me. And if they aren't scared of me, they're terrified of Hawk, and they'll expect him to show up next." I smiled. Being scary wasn't always a bad thing.

"Yeah, that's true. He always has your back."

The way she said it, you would've thought it was an absolute truth, like it had been etched in stone and written in the stars. Too bad that wasn't true, like Xazier had pointed out last night.

The owner of Bewitching was smiling at me through the window, probably adding up the coin I'd spend in her head. Her gaze landed on Bibbi, and there was a curious look but nothing unfriendly.

I opened the door for Bibbi and motioned for her to go first. Bibbi lifted her chin and walked in.

The owner walked right over. "So nice to see you. What can I do for you today?"

"Not her. I'm the one shopping today," Bibbi said with some backbone to spare.

"Of course, what did you have in mind?"

She scanned the room like a kid in a candy store. "I'm not sure, but I think I want to try on *all of it*."

We stepped out of Bewitching, and Bibbi had a bounce in her step.

"Look how it moves," she said, her exaggerated movements making the hem of her jacket flare.

I nodded. "Very nice."

"Thank you. I think so too."

"That blush color is amazing on you."

She flipped her hair as I spotted a group behind her heading our way. No one approached me unless I knew them and they were on my side. At some point since the immigration stories had passed, or maybe the dragon incident—could've been the flashing colors in the alley; I didn't exactly know which story—but people had started crossing the street when I approached, the way they did for Hawk. This group looked angry, and they were heading right toward me.

"Bibbi, we've got problems."

"Yeah, I'd say so. No one is going to be able to stop looking at me in these new clothes. How will anyone be able to work? It's definitely a problem." She kept walking with an extra swing in her step.

I grabbed her arm, hurrying her along with me.

She looked where I'd clamped a hand on her, which was not a Xest thing to do. "Oh, you mean *real* problems."

I glanced over my shoulder again. Bibbi followed my lead.

"Oh. That is a problem."

Her pace finally picked up, but I didn't let go of her arm. This was going to be a battle for sure. How did I fight a group? One on one was a different issue than being surrounded, people coming at you from every angle. Yes, I'd killed more than one before, but it was an accident with a dome and a blast. I needed reinforcements. As much as I loved Bibbi, she wasn't going to cut it.

"Turn right up ahead there. After we turn, you run and get help."

"What? I'm not leaving you. That's crazy. There's ten of them." She glanced back again. "Nope. Make that fifteen."

I pulled her into the alley and grabbed her shoulders. "You have to. There is another group heading in the opposite direction. If you don't get help, I'm dead. If you stay, we're both dead."

She shook her head. "If I stay, you'll have a better chance of fighting them off. You've *got* this."

"There's too many. Bibbi, you have to go get help or we're both dead."

"I can't leave you."

"Bibbi, I love that you're willing to die with me. But *I* don't feel like dying today. They want me, and every second you delay is going to be worse for me. I don't have time to debate this with you."

The group converged at the end of the alley we'd just turned down, joining forces. My urgency went from concern to dead calm.

"They won't follow you. Go before they kill me."

Her eyes opened wide. "Okay."

She took off, and a weight lifted from my shoulders. Now at least the damage would be done to me alone. She'd been right: I would've had a better chance fighting them off with her, but what awaited me was a loss either way. It was either die fast or die slow. Now I needed to stall.

I spun, turning toward the group, listening to Bibbi's running the other way. A few sets of eyes shot to her, as if debating whether to let her go.

"What do you assholes want?" I said loudly, drawing every ounce of attention back to me, as I'd hoped. That was as far as I'd go to provoke them. I didn't recognize most of the faces. They might all be Whimsys, but there were too many.

Three of them took the lead, one man and two women, breaking off from the group to walk closer. The herd quickly closed the distance, not wanting to miss the show or the action.

A lanky guy, probably close to my age, said, "You shouldn't be here. You don't belong in Xest."

"I earned my place here. What have you done other than been shit out?" Probably not the best stall tactic, but no one was looking past me for Bibbi.

If he heard the insult, it didn't show. The boy didn't look quite in his right mind, so focused on me with rage brewing in his expression that could only be matched by one other. Dread felt like this about me. Mertie had warned me.

Dread was getting in their heads, using them against me. Did this kid even know what he was doing, or was he ruled by a rage embedded in him? Was that the case with all of them?

"You're a plague. Evil. An abomination, and we're going to make sure that you are destroyed."

They charged me. All I could think of was how to turn saving myself into saving them. And there were so many of them. Focus on him. Then another. One at a time.

With a leap, I took out the lanky boy with a kick to the head, then tumbled in the air and landed back on my feet. Not a bad start. I swung around to kick an oncoming woman in the chest.

Damn, I was doing pretty good.

They seemed to think so too, because they all came at me at once. I went to leap out of the way, but it was as if I were fighting a monster with unlimited hands. I was tugged down, and the mob devoured me. There was kicking and swinging, and I wrapped my hands around my head, hoping my magic would kick in. I couldn't think of a single rationale that I could use to twist the situation into me saving them.

I hit the ground as I was getting pummeled in every direction. My head took a blow. My ear took the toe of a boot. My stomach was kicked, only to be propelled backward. Bibbi had only had a minute or two lead, and we were on the other side of Xest. How long would it take for help? Would I make it? My vision was getting black spots and my ears were ringing.

A deafening roar filled the alley. A boot was about to hit my nose when it was yanked backward. Another body flew, and then there was the sound of screaming and footsteps retreating.

White paws filled my vision as Bautere knelt beside me. He leaned down, sniffing at my head and grazing it with his nose.

I unfurled my body slowly, each move causing pain. I coughed, some blood hitting the ground and causing a splatter of red on the white. I used my arm to wipe away the moisture from my face.

"I taught you better than this," he said, as if appalled I'd let a horde of deranged lunatics beat me.

"In my defense, I did really well with the first two. Thanks, though. Appreciate the help." I got to my feet and realized one leg wasn't working so well. I put a hand on the building to keep myself up, realizing every movement was going to cause pain somewhere.

"Where are they?" Hawk yelled, racing down the alley toward us, looking much scarier than Xazier ever had.

"They ran off, but I know their faces," Bautere said.

Hawk scooped me up in his arms, giving Bautere a nod. I didn't bother struggling, since I couldn't walk anyway.

"What were you thinking? Why did you send Bibbi away?" Hawk asked as he walked through the door he must've taken here.

"Because it wasn't her fight, and she wasn't going to be able to help anyway." Another person angry at me that I'd been beaten up, but I didn't care. All that mattered was that we wouldn't be walking around Xest for all to see me weak and vulnerable. I had a reputation to protect.

"She would've tried, and when they hurt her, your defensive magic would've kicked in." He kicked the door closed and we were in the upstairs hall of the broker building.

"Is she okay?" Bibbi yelled.

"You can tell everyone she's fine," Hawk said, before he opened the door to his room. After he crossed the threshold he edged the door closed with his shoulder, shutting everyone else out.

"So I'm supposed to keep her around to get beat up so I can protect myself?"

"She would've been fine. You would've made sure of

it." He dropped me onto his bed and went to the trunk he kept his potions in.

"I'm not using her like that." I took a break from arguing with Hawk to try to breathe past the pain in my chest. I shifted left, hunched over, and then tried a different position. Didn't seem to matter how I sat. The pain was still there. "You're not supposed to get angry at the person who was attacked."

He rifled through the trunk as if I hadn't spoken then walked back over with a couple bottles and rags. "Pull your shirt up so I can see your ribs."

I didn't argue, as every breath was another stab of agony. I couldn't be down and out for long. I needed to be in fighting shape, especially if this happened again. This wouldn't do at all.

I lifted my shirt up to just under my breasts, and his anger grew palpable.

"All this magic and what did you do? Curl into a ball like you're defenseless when you're not." For all his anger, he barely touched my skin as he coated it with smelly white lotion.

"I was protecting my head." At the time, it had seemed like the best move.

"You had the upper hand. You rolled over and let them hurt you when you didn't have to."

"I tried to protect myself because my magic doesn't work like that, and won't no matter how you wish it to be different."

"That's a bunch of bull. You can't protect yourself because you don't value yourself. That's the problem here. That's what we keep skating around and avoiding."

He had a lot of nerve lecturing me on self-worth.

Xazier's words, the ones that seemed to be stuck in my head, kept haunting me as he spoke.

"And you helped make me feel like I mattered? All you've ever done was try to push me out of Xest to a place I didn't belong. Don't act like you care." Our eyes locked, my anger boiling as hot as his now.

"That's right. It's my fault again. You just keep finding reasons to hoard and be angry about instead of facing the truth."

"Your truth."

He stood and walked a few steps away from me. I would've done it myself if I could've moved better, but crawling away wasn't the look I was going for.

A minute or so stretched out in silence before he said, "Let me check your—"

"I'm fine. I don't need anything else from you."

He walked closer anyway. "You're so stubborn it borders on stupidity."

"You're so pushy it borders on bullying, so I guess we're even," I said, looking up at him.

He abandoned his room, leaving the door open. Great. I already knew from the throbbing in my leg that I wasn't going to be able to walk. Yelling for help was about as dignified as scooting downstairs on my ass. This was not a convenient location to be abandoned.

I waited until the sounds of his steps had completely faded and then another twenty minutes before I yelled, "Zab? Bibbi? Anyone?"

18

I tried to get off the couch in the back room, but as soon as I put my leg down, the throbbing got worse, like my heart was pumping pain into it instead of blood. Maybe I'd been a little too quick to send Hawk away. It was taking longer than normal to bounce back without him, and could I really afford to be out of commission like this for long?

He might've had something with that "stubborn and stupid" comment, at least this time. I wasn't feeling particularly sharp at the moment, but that might also be because of the blows to the head. At least he'd fixed my ribs before it got ugly.

Either way, Bertha's food might be on the menu, but Hawk's offer to help seemed to be off the board. He'd walked through here several times and hadn't said a word.

After an hour of sitting in bed, I'd hobbled downstairs to sit at my desk and do about as much as I'd accomplished in my bedroom. I'd then hobbled to the back room, where I could elevate my ankle with company.

Zab brought me a plate of cookies. Bertha put another throw blanket on my legs.

Oscar dropped down onto the couch opposite me. "You really know how to take a beating, that's for sure. Hawk couldn't fix you up a little?"

Hawk had left again, thankfully, because there was way too much awkwardness in this conversation already.

"He helped as much as I wanted."

Oscar smiled, finding humor in the darkest of places as usual. "Ah, I get it. I could try to do something, but I might make you worse than when you started. Most of us have gotten pretty lazy and let Hawk handle the hard stuff."

"Don't you touch her, Oscar. I saw what happened to the last person you tried to fix," Bertha said from the other side of the room. "Her splinter turned into a stab wound."

He waved a hand in the air. "See? Not a good idea."

Bibbi dropped down beside me, some knitting in her hands, and shook the entire couch. I grimaced as I resettled my leg.

"Oh, sorry," she said, as she glanced at my leg propped up on pillows.

"It's okay. How's the knitting going?" From the look of the bumps, bulges, and a few holes, not well.

She held it up. "Eh. I thought this would be easier for some reason. Lots of people do it in Rest, you know, so I figured how hard could it be?"

Gillian walked in the back room. "Sorry I missed dinner."

She shouldn't have been. The majority of her roommates were happy she'd given us a few more minutes of peace before she showed up.

"Hawk was late to come and get me," she said. "Now that I'm back to work, it's safer for me to be escorted."

Bibbi gripped the knitting needle, looking like she was getting ready to stab someone.

"Safer, you say?" Oscar asked.

I wasn't sure I wanted to hear any more about it. With Bibbi sitting here with her needle ready to go, it might not be wise. Of course, we were all going to hear it anyway, because that was Gillian.

"You know, just in case I'm being targeted by the grouslies." She was picking at a plate of Bertha's food that had been left out for her, making faces that said it all. "Bertha, amazing as always, but maybe a touch too long in the oven this time?" She leaned back, putting a hand on her chest. "Hope you don't mind me saying that."

"Of course not. We all need a little constructive criticism, right?" Bertha looked about the room. "Oh, dear me, I think I left my glasses in my room."

One gone.

Oscar squinted as he continued to rub his chin. "Gillian, I thought that attack was a coincidence. Why would you be targeted by the grouslies?"

Bibbi was near vibrating next to me, and there was no way Oscar didn't know it.

"Oh, well, since I own one of the most frequented shops in Xest and I'm a figurehead in this community, it only makes sense that I'd be a target of value."

Oscar hummed. "No, that doesn't really make sense to me."

Gillian laughed. "Oh, stop it, Oscar. You're such a teaser. How have you girls put up with him for so long?"

"I don't know. He's a real rascal," Bibbi said.

Gillian kept going, not missing a beat. "I had a chat

with Hawk about how I really didn't feel safe being out and about without protection, and he clearly agreed, because he's walking me back and forth every day. That's why I'm late. He was a bit tardy."

He'd tried to run me out of Xest to "protect me," but with her he made himself personally available. Hawk was escorting her everywhere.

I blocked out the rest of the conversation. There was no need to hear any more. Xazier had implied it. The horde of people beating me had probably been gossiping about it, along with the rest of Xest. I was an idiot.

Gillian's skinny little legs appeared in front of me. I'd never realized how scrawny she was until right now. I glanced around. Besides Bibbi and me, there was no one left in the room. She'd driven them all out, as usual.

"Do you mind?" Gillian pointed to the free spot on the end of the couch, a cup of cocoa in her hand.

"Of course not." I shifted slightly closer to Bibbi, who was rolling her eyes and still gripping the knitting needle with dubious intentions.

Hawk walked into the back room and nodded at Bibbi and Gillian, ignoring me. He grabbed a drink from the corner and then left again, all the while giving me silent rage vibes. It was quite something, considering he wouldn't look at me.

When Gillian was attacked, he felt bad for her. Me? I was a jerk somehow.

Gillian couldn't seem to break her stare from the door Hawk had left from. "Is he mad at you?" she asked. "Is everything okay?"

She tried to act concerned, but there was a hopeful undertone that made me want to gag.

"I don't know. That's Hawk for you."

Bibbi's knitting needle was pointed in her direction. It wouldn't have been bad if I wasn't sitting in between them. I used my finger to steer the point away from me.

Bibbi dragged in a deep sigh and slowly went back to her knitting, in between glares to the other side of the couch.

"This was an excellent batch," Gillian said, then sipped her cocoa. "Neither of you want some? I really outdid myself."

"No, thank you." Bibbi's jaw barely moved.

Gillian looked Bibbi's way and closed her eyes just slightly, as if she were finally picking up on a potential problem.

"I'm good too. Thanks," I said, drawing the attention back my way. Gillian was driving us all nuts. Was she annoying? Yes. Was she a bad person? No. I'd have to have a talk with Bibbi. She was not allowed to kill Gillian just for being alive, no matter how much everyone might enjoy missing her.

Gillian stayed quiet for all of two seconds, seemingly back to oblivion, before she started right back up. "You know, I kind of thought you and Hawk were a thing," she said.

"We're work partners...of a sort."

Bibbi looked back up, this time with narrowed eyes in my direction, as if she were going to use her needle on me instead.

She could think whatever she wanted. A couple of kisses didn't make Hawk and me an item. If you weighed them against all the fights, the scale was near hitting the floor on the enemy's side. I'd called us partners—of a sort. That was about as accurate as it got.

"I don't know. I picked up on this strange vibe, but I

guess I was wrong," Gillian said, failing to hold back the happiness in her voice.

"Yep. You were wrong. Nothing going on."

Bibbi kept looking up at me, as if the words coming out of my mouth were the most shocking things she'd heard in a year. She flashed a look at Gillian and then shook her head, going back to her knitting.

"I guess that makes sense. You're new here, after all. It only makes sense that he'd want someone born and bred in Xest. You know, just how you'd be better off with someone from Rest? You just understand each other better."

"Uh huh." That was all I had left in me.

Gillian, oblivious to the fact no one was interested in what she had to say, continued, "I always thought Hawk was a bit, I don't know, scary, I guess. Since I've come to live here and gotten to know him better, I find myself drawn to him. You wouldn't mind if I, you know, pursued him, would you? I don't want to step on anyone's toes." The sugary sweetness in her voice did nothing to disguise the steel in her gaze. She'd have no problems stomping on toes to get her way.

Bibbi cleared her throat as she continued to knit. It was the loudest "I told you so" I'd ever heard. Now what did I do? Hawk and I might be nothing, but that didn't mean I wanted Gillian to touch him. I'd just gotten rid of one, and now I had another? Although, to be fair, Gillian was a far cry from the evil depths of Belinda.

"There's nothing between us."

Bibbi made a choking sound so loud that Gillian leaned forward to look at her. "Are you okay?"

"Oh, yeah, fine. Jabbed my finger with my knitting needle." Bibbi held up her middle finger. "See?" She went back to knitting as if she hadn't given Gillian the bird on purpose. Did they even do that in Xest, or had Bibbi seen me do it?

Gillian looked at Bibbi's tangle of knitting in her lap, assuming she was just incompetent.

"You're good with my interest, then?" Gillian asked.

Had there been a couple of moments between me and Hawk? Yes. But a couple of kisses weren't exactly a marriage contract, and no one deserved to know what kind of past or not past we had.

"Sure." Now I was ready to choke, and for no good reason. Hawk and I weren't even on speaking terms. How could I not be good with her pursuing him?

Bibbi leaned forward, so she could see past me to Gillian. "You think he's interested in you?"

"I don't know. He did offer to have me live here." Gillian sat a little straighter, letting a dreamy smile tease her lips.

"Yeah, I mean, I guess that makes sense. He let me stay here too, but I work here. He let Oscar stay here, but he's friends with him. Bertha, I guess she's married to Musso. I heard him inviting a few other people, but I can still see how you'd imagine that was something special. It's not like he's invited all of Xest to stay here, after all. Just ten or twenty of us."

Gillian's eyes dropped to her cocoa.

"Oh, I hope I didn't discourage you. I'm sure he likes you. I mean, he likes a lot of people, but it might be different with you." Bibbi's tone was every bit as sweet as Gillian's had been. We were all in danger of diabetes if they didn't cut it out.

"Yeah, well, I think I'm going to head to bed," Gillian said. "I'll see you guys tomorrow. Wish I could stay up with you, but I have to get up early to run my business, after all."

We watched her walk from the room.

Bibbi let out a disgusted sigh. "It's bad enough she's going after him. Can't she at least chill out and be real about it? Even when I was scared of you, I didn't act that fake."

"By the way, you had no reason to be scared of me. I just want to clear that up." The image of her sitting at my table might've soured my mood slightly, but I'd held back pretty well.

"I wasn't scared because I thought you were mean. I was scared because you could do things and I could tell I'd stepped on your toes. I was aware that you weren't always in control of what you did. What if you turned me into a toad by accident and no one ever figured it out and I had to live the rest of my life in a swamp?"

"There are no swamps in Xest that I'm aware of."

"That's clearly not the point of this conversation." She was back to using her knitting needles to knit.

"I wouldn't have left you as a toad. I would've gotten help. I was never *that* out of control."

"Not what I've heard, but my point is, things might've gone bad and I still didn't act as fake as that one does. This night has just wiped me out." She stood, her chewed-up knitting in her hand. "Are you going up or staying downstairs? I can help you upstairs."

"I'm good. I can walk when I try." It might've hurt like someone was stabbing me repeatedly in the leg, but I could. I'd hobble up later of my own volition when no one would witness it.

"All right. If you're sure." Bibbi looked at my leg a few times before finally leaving.

I waited until the place got quiet before I tried to stand. I sat right back down again, pulling a throw blanket over me. In the morning, I'd pretend I'd fallen asleep by accident.

There was a tickling feeling of something with a sharp edge lightly running along my leg, up and down, around it and again. A whispered voice that sounded something like Hawk but not.

I opened my eyes a sliver to see black claws grazing my skin. I looked up further to see a familiar monster.

"What are you—"

One clawed hand moved in a hovering motion over my body. He kept speaking words I didn't understand as the weight of relaxation made me feel like I was sinking deeper into the couch, my eyelids getting heavier.

19

I woke in the back room right as the sky became tinged with light, feeling like I'd slept for a week. I sat up, stretching. Maybe a month.

The room was cozy and warm, too. Someone must've come in and refueled the fire.

I stood up, and then immediately lifted my bad leg so I didn't put more weight on it. But I already had and it hadn't hurt. I cautiously lowered my foot back to the floor, leaning hard into it. Still good. I made it halfway across the room and still no pain.

I tugged up my pants leg; the swelling was gone. It must not have been that bad. Who needed Hawk? All I'd needed was a solid night of sleep.

I made my way to the stash of cocoa supplies brought over from Gillian's shop. Beside it sat one of the tea blends that was *okay*. It had somehow tasted much better before the cocoa had taken up residence beside it. Now it seemed to have a bitterness it hadn't before, an acidic opening note with a lingering blandness that didn't quite satiate.

So would it be tea with no strings? Or the most

amazing cocoa I'd ever tasted but feeling beholden to the she-demon with every sip, the woman who wanted my— boss. Business associate. Whatever.

I was listening to Bibbi too much. This was ridiculous. Had I gotten so much in my head that I couldn't enjoy cocoa without getting crazy?

I had the unfortunate timing of reaching for the cocoa as Bibbi walked over. She looked at my hand on the cocoa, as if I were holding a container of gasoline that would light this place on fire.

"It's *cocoa*." I wrapped my hands around it firmly.

Don't put it down. This is insanity.

"Sure. You can tell yourself that, but we both know better. That's *blood* cocoa." She crossed her arms and tilted her head back, giving me a look of superiority never seen before on Bibbi. She wore it pretty well.

"You mean like blood money? Because I don't think there's blood cocoa. I think there's plain old cocoa that no one died for."

"As far as no one dying for it? If you regard your standards in a rotting pile as no damage done, then sure, I guess that's true." She continued to stare, watching me with that look of judgment.

"You're getting crazy. You do know that, right?" And so was I, because I'd had the same debate internally minutes before she walked in. I'd decided I was crazy, but that was before she'd stared at me, making me wonder if she was right. I didn't want my standards to be in a rotten pile. That sounded absolutely horrible.

Don't put the cocoa down. You want the cocoa. You want it bad.

I couldn't hold out against her looks. They were too

damning, and it was too early for this kind of heavy choice. I put the cocoa down and reached for the tea.

"Well done. I knew you had it in you," she said as if we were running a combat mission together.

"We're going to have to get better tea if this continues." It tasted like sucking on an old penny.

"Agreed." She smiled and raised a mug to me, letting her gaze go all the way down to the two feet I was standing on. "You look much better. The way your leg was puffed up last night, I didn't think you'd be up on it for a week."

"Yeah, I guess I needed a good sleep, is all."

I took a seat at the table, propping my bad leg up on to the other chair, feeling like it shouldn't be this good yet even if it was. Had I taken something last night to help it? There was this nagging feeling in my head that something important had happened. Trying to pin it down felt like roaming around in a pea-soup fog trying to find a cloud.

Bertha and Musso strolled in, with Zab after them and Oscar a minute or so later. The smell of Bertha's cooking began to permeate the air as Zab remarked on how warm the back room was for this early. I'd assumed he'd come down and warmed it, but apparently not.

I leaned closer to Bibbi, who'd taken the chair next to me and was working on her knitting again.

"You ever have an idea or a dream and it's like"—I raised my hand to my head, as if I could pluck something out—"right there? You know it is but you can't quite get to it?"

"Only every day," Bibbi said. "Stop trying to think about it. That helps me sometimes. Then it'll hit you out of the blue. Or it won't, and you'll have forgotten you cared in the first place. Either way, you're good." She went back to her knitting.

I was still sipping my bland, acidic tea. "Bertha, do you have any good tea blends?"

The woman could cook like she was born with a spoon in her hand. She must have some finesse in other areas.

"Oh, yes!" She nearly jumped up and down in her eagerness to prove her skills in the beverage arena. She was putting a mug down in front of me not two minutes later, waiting for me to try it.

Musso was standing behind her, looking at me with fear in his eyes. Nothing scared that man. I took a sip and understood. Suddenly I longed for the bland bitterness of the old stuff.

Then I lied like my life depended upon it.

"Wow, this is...amazing."

Bertha glowed, and Musso sagged, as if he'd just been given a stay of execution.

"That bad?" Bibbi whispered as Bertha went back to cooking.

"Don't ever try it."

Hawk walked into the room, and I forced my attention on Bibbi's knitting so I had something else to focus on.

"You made a lot of progress since last night," I said, pointing to her knitting.

She'd barely made any. Saying anything was better than sitting in silence while I pretended Hawk wasn't in the room.

She held it up. "I mean... I guess?"

Hawk stopped beside the chair where my leg was propped up. He gave me a nod as he looked at it. It was the most interaction we'd had since our last fight.

"It's fine," I said, putting my foot solidly on the ground. But something about him hovering over my leg... There was something there. If it weren't for that damned pea soup.

He took a step away from me.

"Did you..."

He looked back at me, waiting. "Did I what?" He lifted his brows, having no idea what I wanted and sounding like he didn't want to know, either.

So much for being able to have a civil conversation.

"Nothing. Forget it."

20

The weekly meeting, the one that typically put me to sleep or had me hiding in a corner, trying to avoid eye contact, was tonight.

I was wide awake and filled with dread. There'd surely be questions directed my way, and I didn't have a lot of answers to shoot back, which seemed to be the norm. I'd run short on answers the majority of my life. Why should these people get special treatment?

I made my way downstairs, figuring I'd get there early and find a good corner to hide in. The noise of everyone talking made it obvious I was already late. Seemed everyone else had decided to get there early.

The smell of Gillian's cocoa wafted through the packed back room as she walked around, topping off mugs and smiling as if she were hosting this affair.

She spotted me at the door and smiled, holding up her pot of cocoa in a silent offering. I raised my hand and declined with a smile. Never thought I'd miss Belinda's outright dislike of me. At least it had all been laid on the table. Gillian was all fluff and good graces. She might've hated my guts or thought of me as a sister, and I wouldn't know either way.

Hawk was sitting on the edge of the table. He watched me as he sipped cocoa—that was, until Gillian stepped in his line of view, to top off his drink.

Bibbi waved me over, and Zab moved, making a spot in between them. Beyond them was Musso, who was typically hanging near the front of the room, and Oscar, who was always lingering in the back of the room. Bertha was in front of us.

The hand-chosen seat made me feel like I was encased in bubble wrap. Was there a problem I was unaware of? We were all on the same side, I thought. That had been my impression until I'd gotten bodyguards all around, the Xest version of bulletproof glass.

I'd sat by Bibbi because I usually sat by Bibbi. I hadn't sat here for security reasons. This was not the look I was going for. Everyone probably knew I'd taken a beating recently, and now it looked like I was afraid of my own shadow. I glanced around, but there weren't any other free seats to be had. It appeared that I'd ride this meeting out in my bubble.

Hawk stood, glancing my way before he walked to the board. This look I was very familiar with. It was his *guess you're not stepping up again* glare.

I looked to the board, indicating that was exactly what I was doing. There would be no debates, not even silent ones, because we still weren't on speaking terms for the most part.

Hawk tilted his head toward the board with the lists of where everyone stood in this fight. "Any updates?"

There were a couple of murmurs but nothing else.

Guess it had been a slow week for spying. Looking at the turnout this week, I'd expected a bit more.

Hawk called out a woman in the back of the room. "Charuesse, you said you were going to check in with Hendrick. You weren't able to come up with anything?"

"I tried, but they weren't talking," Charuesse replied. "I'd keep them as neutral for now. Not sure how they feel, but they don't seem to have the stomach for fighting unless they have to."

"Any other updates?" Hawk asked, and then rattled off a few more names.

Seemed it was going to be the same story with most of them. People had either picked a side or decided not to pick at all. That was fine. If it wasn't added to the head count of people wanting me dead, I could live with neutral, literally.

I noticed a motion in the corner and glanced over. It was one of Zab's friends leaning against the wall, waving in my direction. His name was Ab and he'd seemed interested in maybe dating, like I had time for that in my life. I hadn't seen him in what felt like ages.

Had he been at the meetings before? This place got so packed, and so much larger, on meeting nights that it was hard to notice everyone, especially as I tried not to notice anyone.

I gave him a nod.

"Ab," Hawk called out.

Ab immediately looked to the front of the room.

"Do you have something you care to discuss?" Hawk asked. "Anything beneficial to bring to the table? I don't believe you've contributed info at all yet, or am I wrong?"

Hawk could get as angry at me as he wanted, but it was hardly necessary to vent it on people who were nice to me. That was some serious grudge holding. We were all on the same team. Even I believed that, and I was in virtual bubble wrap tonight.

Ab's cheeks grew rosy. "No, I haven't been able to yet."

I wasn't sure if Hawk was going to continue to torture Ab, but the protector in me couldn't let it continue.

"Does anyone else have anything to offer?" I asked, standing and looking around the room. "Seems most of us are hitting a dead end, huh?"

If Hawk got annoyed by my interruption, that was his problem. He was the one who'd kept telling me I should be more involved.

Beard raised his hand hesitantly. He and I went way back to an incident at Zark's bar, a messed-up drink and a near burning. We were friendly these days, always giving each other a smile when passing even if I still didn't remember his name. This would surely be friendly fire.

"Just say it. You don't need to raise your hand," Hawk said, when Beard seemed to be waiting for permission to speak.

Beard turned to me, and the rest of the room followed suit. "Is it true you glow the same color as Dread does?"

"Do you want me to handle him? You don't need to answer this," Bibbi said, standing up beside me, pushing up her sleeves as she did. She shifted closer. If she moved in any tighter, she was going to knock me over. Or would've if I didn't have Zab blocking me on the other side.

"I got this. He doesn't mean any harm. We're cool with each other," I said softly.

I cleared my throat, focusing my attention back on Beard. I had the undivided attention of everyone in the room.

"I do glow the same colors, but I don't know why," I said loud and clear, so that not for a second would anyone assume there was anything to be ashamed of. I was so loud that people in the alley behind the building might've heard me.

A unified "ooh" spread across the room. They all looked on as if I were some strange alien in front of them. But not one person looked horrified. Were they too stupid to make the possible connections? No, probably not. After all, the connections were really obvious, and these people weren't stupid for the most part.

They all kept staring as if expecting me to say something else.

"I wish I could say more, but I truly don't know anything else. I'm fairly new to this whole magic business in the first place."

There were a few nods, and a couple of people whispered.

I sat down, and my two guards took their seats as well.

Another person raised their hand, looking at Hawk briefly before turning back to me. I looked at Hawk as well, hoping he'd try to take the reins back.

He locked eyes with me and then settled himself on the edge of the table. Figured he wasn't bailing me out now. He probably loved that I was being forced to accidentally take the lead with this meeting. So much for helping Ab. Next time, instead of trying to help him out, I'd give him a glare. Didn't change the fact that the room was quiet as they waited for me.

"Yes?" I asked the newest questioner.

"Do you think that's why it doesn't like you? Because you have the same magic? Maybe there's some sort of competition or jealousy?"

It was a very good question, and one I'd mulled over myself. "It could be, but I'm not sure if throwing off the same colors does mean it's the same magic, let alone if that's the reason. I really don't know much about this at all."

"Is that why you were able to make that wall it couldn't get through?" a woman in the back asked.

"It's possible, I guess? It would make sense." I'd barely finished answering one question before another was asked.

The questions came at me for a steady fifteen minutes before they slowed down.

We'd hit the end of anything important when a woman with cotton-candy-pink hair asked, "Do you think you could help out guarding my daughter's birthday party next week?"

"Do you think you could use it against it, like the way you made the wall?" a person in the corner asked.

Hawk stood. "Tippi already has a job and her hands full with other matters. She's not available for private parties or personal protection details. If the only thing left is curiosity or appearance requests, this meeting is over. We have other work to do."

Some people looked downward, but I could see the irritated expressions enough to make it clear that Hawk had ruined their party plans.

"That went pretty well," Bibbi said, nodding as she watched people file out.

"Definitely went better than I thought it would," Zab said.

"Yeah, me too," I added, feeling tired already when I knew I had a full night ahead of me.

Bibbi's scowl deepened. "Why do you look like that when things went pretty well?"

"Xazier sent notice for a meeting tonight," I deadpanned.

She grimaced and shook her head. "Oh."

"Yep."

21

"You look nice, if a little less inviting than in your first meeting outfit." Bibbi stood in my door as I finished getting ready.

"I'm not sure he wants to get in my pants as much as he wants to dig around in my head." I tugged my hair back into a ponytail, not caring how it emphasized my unique brand of highlights.

"Oh, that doesn't sound nice at all." She crossed her arms, as if getting ready to fend off an attack not aimed at her.

"It's a bit tiring."

"Don't let him have free rein in there." She twirled her finger toward my head.

"Definitely not trying to, that's for sure." I grabbed the jacket lying on the bed and threw it on, hearing an annoyed chirp. "If you insist on being invisible, how am I supposed to know where you are?" I asked Dusty before turning my attention back to Bibbi. "Anyone downstairs?"

Why I felt like I was sneaking out past curfew every time I met Xazier was beyond me. But I did.

"No," she said. "I haven't seen Hawk since the meeting, and everyone else went up early."

It was strange how that seemed to happen on Xazier nights, as if no one could quite stomach my interaction with him. It made what was to come somehow lonelier, even if that was the most absurd thought. I didn't want to make a big thing of it, and yet the loneliness was killing me. What did it matter if most of them didn't want to be there for my departure?

I threw on my jacket as Bibbi moved out of the doorway.

"Good luck, and keep your mind closed," she said.

"I will." I hoped.

I walked down the stairs, not caring if they creaked. The office was dark but the smell of cocoa still lingered, as if I needed salt in the wound. Would Gillian have stepped up and offered herself to buy Xest time? I doubted it. It was surprising she hadn't asked for a chariot to bring her back and forth across the street yet.

Helen's gears ground.

I looked back at her. "Thanks. I'll need it."

A wet nose wiggled its way in between my boot and pants. I reached down, giving Dusty's head a pat. I hadn't realized it had followed me down. "I'll be back soon."

I walked from the office. No one stopped me on my way to the square or fell into step with me. Xazier was right: I was a schmuck. I'd done this for Hawk and them, and they hadn't wanted me to.

No, that wasn't entirely true. I hadn't done it just for them. I'd done it for me, for Xest, this magical place that had made me finally come alive. I'd done it because it was the right thing to do. I didn't want to die knowing I hadn't stepped up, left it all on the field, when it counted. If everyone else thought my actions had been a mistake, or couldn't come to terms with it, I'd accept that because my motives had been pure.

Xazier was waiting for me, smiling. He glanced at my outfit. "That won't do for where we're going, but I'll take care of it." He held out his arm and we were in a nightclub. I didn't know where, but it felt distinctly European.

The place was so dark and crowded that our appearance out of thin air was barely glanced at.

My outfit was replaced by a velvet dress with one shoulder bare and a hem that nearly grazed my hip before descending on the other side to barely respectable. And again, the most useless little straps of leather held spikes onto my feet, as if he were hoping I'd fall and die on the next set of steps we encountered.

He motioned us toward a roped-off corner where a booth awaited us. A bottle of iced bubbly was on the table in front of it.

He poured me a glass of champagne, not bothering to ask if I wanted one. I took it, knowing I couldn't let myself have more than a sip or two. At least here, it would be hard to talk with the music blaring so loudly.

He leaned back in the booth beside me, and suddenly our small little area quieted. Everyone else kept on dancing as if we were alone in our quiet spot.

"I heard there was an incident, but you seem well. I'm glad." He smiled, his human facade looking perfect.

"It wasn't much of anything." I would've loved to know who his sources in Xest were, not that there'd be a short supply when half the place wanted me dead.

"You know I could help you if you let me. I wouldn't take over Xest. We could form a partnership of sorts, but a partner who wouldn't try to control you and then abandon you." He leaned in closer, laying his arm along the back of the booth behind my shoulders. "I can be very loyal to people who are worthy, and you, my dear, are most certainly worthy. I would treat you the way you deserve, unlike some others."

"Something to think about." I tipped my glass in his direction before taking another sip of champagne. I wouldn't lose any sleep thinking over his offer. I'd spend more effort in counting my sips, knowing I couldn't have too many.

"Have you made any progress? Word is you haven't. I'm hearing you don't even have a plan. Making a deal with me would be a way to save Xest. You want that, don't you?"

"We'll figure something out." Did he have someone on the inside, or was it blatantly obvious to everyone in Xest that we were a lost cause?

"This deal won't be on the table forever. There'll be a price to pay for making me wait until the end. Would it really be that bad to work with me? Forget all that nonsense you've heard in Rest about hell and roasting bodies. Truth is we're simply another plane of existence, no different than Xest."

"As I said, I'll need some time to consider it."

"Some, yes." He sipped his champagne. "So how did this attack the other day happen? I heard it was fairly vicious."

"It wasn't that bad." He'd probably salivate if he heard the details, and tonight was bad enough already.

"No one was there to help you? Curious, because I've heard Hawk is personally guarding some witch named..." He shook his head. "I can't remember the name. All I heard is she makes candy or some other frivolous thing.

Some bit of fluff, from what they say, but I guess she must be important to warrant his attention."

Had to hand it to Xazier. He was a master at pushing my buttons and obliterating self-esteem. I took another few sips then let him refill my glass. I wasn't going to make it through this night without liquid help.

The office was dark when I got back, but this time it wasn't empty. Hawk was waiting, standing in the door of the back room. Whatever the situation was with Gillian, he still cared enough to see if I made it back alive. No matter my mixed feelings, I was relieved to not be alone for a few moments. Meetings with Xazier left a chill in my blood that was hard to shed.

I let the jacket slide off my shoulder and then hung it, fully aware of how my new outfit clung to me. Had to give Xazier credit. He definitely knew how to bring out the best of my features. I certainly didn't look like the tomboy I'd always been. After our meetings, I came back looking like my much more sophisticated twin sister who oozed sex appeal and confidence.

Hawk took in every inch, making no attempt to hide the perusal. "Nice outfit."

His tone didn't have anything nice or civil about it. It was nearly primal. If I was exuding sex, he was meeting it with pure testosterone.

He straightened from where he was leaning and walked closer, his nostrils flaring as he took in my scent. I might rival him with magic, perhaps beat him out in certain areas, but he had senses I'd never match.

"You shouldn't let him touch you. You don't know what he's capable of."

"I don't think he meant to," I said, remembering the way Xazier's arm lay across the top of the booth behind me. How many times had his hand grazed my shoulder while he talked?

"Trust me, it was completely intentional. Don't let him twist you up, Tippi. I know him. I know how he operates."

He was standing as close as Xazier had, but when Hawk was near me like this, I had a hard time keeping my heartbeat steady, my breathing regular—thinking at all became a problem.

He dipped his head lower, toward my bare shoulder, his lips a hair away from grazing my skin. He brought his hand up, his touch hotter than normal as it moved along the skin that Xazier had brushed. I wasn't sure what Hawk was doing, but the chill of Xazier was slowly melting away, and for that reason I couldn't bring myself to stop him.

He feathered his hand down over my arm before moving it back. I'd never thought of the arm or shoulder as an erogenous zone until now, as his fingers moved over me, working its way back along the crook of my neck.

My head dropped back. "He didn't touch there," I said, in case there was a purpose to this I didn't know.

"I like to be thorough," he said as his hand continued until it was at the back of my neck, and then at the base of my skull, threading into my hair, tugging at it until it fell from its loose ponytail, slipping down about my shoulders.

I couldn't get control of my breathing or the thudding in my chest. It didn't matter if we were barely talking or if I thought I hated him. I wanted him to touch me, kiss me. I couldn't bring myself to make the first move toward him, but all I wanted was to feel his hands on me. If Xazier had made me feel even a touch of this, I shuddered at what I might've already given away. I'd probably be setting up shop in hell right now.

He was close enough that his shirt brushed against the front of my dress as he lifted me by the waist to sit on the desk in front of him. He leaned his hands on either side, forcing me to bend back as he hovered over me.

"Did you let him kiss you?" His voice was low and gruff—raw.

We'd barely spoken to each other lately, and when we did communicate, there was nothing civil about it. I should tell him no. Stop this thing we were doing. But then he might step away...

Tell him no. Tell him.

He probably only wanted me because he was territorial. Maybe I only wanted him because I was too. Every time I saw Gillian near him, I wanted to jump in between them.

Still I said nothing, as my back arched in his direction and my lips parted, nearly beckoning him to act on the invitation.

He moved until we were flush against each other, and then his lips were covering mine and I was opening to him in a way I'd never done before, with anyone. His flesh was on fire as his tongue dueled with mine.

The stairs creaked as someone stomped down the stairs. I pulled back right before the door opened.

He countered by stepping away, our gazes locked.

Gilli walked in the room. "Oh, I'm sorry. Did I interrupt something?" She took a tentative step forward.

Hawk didn't answer but continued to look at me, waiting. What did he expect? Was I supposed to tell his favorite that he was busy with me and that he'd get to her later? If she was interrupting, he should be the one to step up and say it. I wasn't the reason she was sneaking down here at the first sound of anyone. He was.

But he didn't. He stood there, waiting for me to say something.

"You're not interrupting anything." I straightened my dress almost aggressively as I stepped around him, in a fouler mood now than after I'd left the demon. It hadn't seemed possible.

Hawk glared, as if I'd done something wrong. I walked to the door.

"I was just coming down to get a late-night cocoa. Couldn't sleep. Care to join me?" Gillian asked.

I headed upstairs, refusing to linger even a second. If he started up with her next, I didn't want to hear it.

22

Gillian walked into the office, with no sign of Hawk, and headed over to my desk. She had two cocoas in her hands. I refrained from asking how she'd managed to cross the street alone.

Instead, I focused on the cocoa she placed on the desk in front of me and noticed the lack of extras. I took it for what it was, which wasn't that I held a special place in her heart. She was keeping her enemies close. She didn't need to bother. If she wanted to chase Hawk, I wasn't going to stop her.

"Thought a hot cocoa might hit the spot today." Gillian's simpering sweetness was stomachache-worthy.

Zab was staring at the cocoa in front of me, trying to figure out why I was getting special treatment. He hadn't been in the office last night when Gillian interrupted. Bibbi was narrowing her eyes as if the cup held poison. Her interpretation, although severe, was closer to the truth. If I could meld the two of them together, they'd make the perfect confidant instead of Zab being clueless and Bibbi wanting to kill everyone.

"Thanks." I tried to remain civil. It wasn't Gillian's fault I'd left when she came in. She *had* asked if she was interrupting. Whatever happened or didn't last night, it was on me. Or Hawk. If he wasn't holding her hand and walking her to her shop every day, maybe she wouldn't have feelings of ownership, which she seemed to be developing. If you lead someone on, you can't expect them to not think they're going right where you're bringing them.

"You know…" Her words died off as she glanced around the room.

Zab dropped his gaze back to his papers. Musso hadn't cared what we'd been discussing before and still didn't. Bibbi's lids lowered into more of a glare.

"I was going to step in the back for a second. Would you come with me? Had something I wanted to ask you."

There was a sigh building in my chest that would've taken an hour to let out. But again, as annoying as she could be, her cocoa was so good.

"Sure." I got out of my seat as quick as my lack of enthusiasm would let me and followed her into the back.

The room was empty, but Bertha had been hiding out upstairs lately. From the smells that occasionally wafted down from the third floor, I suspected they'd installed a kitchen up there.

Gillian glanced around, making sure she was alone before switching her attention fully back to me.

"I know you said that nothing was going on with you and Hawk, but I thought I picked up on something last night." Any sugar that had been in her tone had turned into something blackened on the bottom of a pot.

Now I understood exactly what this was, and it wasn't a peace mission. It was a fact-finding mission disguised by a cocoa offering. Had she realized exactly what had been about to happen on that desk last night? And still she stayed, interjecting herself where she wasn't wanted. Well, she wasn't as dim as I'd feared. Delusional, though, if she thought her cocoa was good enough to pry private details out of me.

"You did?" I asked, playing as stupid as she occasionally did.

"It was a vibe I picked up on. I know I asked you this before, but you're sure there's nothing between you two?" She sipped on her cocoa as if she wasn't white-knuckling her cup.

"Don't worry about my situation. You need to do whatever you feel you should." That was as good as it was going to get, in spite of what I thought she might want, and that was a guarantee nothing was going to happen. Even if there wasn't, it was my business.

Hawk walked in the back door, startling us both.

His glare made the gust of wind at the door opening feel downright warm. Great. He was probably mad about last night, like I'd swindled him into kissing me again.

I turned, going back to my conversation with Gillian, or the new one I was going to pretend we were having.

"So you're back to work full-time again?" I asked.

She was smiling in his direction. "Yes. I hate to leave the shop for too long. With everything so slow, I've been tinkering with recipes. I made this amazing white chocolate caramel swirl this morning that is going to drive everyone crazy. I'll bring some home tonight." And the sweetness was back.

It was a good thing I wasn't drinking, or I would've choked. Home? She was calling this place home? That was wrong on so many levels.

Hawk walked past us and into the office, and her attention went with him.

"I'm sorry, but do you mind? There were a couple of things I needed to talk to Hawk about. He's been such a help to me."

Before I could answer, she was gone, shrugging off her coat on the way.

Maybe Bibbi was righter than I wanted to give her credit for. I looked at my cocoa and then tossed it in the fireplace just in case it was laced.

I let out a long sigh, reminding myself that I couldn't keep telling Gillian it was okay to go after him and then be annoyed by it. That would make me crazy, and in a different way than I normally was. Hawk and I could barely tolerate each other. What did I care if she chased him like a puppy dog?

"What's with the long sigh?" Oscar asked, walking in the back door.

"Nothing. Just tired today."

"How'd the date go? Late-night partying with demons can make you really tired."

"It wasn't a date," I said, walking back toward the office. I stopped right at the doorway, teetering between wanting to watch or just run out of the building, as was my fallback position. It made me wonder why I'd given up on running. It was such an easy way to be. There were none of these issues if you stayed on the surface with everyone and everything and took off when things got too deep.

Oscar walked over and leaned near the door beside me. He paused, his eyes narrowing on the same scene I was watching. The sight seemed to have frozen him.

"What's going on over there with them? Is this actually

becoming a thing?" Oscar whispered, staring at Gilli and the way she leaned just so, making it appear like her breasts might tumble out of her shirt at any moment. Hawk laughed at something she said.

"I think it's fairly clear what's going on. He doesn't look as if he's swatting her away either, so it must be mutual." I never should've had a sip of her cocoa. My chest was burning like it had been laced. Was I going to drop dead? Maybe she *was* going to try to poison me.

"*No.*"

Oscar's tone drove my attention away from dying. His eyes were hard, the lines of his face stark enough that I wondered if he was afraid of some bad cocoa too.

Oscar pointed toward Hawk and Gillian. "That is not happening. I'm going to have to step in again, because you're blowing things up. The work I'm putting into this, and you keep on wrecking it."

"What are you talking about?"

Oscar's attention was fixed on the duo with an alarming intensity. "Hawk's as close to a brother as I've ever had. He's saved my ass many a time, and he's going to be in my life until I drop dead, which means I better damned well like whoever he ends up with." He pointed in Gillian's direction. "That one annoys me."

I shrugged. "She annoys everyone, but that doesn't make her the worst person ever."

Even the way she was flipping her hair right now was annoying. What was wrong with her? She looked like she had a crick in her neck. I wanted to walk over and give her a not-so-gentle adjustment.

Oscar shook his head. "She's too nice, but she's not nice at all. She never says anything explicitly bad, but nothing very nice either. She never gives anyone dirty looks. She's like a plain scoop of vanilla with something rotten on the inside. I would rather have Belinda back." He broke his gaze from them to give me a sly nod in their direction. "You killed the last one. Any chance?"

"I didn't mean to kill Belinda. It just happened." I glanced at Gillian. "She makes the best chocolate in town."

"I'm telling you, a week with her and you'll be looking to drown yourself in her cocoa. No. This won't do at all." Oscar shook his head and groaned. "He can't be interested. That woman couldn't get a sail up in a tornado."

"Are you saying she can't get a man hard?" I asked.

"Yes, Tippi, that is what I'm saying. It's your fault if he ends up in a relationship with her. Then we'll all get stuck with her. And don't act like you're okay with this either. I can nearly feel the anger rolling off you."

"I *am* fine." Hawk could do what he wanted. I'd come to terms with that, and Oscar would as well. But if this continued, I'd have to find a new place to live. No way could I stay here.

Oscar was still shaking his head. "It'll be Belinda 2.0. Instead of a raving bitch, we'll be bludgeoned to death by boredom and bravado. I'm telling you right now, I'm not having it."

"There's nothing you can do. If they have something, that's between them."

"You really think that those two fit?" He was smiling now, in spite of how annoyed he was a second ago. "I don't think so, and there's plenty to be done about it." He pushed off his side of the doorframe to lean on mine, resting a hand over my shoulder and then dipping his head, his cheek grazing mine. "I'm telling you now, I'm not giving up easily, and I can fight dirty."

"What are you going to do, Oscar?" There was a gleam in his eye that made me think of masked men sneaking about at night.

Hawk's attention shifted in our direction, his gaze lingering on Oscar, almost as if he could smell something afoot. Oscar's gaze was still on me as he leaned in closer, his broad shoulders blocking my view.

"I think we're going to have to take some drastic steps." He smiled, his tone flirty.

"What are you doing?" He was cranking out sex appeal the way Gillian cranked out cocoa. It was enough to make my body waver over whether this was real or not.

"You know what I'm doing," he said.

"Do I?"

There was a flicker in his eyes. "I think so, but I might be open to diversions from the plan."

"Hawk, are you walking me?" Gillian called out across the office.

There was no response.

Oscar's smile grew as his shirt brushed mine.

"Hawk?" Gillian called again.

The door shut loudly a few moments later.

I glanced over in time to see Gillian and Hawk crossing the street, my heartburn making a return.

I turned my attention to Oscar, who was still standing a hair away from me.

Oscar's gaze lingered on my lips. "If I wasn't so sure I'd be runner-up, the things I would do..."

He broke away before I had a chance to argue that he was wrong about my feelings for Hawk.

23

The door to the office opened. Zab, Bibbi, Musso, and I all turned to see who was walking in. We had so few people coming in these days that any activity had everyone's attention. I immediately dropped my gaze again. This wasn't a visitor I was interested in seeing. The visits from Xazier were enough of an issue. Someone else could handle the high ground.

Lou continued into the office and no one said a word in greeting. If I had the nerve to glance up, I'd imagine all their heads were down as well.

The footsteps continued until he was standing in front of my desk. I ignored him for another few seconds, because the bottom line was that a representative from "up there" was as scary as one from below.

Not able to take the tension a second longer, I broke and looked up slowly.

He was grinning. "So glad I caught you here. I wasn't sure if this would be a good time."

"For me?" I couldn't stop the urge to glance around.

There had to be someone else here he'd be more interested in talking to.

He followed suit, looking about the office before
looking back at me.

I reshuffled some papers on my desk, acting as if I
were so busy. "Maybe you'd want to talk to..."

His perpetual grin and shaking head made it clear. He
was here for me, for better or worse.

"Do you have somewhere we could talk alone? I have
an issue that I'm hoping we could come to an agreement
on," Lou said.

Oh God, the scary-ass angel wanted to talk to me
alone. Musso, who wasn't scared of anyone, was getting
out of his seat in case he had to run for help. Bibbi and
Zab were shoulder to shoulder, and people in Xest didn't
like to touch, even through clothing.

"I'm really not in charge around here. I'm not sure I
can help you," I said, trying to pass the buck.

"Oh, no, you are the exact person I need to talk to." His
smile was practically a spotlight on me.

Could you say no to an angel? Well, I shouldn't be
presumptive. Maybe he was from there but not an angel at
all. Every organization needed a bad guy. Although wasn't
that hell's purpose?

He took a step backward, waving his hand for me to
follow. "This will only take a few moments."

Shit. Shit. Shit.

Why had I wanted to stay in Xest? Salem had been
such a simpler life. Now I was selling my soul to one
demon while an angel wanted to have a private chat with
me. Nothing would ever be fine again.

As Lou continued to wait, I got out of my seat and
motioned to the corner. "I'm going to grab my jacket."

Didn't want him to think I was making a run for it and have him hit me with a bolt of lightning. Word was it was their preferred weapon.

I grabbed my coat and tried to wipe moist palms on my pants as Lou headed toward the front door, never losing sight of me.

Zab had his hand on a pile of newsflash papers, waiting for the sign to call in the cavalry. I shook my head slightly. The last thing I needed was Hawk making this into an even bigger to do. I'd held my own with a demon. Would the angel be that much worse?

"I'll be back in a few minutes," I told the rest of the room, waiting to see if Lou would disagree. He stood silently by the front door.

"Shall we have a bit of a walk?" he asked, as if I had a choice in the matter.

"Sure." I pretended that I did as well. Pretense was better than finding out that there were no other options.

The second we started walking, it was clear that something was off. People were crossing the street and moving out of our way, but no one was looking at me, not the people who hated me *or* liked me. It was as if I wasn't there at all. As if something drove them away from us without them being aware of why. If things took a dire turn, would anyone hear my screams? This was getting freakier by the second.

"I did a little digging, and it turns out you weren't exactly forthcoming with me on our first visit. I have to say, that was a great disappointment." Lou sounded like he'd mastered the *you should've known better* voice a decade ago.

I'm dead. The creepy angel knew I'd lied to him.

Would compounding it with another lie make a difference? Was one lie forgivable but the second a capital offense? I stayed quiet.

I should've refused to come with him. I was so over my head that I didn't know which way was up anymore.

"No need to worry. I don't take offense. I merely mention it because, going forward, I'm going to need your complete transparency. No secrets between us." He was back to beaming at me.

"Going forward?" The words came out a little rough, like I'd been doing shots of crumbled cement.

"You have to understand that Xazier and I go back a very long time. I know him better than anyone, and he has a tendency to get a little sneaky at times. It's fine, because I keep him in line, but I need to be aware of what he's up to or he could cause a lot of problems. I know he's trying to make a move on Xest right now."

He looked at me to agree. Was this going to get me caught in some war between heaven and hell? Lou already knew, and I hadn't been sworn to secrecy by Xazier. I was collateral, but there hadn't been a nondisclosure agreement. This should be safe territory, even if it felt like jumping into a pool of water and not knowing where the bottom was or whether it was boiling.

"I do believe he would like to make his presence here known in some way." That was fairly diplomatic and vague.

He stopped walking and smiled. "See? Was that so hard?"

I didn't respond and merely smiled back.

He began walking again. "Tippi, you have to understand, it's much better to be friends with me than enemies. I can help you. You don't have to fear Xazier if

I'm your friend." He laid a hand on his chest and stopped, again, seeming to wait for a response.

"That's good to know." Was it normal that the one from heaven seemed worse than the one from hell? At this rate, I was never going to be able to die in peace. On some level most people are afraid of dying, but this brought a whole new element to it. Up or down, didn't matter if I was blacklisted by these two.

"Do you plan on speaking to Xazier again? I've heard you're meeting with him weekly until you get this little problem you have sorted out, which should be a priority, considering what is at stake."

Now what to say? How much did he know?

"I do believe he will be back to check up on things, but I don't call the shots. It's at his discretion." Again, all true but a bit vague. I was definitely getting the hang of this.

"The little problem you've been having, we've been aware of it as well, and it is an issue. I might be able to help you out if you're willing to make certain concessions. I'd have to make sure that if I tipped the order of things one way or another that you'd be willing to repay my kindness. Roads must lead in both directions, after all."

Oh, no. I already didn't like where this was heading. What was the point of getting help to swap out one takeover from another?

"We're still exploring our options right now, so I'd have to get back to you on that." These bogus lines were really flowing now. If I'd stayed in Rest, I might've been able to get a job in PR.

"That's fine. We have a bit of time." He smiled and shrugged in a way that made me wonder if there might be something he knew. "You'll need to make sure to call me after your next meeting with Xazier, though. Just step outside and say the word 'Lou' into the fifth wind. I've got you tagged as a VIP caller, so you'll get right through. But you must realize how important it is to call. If we're friends, you'll call. That's what friends do." He stopped walking and turned to me. "We are friends, aren't we? I wouldn't want to not be friends. That wouldn't be good for anyone."

It was about as thinly veiled a threat as you got. Any thinner and there'd only be air. If I agreed to being friends, was I locking myself in magically? Why had I agreed to talk to him at all? That was right. I'd been too chicken not to.

"I'd like to be friends if possible," I said, being as evasive as I could pull off and hoping he'd take it.

He smiled and then turned on his heel, directing us back to the office. "That's good. Come. I'll walk you back."

"No need. I'm sure you have a busy day," I said, risking a faster pace.

"Not at all," he said, walking faster with me. "So, you came from Salem, I hear? Interesting how you ended up in Xest."

"Yes, I guess. Never really thought much about it myself." This was getting oddly familiar. Demon or angel, they were starting to merge in my mind.

"Was your family witches?" he asked.

"My mother was a witch." He probably already knew that. He probably knew a lot of things—more than I did, if I had to guess.

He hummed. "Was she strong?"

"I hate to admit it, but I'm really too ignorant to say."

"And your father?" he asked, not letting a second lag between questions.

"Can't say. I didn't know him." Finally, I could give him a truth.

There was more humming. I could see the broker building up ahead. Just a little bit closer and I'd be away from him.

"I find you so very peculiar. There's"—he put his hand out, twisting it back and forth like a seesaw—"something."

"I'm a weird girl, is all. Nothing overly interesting about me." Few more steps. Almost home free.

"Well, here we are. Don't forget, I'll be waiting for your call."

"Definitely won't forget." I gripped the front door.

Lou smiled again, and then he was gone.

The door to the broker office swung open and Hawk was standing there.

"Where the hell have—"

I clapped a hand over Hawk's mouth and put a finger to my lips. I looked about the office, making sure they were all getting the message, and then made sure the door was shut completely.

"I think he can hear things through the fifth wind, so no talking about any matters if the doors are open," I said, making sure everyone was listening.

"Where did he take you? I've been looking everywhere," Hawk said.

"We were walking around Xest, but I don't think anyone could see us." As angry as I was at Hawk for varying reasons, knowing he had tried to find me gave me a warm feeling. Besides, this mess superseded any fight.

I shrugged off my jacket as I came to terms with this new issue. I walked until I was in the back room, pouring tea and settling on the couch, trying to unfreeze my brain from a stalled position.

Hawk followed me in, with Zab, Bibbi, Musso, and Bertha trailing behind him. How exactly did I tell them that, in a nutshell, I'd become the knot in a tug of war between heaven and hell and was beginning to suspect this fight was over more than gaining control of Xest.

Hawk stepped closer. "Tippi, what happened with—"

"Don't say the name." I nearly choked on my tea. I'd just gotten rid of the guy. I didn't want him back now, and even inside, I was afraid his name might trigger an appearance.

"What happened?" Hawk repeated.

Bibbi came over and topped off my tea, even though I'd only had a couple of sips. "It's all right. Just take your time."

"No, it's not all right. I need to know what happened," Hawk said, coming closer.

Bibbi gave me a smile, silently telling me to ignore Hawk. Had to give it to the girl. She was really coming into her own these days. She'd been hiding a pair the size of watermelons under her new outfits.

Zab, Bertha, and Musso stared and waited as Oscar rushed through the back door.

"You found her," he said, stopping short.

"She came back on her own," Hawk said.

"What happened with—"

"Don't say the name," Musso said, throwing up a hand.

"Okay, well, what did *he* want?" Oscar asked, becoming part of the circle of people staring at me.

"He said that he's heard about my prior meetings with the one from down below." I wasn't taking a chance naming any names.

"That's not really where it—"

"No one cares, Zab. Do the geography lesson another day," Bibbi said.

"Keep going," Hawk said.

"So, the one from above wants to be informed of what's happening with the one from below. That he wouldn't consider us friends if I didn't cooperate." I leaned forward, putting my tea down, because if I didn't, I was going to spill it on myself. The more reality hit, the more my hands were starting to shake, and that wouldn't do.

"Was anything else said?" Hawk asked. "Don't leave a single detail out."

"He asked about me a bit. My parents, where I came from."

Hawk moved closer. "What did you say?"

"That I didn't know much but I was basically a girl from Salem."

"Did he buy it?" Hawk asked.

I was so past the realm of normal, even in Xest, that no one skipped a beat at that question. All they were focused on was if I'd sold him a bill of goods about being common. Well, they were all going to be disappointed.

"I doubt it." I sat on my hands in a show of warming them, which had the added benefit of hiding the tremble.

"This is not good. First we've got one involved, and now the other? What happened to Xest having autonomy?" Musso said, shaking his head. Bertha moved in closer, patting his back.

"Are you okay?" Bibbi asked, sitting beside me.

"I'm fine. I'm just going to drink some tea and unwind for a few minutes, and then I'll be good."

Her eyes suddenly seemed to glaze over. "Okay. Well, I'm going to get back to work." She got up as if nothing strange had happened.

"Yeah, I've got some stuff to finish up as well," Zab said.

"Oh, I've got dough I need to get in the oven," Bertha said, and then Musso followed her out.

"Shit. I forgot to run over to Zark's and give him something. I'll be back," Oscar said, then hurried out the door.

One by one, they all remembered something else they had to do. The only one left standing in the room was Hawk.

"What did you do to them?" I asked.

"Gave them gentle reminders they needed to be somewhere else. They'll probably realize it by tomorrow and be angry." He sat across from me then leaned back, his stare fixed on me. "Now that we're alone, what *aren't* you saying? How bad is it?"

I weighed my options as I stared back.

Even if I didn't want him to be the person I confided in, I wasn't sure anyone else could handle what I was about to say. The weight of it might crush a weaker soul. Hawk had a lot of flaws, but no one would dare call him weak. I had to face it: whether I liked it or not, he was still my strongest ally right now in this war, even if he did play dirty. Or maybe because of that. Jury was still out.

"They're both trying to get me to agree to be indebted to them, like they know something about me, or at least suspect something. There's something beyond Xest at play here. They want something from me, and I don't know why."

I leaned forward, feeling a smidge better for getting it off my chest. I wrapped my hands around my teacup, steady enough to not splash myself as I waited for him to say something. When he didn't, I looked up.

Hawk's eyes had hardened, the lines of his body tense and coiled.

"It doesn't matter. They're not getting you," he said, with an eerie calmness.

If he wasn't an ally, I might've run from the room right then, new resolutions of not running be damned.

24

I lifted my head back, sniffing the air. It wasn't that it was easy to smell grouslies, but once in a while, when I took a deep breath, it was as if I could feel their presence nearby. The only smell on the air tonight was the stink of Mertie's weird tobacco blend. Sure enough, a cigarette glowed in a nearby alley.

She poked her head out, glanced around, and then waved me closer.

This time there was no hesitation joining her. I'd never thought I'd count Mertie in my list of assets, but that was exactly what she was becoming. She grabbed my jacket, yanking me farther into the shadows with her.

"If I get caught talking to you people, my reputation will be in shreds. It's bad enough you've got the whole rainbow on display, but could you try to be a little less conspicuous?"

"So nice to see you too, Mertie. It's always such a pleasure." I tucked some *rainbow* behind my ears.

It wasn't worth arguing with her. Both Hawk and I were known to attract attention no matter what precautions we took. What she was asking for was nearly impossible. Although if she'd given me some warning, I would've put on a hat.

"Did you get me information on that person?" I asked. "I'm assuming you're hiding in the shadows for a reason and not a lingering habit from your previous occupation."

She was looking out of the alley, unfazed by my return jabs. The fact that she could take it as well as she dished it out was redeeming, even for a past demon.

"Some, but I want to go over our agreement again. If things get ugly, I get to move into the broker building, right?"

"Yes, that is the deal." The way Mertie kept looking for guarantees was making the long shot of her actually moving in seem more and more likely. I was lucky Hawk wanted me alive but wasn't sure how well the rest of my roommates would take it. Gillian would clash with Mertie being there on day one, and my coin would be on Mertie winning.

"What? Why are you smiling at me like that?" Mertie asked.

"Just glad to see you."

"You're so odd." She dragged out the sentence as she tilted her head. It wasn't the unkindest thing I'd heard from her.

"I've been told. What do you have?"

She stuck her head out of the alley again before she spoke. "I went through the records. Your person *was* a worker at the factory, like you suspected. Middle-of-the-road Whimsy, nothing special, maybe a little more staying power than some but less than others. Only thing that was of any interest was that she could jump puddles, which is unusual. A lot of Middlings can't. Other than that, nothing surprising."

My mother could jump puddles? She was a Whimsy and she could puddle-jump and yet I couldn't? How was that possible? Why couldn't anything ever be neat and tidy?

Mertie turned to leave.

"Wait. What happened to her? Did she get fired from the factory or something?"

"No one gets fired from the factory." She let out a laugh, as if that were the most ridiculous thing someone could utter. "Our records indicated probable death, but it had a bunch of question marks beside it, which means she somehow disappeared on her own. Marvin doesn't like there to be written records when someone manages to save themselves."

"How long ago?" Had she conceived me here or in Rest? Was my father a warlock or some human she'd hooked up with afterward?

"Around nineteen years ago, but I don't have anything more specific. It might've taken a while to notice her gone as well. Like I said, Marvin doesn't like to keep those kinds of records. I wasn't employed there yet, and any Whimsy that knew her is long gone by now." She lit up another cigarette. "You're not going to back out on our deal, right? If you're even thinking about it, I—"

"I gave you my word I wouldn't." It was beginning to be obvious that it wasn't *if* Mertie was going to come, but when. But why? If I'd had a true idea of the odds of having to pay up, I would've negotiated a little harder. "Tell me one thing: if things get bad, why would you need a place to go? Why can't you stay where you're at?"

She shrugged and rolled her eyes, as if annoyed I'd

asked. When I continued to wait for an answer, she finally huffed. "I told you the witches and warlocks at the factory are getting weird. What else do you need to know?"

I leaned back on the side of the building. She didn't like Dread either? I'd thought she was impartial, but this was just...

"Dread unsettles you too?"

She shrugged.

Mertie got the same bad vibe we did. That was interesting, and maybe a little nauseating. I'd thought it was a given that this thing was evil, but wouldn't an ex-demon like it, then? What did that say? Or maybe that was why she was an ex-demon. Maybe she hadn't been cut out for the job? Was Mertie as lost a soul as I'd been living in Rest?

"Look, one way or another, we'll make room for you. You'll have a place to stay."

She gave me a half a nod. It was the nicest gesture she'd ever given me. Maybe the nicest gesture she'd ever made?

"I gotta go," she said, and then took off, as if that in itself had been a little too much niceness for her to stomach.

25

There was a towel over my eyes; I was trying to ease the ache of eye strain from poring over every book I could find in my search for a solution to what was coming. It felt as if most of my day was spent hunting an enemy I couldn't find or mentally roaming around in pea soup without a clue, and begging people to dig for details of my origins, in some hope it might lead me to what Dread was.

"You're not going to find answers in that book," Oscar said.

I lifted the rag off my eyes and surveyed the room. Oscar was hogging the other couch. Bibbi had a pile of slips at the table she was sorting and Zab was sitting on the other side, eating again, feeding his anxiety, as Bertha tried to cook hers away.

"It's better than doing nothing," I said, eyeing Oscar up.

Point was, none of us knew what to do at this point. We'd once again hit a brick wall, and the clock was ticking louder every day.

"It might appear as if I'm doing nothing, but I'm quite busy thinking." He tapped his head. "Tell me what Mertie said again?"

I relayed all the information that was pertinent, which excluded her moving in. This was not the day for that conversation. That day would happen when she showed up.

"I have to say, it's very strange you were born to a human and a Whimsy witch," Oscar said. "It doesn't seem possible."

"Why do you think that? Maybe my father was a warlock?"

"Odds of a warlock of any kind of serious power being born as a pop-up in Rest is very unlikely. And you weren't conceived here, or immigration wouldn't have been able to boot you." He was scratching his jaw as he went back to his heavy thinking.

"That goes back to conception?" I asked.

"Yes. Why? Did you think maybe Zark was your long-lost daddy or something?" He laughed even as I threw my wet rag at him.

"You're not funny most of the time. I hope you know that," I said, leaning my head back again.

"That one was actually pretty funny," Zab said. No one else disagreed.

"Can I have my rag back?" I held up a hand, and the wetness smacked me in the palm a second later, all nice and toasty again. "Thanks."

"You're welcome," Oscar said. "You should really work on learning some more fundamentals, especially since everyone is looking at you like the savior of Xest. They'd find your lack of basics startling."

"For your information, that position has already been

taken," I replied. I didn't need to say what cocoa-serving pain in the ass had stepped up to fill it. We all knew, evidenced by the lack of follow-up. Gillian was going to change the world, one magnificent cocoa at a time.

A chair scraped against the floor. "I'm going to need at least two pots of tea to get through all these requests," Bibbi said, sounding frazzled. "You'd think Marvin had completely closed up shop the way these smaller requests keep piling up lately. Why are they even coming here?"

"Maybe Marvin is looking to cut back," Zab said. "Such a greedy jerk that I didn't think I'd ever see the day, but he's been getting lazier and lazier every month, it seems."

A tingle spread over my skin.

"How many do you have?" Hawk asked.

"Oh, I hadn't realized you were back," Bibbi said.

No one probably had. No footsteps, no smell. It was as if he could disguise his entire presence when he wanted, except somehow I still sensed him.

"Too many to count," Bibbi said.

I kept my head back, rag on my eyes, focusing so hard on ignoring his presence that it was nearly all I could think about.

Stop it. Why do you have to focus only on him if he's anywhere around? It was embarrassing. I was a pathetic loser, and there were important things to ponder, like angels and demons who seemed equally evil, invisible monsters, and people long dead.

Dead people. Everyone that had worked with my mother was long gone, and there were very few witches and warlocks that were born in Rest. And pop-ups, as they called them, typically didn't have a lot of magic.

So how was Marvin keeping the factory stocked with

enough witches and warlocks? Or had he kept it stocked before, when, from all appearances, he was losing ground now?

I yanked the rag off my eyes, sitting up. "Whimsy witches die young, typically. That's established. And pop-ups aren't that common, right?"

"Yes," Hawk answered.

The entire room settled their attention on me, as if they sensed something was coming.

"How many Whimsy witches and warlocks are typically born in Xest?"

There were a few head shakes, as no one had an answer.

"I don't think that many," Hawk said, walking closer.

"So if they aren't getting imported, and there aren't that many to begin with, and they die young, how's he been keeping that factory stocked with enough magic? Has there been an influx of pop-ups, or has Marvin been doing something else?" I asked.

Everyone was sitting upright.

"If there's someone sneaky enough to steal magic somehow, it would be him," Musso said, walking in the room. "I never did trust that guy."

"From what I read, Xest has a certain amount of intrinsic magic that's inherent to the place, correct?" I asked.

"Yes, it does." Hawk was right by the couch now. "And there's typically been a balance. *Dread* is not balanced."

"Maybe Marvin did something that threw off that balance?" I looked about the room, trying to read the reactions. No one was saying much, and no one looked overly sold.

"Is he smart enough to pull off something big enough

to shift the balance in Xest to create a monster like that?" Zab asked.

"It's a long shot, but we don't have anything else," Hawk said. "Zab, send out a newsflash to those two idiot brothers. I want them here in the next twenty or else."

Hawk walked into the office, Zab right behind him.

"Who are those two idiot brothers?" I asked Oscar, who was standing and getting ready to follow as well.

"You call them Spike and Braid—they're the two that brought you over. They do most of Marvin's collecting. They'd know how many pop-ups have been coming in. They're idiots, but they puddle-jump really well for low-level Middlings."

Spike and Braid were outside the office nineteen minutes later, arguing with each other.

"What do you think they're fighting about?" Zab asked. The two of us stood in front of the plate glass, watching the brothers as they shouted and did a lot of finger pointing.

"Not sure, but it does give the appearance of guilt. Problem with those two is they might be guilty of so many different things that it could have nothing to do with this." I sipped some tea, since I didn't dare drink cocoa within sight of Bibbi these days, even though Gillian was still at work and it was probably poison-free.

"They better not have screwed us over," Bibbi said. "I say we leave them out there for a while until one of them freezes and the other cracks."

I glanced back at Bibbi, so nice and innocent when I first met her, and saw the glint of rage and steel in her eyes. She might've been one of the toughest people in Xest, masquerading as this cute chick I called a friend.

"She's a little scary, isn't she?" Zab whispered, noticing my attention.

"Just a little, but she likes us, thankfully. We probably don't want to get on her bad side, though."

Bibbi just laughed, thinking we were kidding. Or maybe not.

Hawk walked back into the offices, scanning the place until his gaze narrowed on the window. "What are those idiots doing?"

"They don't appear to want to come in," Zab said.

We'd been watching them bickering back and forth for a good five minutes already.

Hawk walked to the door and held it open for them. They stopped talking the second he did. Braid nodded to Spike; Spike then nodded to Braid, as they silently argued who was going to go inside first.

"Inside." Hawk pointed at the bench along the wall.

Braid lost the fight, walking in first. The two of them took a seat, whispering things to each other that appeared to be a continuation of their argument, if their wrinkled-up faces and jerking movements meant anything.

Hawk let them continue to fight it out for a minute until Braid turned to Hawk, his eyes scanning the rest of us, as if he were determining how bad their odds were.

"I don't know what you were told, but we didn't do anything. We had nothing to do with her." Braid pointed to me. "Or the gangs or any of the evil shit happening. We know our place. We stick to the small stuff. *This* ain't small stuff."

"This is going to be easier than expected," Zab said.

"How many Whimsy witches and warlocks have you brought over in the last six months?" Hawk asked.

"That's why we're here?" Braid squinted.

"Answer the question," Hawk said.

They went back to looking at each other, as if there was a trap here that they couldn't spot yet.

"I don't care if it's two or twenty. There is no wrong reply. Just answer," Hawk said, stepping closer to them.

I was itching to get into the fray and start interrogating them myself. Their fear seemed to be focused mostly on Hawk, and my instinct told me to let it stay there. There was plenty of talk around Xest about Hawk, not that anyone whispered the rumors to me. There were reasons Hawk cleared the sidewalk like no one else in this place, even if I didn't know them.

What the hell was Hawk that he could call anyone in and they'd come running? He wasn't completely human, as evidenced by the creature he could become. This was a very good reason why I should never have kissed him and enjoyed it. It was always a good idea to know if the person you were clinging to like life depended on it was even a human.

The two of them were back to the silent debating. Braid shrugged and Spike nodded, as they came to some agreement.

"Should we count the two times we brought her over?" Braid asked, pointing at me again.

"No," Hawk said.

"Then none."

"If you're looking for more Whimsy witches, it's not our fault. It's been slim pickings," Spike added. "We've been trying."

Braid nodded, completely missing the point of this

conversation. We didn't care if there weren't more witches and warlocks, only that nothing was adding up. How had Marvin kept the factory running?

"What about the last couple of years?" Hawk asked.

"A handful. Maybe four?" Braid said right away. After they hadn't gotten beheaded for the first answer, they clearly didn't feel the need for another debate.

I didn't know the math, or how many Whimsy witches were born a year, but that didn't sound like enough to keep the engine churning at the factory.

Hawk waved toward the door. "You can go."

"We can? That's it?" Braid asked.

"That's it."

Instead of running out of the office, they both got up like they'd just finished a marathon and all their energy was depleted. They looked about the room, as if they were stupid enough to think someone was going to fill them in on what was afoot.

Hawk cleared his throat and then pointedly looked at the door.

They nodded and headed in that direction with a bit more speed. I followed, smiling as I showed them out.

I held the door open as they left and then kept it open a few inches as they walked away. They didn't bother looking back as they started talking.

Braid turned to Spike. "You know, considering the lack of pop-ups, I wouldn't be surprised if Marvin gets desperate enough to use the hill again."

"I don't think he'll do that anymore."

I flattened my palm on the door, pushing it wide open. "What's the hill?" I yelled.

They turned, their faces stark white and the urge to

run in their twitchy gazes. As a former runner myself, I was a master at spotting another.

"Hawk," I called inside, grateful I had some backup on hand. Last attempt I'd made at questioning one of them had led to a merry chase first.

"I'm right here," Hawk said from behind me. "We need these two still?"

"Yes."

"Well," Hawk said, "you heard her. We need to talk some more." He had one hand on the door, holding it open while he waited for them to turn back around.

They were cursing under their breath as they walked back in.

Spike turned to Braid. "You call me the stupid one, but you're the one always gabbing away. Can't keep your mouth shut for nothing."

"Shut up or I'll shut yours for you." Braid elbowed him.

Hawk tilted his head back to the bench. I didn't wait for anyone to tell me to take the lead. They'd have to fight to take the reins out of my hand.

"What's the hill?" I asked.

"We don't know." Braid couldn't sit still.

Spike stared at his shoes, saying nothing.

"You *just* talked about it," I said.

"That doesn't mean we *know*." Spike looked up, even as he kept his head down.

Braid shook his head. "We really don't know. We hear shit. No one tells us anything."

"And what shit do you hear?" I asked, as Hawk stepped closer.

"We can't talk about it. You don't understand. *He'll* kill us."

"You think I won't?" Hawk asked. "Don't tell me you haven't heard the rumors. Trust me when I tell you that not only will I kill you, but I'll enjoy it. You two have been nothing but a pain in my ass. I'd be happy to kill you."

Bibbi walked over and stood on my other side, a letter opener in her hand. "Let me have a chance at them. We'll see what they know."

I swung an arm out, stopping her from getting too close. "Hang on there. I think we should give them a chance to talk first."

"Fine. We can give them a chance. But for the record, I don't have a lot of patience." She dropped her hand only enough so it was no longer level with their necks.

Braid and Spike's faces were white enough that you couldn't help but wonder if they had any blood left.

Braid said, keeping his eyes on Bibbi's letter opener, "Marvin mentioned in passing once that we either found him more pop-ups, ones who weren't totally useless—"

Braid elbowed Spike in the ribs. Braid seemed to catch his error and looked at me, shaking his head. "I didn't mean to say you were useless. Just most pop-ups are weak as hell, and—"

"I don't care. Keep going. What else did he say?" I asked.

"He'd have to go back to 'the hill,' and he didn't want to do that again. That's it," Braid answered, putting up his palms.

I kept staring at him for another few moments, trying to smell a lie. They squirmed a bit, but nothing worse than what I'd expect with a rabid Bibbi ready to gut them.

"Don't move," I told them.

"I'll watch them. They won't go anywhere," Bibbi said.

I walked to the other side of the office. Everyone

followed me but Bibbi, who stood in front of them, flipping her letter opener end over end.

"Do you think they're telling us everything?" I asked.

"I do," Hawk said.

"Yeah. Me too," Oscar said.

Musso and Zab agreed. It was unlikely we were all wrong.

"Bibbi, cut them loose," I said.

She turned toward me. "Really? Do I have to?"

Braid and Spike took off. Bibbi let out a grunt as she watched their backs. They were lucky she wasn't giving chase.

Musso hummed. "What hill could they be talking about? After all my years here, I thought I was aware of every nook and cranny in Xest."

"Maybe the hill behind the mailbox?" Zab asked.

"I think I might have a lead on the hill," I said, remembering the place Bautere had brought me. It had seemed like nothing, but it might be the only lead.

Hawk turned back my way. "You do, do you?" There was no need for him to say anything further.

"I wouldn't get all judgmental if I were you." I went and grabbed a jacket, and everyone in the office went to do the same. "Um, I'm not sure if we should all go. It's in Bautere's..."

I didn't have to finish. They were already putting their coats down. That was easy enough.

Hawk walked to the stairs, waiting, the only one who didn't mind going into Bautere's territory.

26

It was more of a mound, and that was a generous description. This thing wouldn't trigger a deep breath if I ran up it hard and fast. But this was the place Bautere had said seemed odd. It was our one and only lead at the moment.

Hawk walked cautiously around it, giving it much more respect than I did. He circled in tighter and tighter rings as he approached.

"Bautere said there was something off about this place, but...I don't know." I took a few steps closer, thinking that a cup of tea in the back room might've been more worthwhile than this trip.

Hawk didn't lose an inch of intensity. "Don't judge anything by appearances. The most lethal witch I've ever met had a bun and wore an apron. She baked me cookies right before she tried to kill me."

Glad he was impressed by this lump of snow. "Were they good?"

"Best I've ever tasted."

His wannabe girlfriend would lose her mind if she

knew someone had outdone her in the sweets department.

"Don't let Gillian hear that." I let out a half laugh, realizing belatedly that it sounded more like a cackle. Did that sound bitter? What was wrong with me? I didn't care what happened with him and Gillian. There was a job to do, a hill to find. How Gillian felt about someone else's cookies was the least of the problems facing all of us.

After this new perusal, it might not qualify as a mound. I took a few more steps toward the clump of snow.

"This place seems pretty normal. This doesn't seem to be the place." I pulled my collar up as the wind kicked up.

Hawk kept walking around intently, like a dog on a scent. He didn't appear to be ready to leave anytime soon.

Out of sheer boredom, I made my way closer. A weird feeling made my insides tingle. I took another step. The feeling grew. I took another few steps, single-mindedly heading in the direction of the feeling. It was unlike anything I'd felt. Maybe it was because I was closer than last time, but I felt like I was a magnet being pulled toward something much larger than myself.

The closer I got, the more I felt I couldn't retreat, until I was nearly glued to one spot on the ground.

"Hawk?"

"Yeah?" He was kneeling, laying a hand on the ground.

"I need…" I crashed to the ground, hitting my knees and then my palms.

"Tippi?" He headed toward me. "What is it?"

"There's something here. I feel…strange. I don't know if I can move."

I didn't have to say another word before he tossed me

over his shoulder and took off. He didn't stop until we were a good hundred feet from the mound.

He dropped me to the ground, kneeling beside me. "Are you okay?" He moved my scarf away and laid his fingers on the side of my neck. He ripped my glove off next, feeling my wrist.

"I'm fine. It was just unsettling." I stared back at the hill, and I'd give it enough respect to call it at least that now.

"What happened?" he asked, sitting back on his haunches, watching me as if I were going to tumble over.

"I don't know. I felt a pulsing of sorts and couldn't seem to move. I've never felt anything like it before."

"How do you feel now?" He put his hand my neck again, as if he wasn't convinced things were okay. "Your magic feels strong."

"Fine." I couldn't stop looking at that spot. What was there? The only thing I was sure of was that this was *the* hill.

"I'm going back over there. Stay here." He stood, watching me.

I nodded. There would be no fight on this one.

He walked back to the spot, and I looked around for a big stick. What if it was like being electrocuted and he got stuck? I'd need something to push him off.

There was a nice five-foot-long stick not far away. I hurried and got it, then returned fast. I watched, waiting to see what would happen.

He kept walking back and forth over the area I'd gotten stuck in. He did it another ten times before he canvassed the rest of the mound. By the time he was done, I was huddled in a squat with my branch beside me.

"Are you planning on hitting me with that?" Hawk asked as he walked back over.

"For your information, I was going to use it to save you." I threw it to the side, since the hill hadn't wanted any part of him.

"Whatever is there, I can't feel it." He sighed as if frustrated he couldn't get a read on it.

He looked back at the spot and back to me. Another thing piling up, not making sense, like so much else. It seemed that the more information we got, the less we knew.

"Either way, we need to get going. There's a storm coming."

I held up my bare hand. "It feels calmer than ever." The air felt colder, but the constant wind had gone away for maybe the first time since I'd been in Xest.

"That's how you know a storm is coming. The calmer the wind, the worse it'll be." He looked in the direction we'd come, his eyes narrowing. "This isn't good."

I turned around. "Where'd the door go?"

Bautere walked across the snow until he was standing beside us. "Heard you were in these parts."

"You told Tippi that there was something wrong with this place. I wanted to check it out, and then our door disappeared." Hawk waved to the place it had been.

"Magic has been acting weird in this area for a while now." Bautere raised his head in the air, his nostrils flaring. "You're not going to be able to get back, not with the storm brewing. You'll have to stay the night with me."

Before we answered, he turned and began walking back in the direction he'd come from. With no options, Hawk and I followed. It was better than getting stuck in a blizzard. Xest's weather wasn't kind on a good day. There was no way we'd make it back on a bad one.

There was a fire, but it barely warmed the area. I bunched the furs around me again, trying to trap every smidge of body heat. It was a losing battle that I'd been fighting for a good hour.

I had my back to Hawk, who was on the next pile over. He wrapped an arm around my waist and dragged me up against him.

My instinct to push away lasted a half of a second, maybe even less, because that was how long it took to feel how warm he was. My thoughts soon shifted to how I could maneuver myself closer, without literally draping myself on top of him. I settled for mounding up the furs around me and him, barricading his heat in.

"Just so you know, this doesn't mean we're on good terms," I said. "I'm only sleeping next to you because it's cold and it's a necessity. Same reason I'm talking to you. Only as needed."

"Noted," he said, his eyes remaining closed.

I maneuvered slightly so that my head was in the crook of his arm. If I was going to sleep next to him out of necessity, it made sense to get as comfortable as possible. He was like being pressed up against a wood stove that was continuously pumping a slow heat.

"How is it that you're warm when I'm freezing?" I put my hand on his side because there was no other place for it, and if there was a sudden attack, warm fingers functioned better. Again, it was all about survival.

"I'm a shifter," he said, as if that in itself explained it all.

"And?"

"I have two different cells trying to occupy the same space at all times, almost warring with each other for dominance. That generates more heat."

"Oh."

He hummed, not sounding interested at all. I closed my eyes, trying to let sleep come the way he seemed to have managed. Finally warm, the sound of the storm blowing outside, I was snuggled up to a man I hated most days.

So why couldn't I stop thinking of sex?

I closed my eyes, shifting a bit, trying to get comfortable, moving my leg slightly over in my quest to sleep comfortably. I'd never noticed men's legs before, but he had the kind of thick, muscled thighs that were hard not to notice, especially when you were right up against them.

Hate him or not, he was a good-looking man. It would be hard to deny that. I was a hot-blooded woman who hadn't had sex in a long time. Of course I'd be attracted to him.

I needed to think of something else so my heart slowed and my breathing normalized before he noticed. Although he was probably asleep already, he was so still.

"Tippi..." His voice was guttural, drowning me in testosterone.

I tilted my head back so I could see his face. His jaw was tense and his eyes were blazing as they looked at me.

"Did I wake you? I was just trying to get comfortable." My voice didn't sound right. Probably because my heart still hadn't stopped racing.

His chest nearly rumbled before he rolled over, taking me with him. He molded himself to my body from his lips, to his chest, to his hips, where his leg found purchase in between mine. For all my big talk, all I could do was arch and moan as his tongue delved into my mouth. Logic was gone, replaced only with need. I gripped his hair, keeping his head close, wrapping my free leg around his.

He reached down, dipping into the waistline of my pants, skimming over my wetness. He froze, and I arched into his hand. Instead of starting back up, he pulled back his hand.

"What are you doing?" I sounded flustered by any measure.

"Sorry to interrupt. Heard about your visit to the hill," an older female said.

Hawk tugged down my shirt and then rolled off me.

The older female, Bautere's leader, was standing there.

"You shouldn't be out in this weather," Bautere said, walking in from the other room.

"I'm not out anymore. I'm here, and I had to come." She waved a paw at him and then turned to us. "I need to know what's going on. I need to know what is being done. You've got some bad sorts around and still no answers?"

"We're trying," Hawk said.

I was glad he took the lead, as I was still trying to gather myself.

She stamped her cane. "It's not enough. You need to get this handled, or all of our existences are at stake."

"We're aware of that," Hawk said, keeping his calm.

She turned to Bautere. "I need some of that hot bark brew you make. That'll warm my old bones as I get all of the details." She waved him back with an imperial flick of her hand.

She settled in and didn't look like she'd be leaving anytime soon.

27

Hawk and I walked back into the office the next morning. Musso, Zab, and Bibbi all looked up, scanned us, and nodded.

"Glad you're not dead," Bibbi said.

"You were with Hawk. I told her you were fine," Zab said.

Gillian ran out of the back room, past me and right to Hawk. "Where have you been? When you didn't come get me at the shop last night, I was worried sick that something happened." Her hands fluttered to her chest.

I drifted away from the little scene, not that Gillian noticed. After all, it wasn't me that had made her run across the room. Hawk walked into the back room with her nipping at his heels.

"What happened to you guys?" Bibbi asked.

"We got stuck in the storm. Had to stay at Bautere's place." I kept it short and simple, but my cheeks still burned, as if somehow they'd know something.

"Oh, well, that's interesting." She was getting a sly look about her.

"It really wasn't." It might've been, but that had crashed and burned, and I was glad for it.

I didn't look toward the back room. I didn't want to know what was happening there. I'd gotten very close to opening up, giving everything to a man who'd tossed me aside more than once. And why? Because it would've felt nice? Maybe better than nice. Maybe *amazing*.

But that didn't matter. Right now, he was talking to Gillian in the other room, calming her worries. Any *amazing* feelings from last night would've been washed away with acid and a steel brush. Instead, my head was on straight as I made my way to my desk, checking over anything pressing. Nope, nothing painful about this.

The cocoa wasn't tempting me as I made tea.

Hawk walked in the back room. He'd been in the office more often than normal today, which made it a little harder to act like nothing had happened between us, but damned if I wouldn't.

He walked over and reached for a cup and then the kettle, saying nothing. No one would know, as I stood inches from him, that we'd had our bodies plastered together less than a day ago.

I stood silently, refusing to give up ground, even if that ground was in the back room. I wasn't talking, either. I wasn't sure whose choice that was, his or mine, but I'd taken part ownership at this point.

He stood beside me, drinking his tea instead of leaving, both of us silent. If someone walked in and looked at us, we would've screamed "awkward moment." Luckily, no one did. Or maybe not so lucky. It seemed people were beginning to give us a wide berth when we were together, except for Gillian. She homed in like a heat-seeking missile when Hawk and I neared each other.

I took another sip of my tea.

He drank some of his.

"I'm going to go talk to Marvin this afternoon. I want to question him about the hill," he said. "Do you want to come, or would you like to sit this one out?"

I pulled my gaze away from his lips, as it took me a few moments to respond.

"Tippi?"

Marvin would be at the factory. A month ago there wouldn't have been a hesitation. That was before I'd been overtaken by a horde of people kicking and punching me, trying to stomp my brains out. But there was no way I was sitting this one out.

"Of course I'm coming. Why would I want to sit that out?" I took another sip of tea, reminding myself that I could handle anything.

"Be ready in an hour."

I glanced out the window at the darkening sky. "You sure you want to leave that late? You might not be back in time to walk your girlfriend home."

Well? Would he confirm it or not? Was she his girl-friend, or did she only act like she was? Or did he run around and kiss all the girls, as I was starting to fear?

His eyes narrowed and then he let out a deep laugh. "See you in an hour."

Glad he found the situation so amusing. That did nothing to answer the question, though.

When Hawk walked into the office a little while later, I was seated at my desk with my best ass-kicking outfit and a warrior braid. Technically it was a French braid, but it made it a lot harder to grab my hair if I had to throw down with someone.

Hawk paused in front of Zab's desk. "I need you to walk Gillian after work tonight."

Bibbi might not have looked up from her work, but the corners of her mouth definitely went up.

"Oh, uh, I don't think that's a good idea." Zab immediately leaned back in his chair, shaking his head and putting up his hands, as if begging for mercy.

"It's fine." Hawk took a step away.

"I'm not good with...*protection*," Zab continued, his gaze following the retreating Hawk's back.

"You'll be fine," Hawk said without glancing back. He turned to me. "You ready?"

I got up from my seat and grabbed my jacket. Bibbi was still smiling wide, and Zab looked like someone had dragged him out in the alley to shoot him.

"Your girlfriend might be a bit upset with you tonight," I said as we left the office.

"Gillian will adapt," he said, without hesitation.

Did that mean she was his girlfriend or not? Considering how he was all over me last night, I wouldn't answer in his place either. Was he the perpetual playboy? Or did Gillian think they were together and he was a cheater? Neither was good. I'd better remember this next time I got all hot and bothered.

The factory came into view up ahead, filling me with another unsavory feeling. I kept my pace, refusing to slow or show any fear.

Mertie was on the stoop, smoking a cigarette as we approached. I gave her a single shake of my head. She got the message loud and clear, turning away from us and singling out a Whimsy witch working on the outside of the building.

"What are you doing? That's not the way to do that. Do I have to show everyone *everything*?" She walked toward the Whimsy, leaving her spot by the front door and giving her back to us as she made a show of grabbing the trowel and shoving cement in the line between the stones. "See? That's how you do it. I'll do a few more to make sure you really understand."

Hawk pushed open the door.

"Do you have a plan?" I asked.

"Walk in and ask. If Marvin doesn't answer, hurt him and ask again."

That was it?

Seemed to be. And here I thought the man couldn't do simple.

"Sounds good to me." It was fairly close to what I would've suggested.

As soon as I was in the building, meaning to or not, I fell a few steps behind Hawk. Taking a couple of deep breaths, I felt for the knife in my pocket and forced myself not to fall too far behind.

I didn't remember the factory that well, but it seemed as if we were going the long way to Marvin's office after a couple of wrong turns.

"Do you know where you're going?" He'd been in Marvin's office before. Had the rooms been reshuffled? Did he know something I didn't?

"Yes," he said.

But then he slowed down in front of every door,

looking for Marvin. Typical man—he didn't want to admit he was lost.

"I think we should turn around and go back the other way," I said, as he kept stopping at every door.

He glanced back at me. "I know what I'm doing."

I'd never been called slow, but I might've been a bit duller today. It took three hallways before the truth of what was happening sank in. He was stopping by every room, letting them see us together, to send a message.

"You don't need to do this," I said as we passed another door. "I can handle myself."

"I'm not doing it for you. I'm doing it for them." His tone was all business.

"How's that work?"

"You're with me, and they should know better. I don't feel like killing more people, and I'm sure they don't feel like getting killed." His grim reply left no doubt how serious he was.

Kill more people? Had he already killed some of the ones who'd attacked me? Or was he talking about other deaths? Was that better? I'd probably lost the high ground when I killed Belinda and Raydam. Although that hadn't been intentional. There might be a little leeway for some judgment left, even if I couldn't seem to dredge any up.

Had I recognized any of the faces from the alley? It wasn't like I'd memorized them that day when they were beating me to a pulp, but still, I didn't think I'd seen a single one since walking into the factory.

I was in the process of trying to remember when Hawk kicked open Marvin's door.

It might have been unlocked, but it was an effective entry, judging by the startled look on Marvin's face.

Marvin got to his feet. "Mertie! Mertie!"

"She's not out there." Hawk walked around his desk and sat him back down with a hand on his shoulder.

Marvin's eyes flickered to me as I attempted to close the door, with hinges that weren't working as well as they had been a few moments ago.

"What do you want?" Marvin asked, his eyes bouncing back and forth.

"What's the hill?" Hawk perched himself on the corner of the desk, leaning over Marvin.

I walked to the other side, staring down at the warlock.

"What hill? There are hills all over the place. How am I supposed to answer an idiotic question like that?" His forehead was looking a little moist and his bony hands were gripping the chair like it could save him from drowning.

I gave his chair a little kick until it was flush against the wall. "Marvin, we're not leaving until we find out. You either tell us now, or he'll torture you and then you tell us." I tilted my head toward Hawk.

"I think you know what I'm capable of when crossed," Hawk added calmly.

"We have a way we do things. A balance here in Xest. A mutual respect," Marvin said.

"There *was*, but that's over. Xest is going to hell, and I've got a feeling you had something to do with it."

Hawk's voice was deep and rough, and somehow reminded me a little of how he'd sounded the other night. There was never a good time to think about that, but this moment was definitely wrong. Very, very wrong.

I kicked Marvin's chair again, pulling his attention to me. "We've got an angel and a demon breathing down our necks, ready to take over. You think you're going to get to keep your little labor camp here if they step in? You won't.

And you know why? I'm going to be the first person pointing at this place and telling them to dismantle it stone by stone. If you know something, you better spill it now, because you *will* be going down with the rest of us if they take over."

He slumped back, almost as if he'd realized he'd lost a war he'd just discovered he was in. "So the rumors are true?"

"Yes," Hawk said.

Marvin's shoulders fell and he looked like he'd just aged a decade. "There's a hill, but I don't know what it is. I stumbled upon it and realized something was different."

"Keep going," I said.

"I used to buy furs from Bautere and some of his people. Everyone knows they have the best pelts. Sometimes I'd bring another witch or warlock with me to help carry them back. I noticed that the Whimsys I brought with me on these trips seemed to live a bit longer, but only if we went one particular route, by this hill area." He shrugged. "So, I started only going that way, and maybe I bought more furs than I used to. I didn't realize there was a problem until things started to get weird in the unsettled lands. I still don't know if it had anything to do with me, but I stopped then and there."

He slumped in his chair, looking as if he had no fight left in him at all.

I might never get a better chance to ask.

"Did you know Jossi Tudor? She was a Whimsy witch here. Did you bring her to this place?" I asked. It would tie it all together. Had she somehow gotten this magic and then passed it on to me?

His head jerked back as he stared at me for a second. "No. I never took her there. I found her too irritating to be around. Why? Who's she to you?" Marvin took a hard look at me as if trying to connect this with the present.

"No one," Hawk said, stopping me from answering.

If Marvin believed Hawk or not, he didn't have any desire to fight. "That's all I ever did, and I stopped before things got crazy."

"Yeah, I'm sure you stopped the very second," I added.

Hawk stood and nodded to the door.

I stayed put as he made his way out and then stopped, waiting for me.

I looked at Marvin and then back at Hawk before joining him outside the office.

"That's it? We're leaving him?" I asked, as he took another few steps away.

"Yes." He kept walking.

After a few seconds of debating, I followed him.

I waited until we were away from the building before I said, "As far as an interrogation goes, that sucked."

"He was telling the truth."

"So? I think he deserved a few punches anyway." I might have to consider trading Hawk in for Bibbi.

"I'd rather leave him alive in case we need him for something later." He kept walking.

Alive? I hadn't planned on killing the guy. Only rough him up a bit.

"Well? What do you think? Any thoughts on our next move? Because that didn't seem to help matters." I hoped he had something, because I had zero ideas of where to go from here.

"Other than I think there's a connection? No. But maybe we should at least confirm there *is* a connection with the hill."

"Bibbi style? We bring the stone to there?" I pulled my

jacket closer as the few people out and about crossed the street a few blocks away. The buffer zone had definitely grown in the last month.

"Yes. We bring the stone to the hill as soon as I get it back," Hawk said.

Back from where? Did he really need to lend it out? Did he not know it was sort of important?

No. It was his stone, and I was not telling him how to use it because no matter what anyone said, I wasn't controlling, not the way he was.

"Is there a problem?" He stared at my crossed arms and fisted hands.

"Of course not."

He smiled, as if he knew I was lying. I wouldn't give him the satisfaction of saying a word, and it was killing me.

Bibbi glared across the room at where Gillian had taken a seat next to Hawk on the couch, who was reading over some papers.

"She never stops," Bibbi whispered. As much as I wanted to stay and commiserate with Bibbi, I'd rather pull my eyeballs out of my head than remain here. How long was I going to deny it? The disgusting truth was that I had a thing for Hawk. Some messed-up part of my brain wanted him, and there was no getting past it. I'd have to bear it while waiting for the feelings to fade away. It would definitely happen next time he did something else high-handed, but I'd had enough torture tonight.

I got up and grabbed my jacket off the hook.

"Where are you going? Do you need a buddy?" Bibbi asked.

Hawk's attention shifted to me. I pretended not to notice him or Gillian.

"I'm going to do a perimeter run. I'm not going to be long, and it's better off if I go alone."

"Are you sure that's a good idea?" she asked.

"Where are you headed?" Oscar asked, walking in the back room.

"Just going for a walk," I said, trying not to let the desperate need to escape leak out into my voice. It was hard when I couldn't get out of the building without having to answer to every person in the place.

"I was heading to Zark's. I'll head out with you. It'll be a nice little moonlight stroll," he said, smiling at me as he put on his act for the room.

"Sounds lovely," I said, not caring how it sounded as long as I got out of that room.

I felt Oscar's hand on the small of my back as we walked out. "Where are we heading?" he asked. His hand dropped as he switched back to friend mode when we hit the streets.

"Anywhere but there." I walked, not caring where I ended up right now. "You know, if you keep going with this little charade, people might start to believe there's something going on with us." At the moment, it seemed like a nicer reality than being the girl who was always watching Hawk with someone else.

"That's the point. I hope he does. He's being an idiot, and I'm enjoying this. Did you see his face when we left?" He smiled like a man who'd tasted triumph.

"No."

"Good. It's even better that you didn't look back. But

just so you know, it was burning him up." Oscar laughed. He might've been the only man in Xest who found it amusing when Hawk was annoyed with him.

"Trying to drive us together isn't a good idea, because I don't want him," I said.

Oscar laughed harder. I glared at him. He *kept* laughing.

"Fine. I'm attracted to him, but I don't want to be."

"You want him and he wants you, and I want you to be with him. It's got to be you. There's no one else like you. He can't be with someone weaker than him, especially not from Xest. They'd idolize him, and he'd eventually run roughshod over them because it's who he is. If you don't stand up to Hawk, that's what happens. It's not to be mean. His tendency is to run the show and call the shots." Oscar shrugged as if it wasn't a big deal.

I picked up my pace, wishing I'd gone alone. "So I get to be the lucky person because I tell him to go to hell?"

"It doesn't hurt that he wants you more than I've seen him ever want anyone." His voice had lost every shred of humor.

"That's not true." I picked up my pace even more.

"I know him. It is," he said as I left him standing in the street behind me.

28

Hawk walked toward me with a purpose, not stopping for any niceties with the rest of the room as they finished breakfast.

"You ready?" he asked.

I still had a half a cup of tea and a full biscuit left. For what needed to be done, and I was certain it was the hill, I'd finish later.

Gillian was calling his name and rushing over before I had a chance to stand. Bibbi glared across the room. Someone needed to take the butter knife away from her.

"Hawk, you're not walking me to work?" Gillian asked.

"Zab will do it."

"But—"

"It's fine. He can handle it." Hawk walked away from her before she could continue her damsel-in-distress act.

Gillian was frozen in her spot. I made my way around her, trying to not look in her direction.

Zab was slumped in his chair, looking as happy as Gillian was as I left the room.

. . .

We stopped in front of the hill as if planned. I had clear reasons to be nervous about walking on it. Last time hadn't been bad exactly, but not normal. Hawk's issues weren't as obvious. He was staring at it like he'd been the one that had been nearly stuck to it.

We both continued to watch it for another few minutes of silence.

He was still staring at the hill when he said, "I'll release you from your work agreement if you leave Xest. I'm not sure I'll be able to hide you, not even in Rest, but I'll try if you go."

Shoved out again. The guy was trying to make a career of getting rid of me. What he wanted didn't matter. It didn't. He was a stupid man, and an ass to boot. What did it matter what he thought?

But I couldn't keep it all buried anymore. I turned and swung at him. I missed and swung again as he kept dodging my strikes. I struck out another handful of times.

Worst part was that when I finally stopped, he was eyeing me as if I were crazy.

"Are you done?" he asked.

Just for that, I swung again. Damn he was quick.

"Stop trying to get rid of me. I'm not going anywhere," I screamed.

"I'm not trying to get rid of you," he replied, the veins popping in his neck.

"Except you are at every turn." I swung again, and this time he caught me in his arms.

The only good thing about him holding me was my arms were still free and I was able to hit his back, although not very effectively.

"You know, I'm beginning to understand why you lose

so many fights," he said, then held me firmer as I renewed my attack on him.

Or tried. It was a pitiful effort. Good thing Bautere wasn't watching, because this was not my best showing.

I stopped hitting Hawk and pulled away. He didn't try to stop me.

He watched me for a few moments as we both went to our proverbial separate corners. He tilted his head back and let out a sigh.

He was acting like *he* was having a bad day? I didn't say anything. If I talked, I'd argue. Then I'd start swinging again.

"You think you know the way things should be, but you don't even know the way they are," he said.

"Please spare me the condescension. Stop trying to turn this into you trying to be the good guy when clearly you just want me gone. I didn't arrive in Xest yesterday. I've been around the block a few times now, and you know damn well I can handle myself...most of the time."

"I don't think you realize the risks."

"Yes, I believe I do. I'm not saying that there might not be some surprises here and there, but show me a life lived fully that doesn't have a few. And stop trying to turn this around into something it isn't. This isn't about me. It's about you. Why don't you tell me why you're so obsessed with getting rid of me?"

He shook his head, nearly as angry as I was. He took a few steps away from me before rounding back, as if he were ready to hash this thing out. Good. I'd been ready for months.

"If you put our recent disagreements aside, just going by when you've been in a tight spot, would you say I've been one of your strongest allies here?"

"Recent disagreements and hazy future to the side?" I waited a few seconds, letting those parameters sink in. "I say we've both helped each other out a fair amount."

"Have I ever put you in danger or not tried to keep you alive?" he asked, ready to fight the point.

"Yes. You seem to want me breathing. Very gracious of you."

He reached into his pocket and drew out the box that held the stone. He opened the box and picked it up off its bed, then looked at me, holding up between us. I'd lain it in its bed more than once wondering what color the stone would flash if Hawk ever touched it. It didn't flash anything. It turned matte black.

"By your own admission, I'm your ally. The way I see it, I'm the best one you have, and yet you don't even know what kind of threat I am."

"Do you think that's going to scare me? Is that the purpose of this demonstration?" I stepped closer and wrapped both my hands around his. "This proves nothing. Do I know what you are? No. I make no claim to that. Most days I don't know what *I* am, and I'd bet it turns out to be a hell of a lot worse."

I grabbed the blackened stone from him, and it immediately came to life. If he thought his little trick was going to scare me, he didn't know the thoughts that kept me up at night.

He was looking at me, as if something had finally stunned him in his long life of knowing it all.

"Guess it's your day to be surprised?" I asked, laughing. He really thought he'd scare me. After what I'd seen, it would take a lot more than a black stone.

"I won't ask you to leave again." He was straight-faced,

but sounded relieved, or maybe even happy? It was more likely my own delusions.

"Good, because I'm tired of that question. You were getting a tad boring about it all." Gem in hand, I took a step toward the hill before I lit up the entire countryside with my rainbow. "I'll let go of the gem once I hit the spot."

I took another step toward the hill, thinking about how I'd tried to beat up the only backup I had. I stopped walking and turned back to him.

"You're ready to pull me off, right?" I waited for his agreement. This wasn't the hill I wanted to die on.

"Have I left you for dead yet?" His eyebrows rose, as if my question weren't worth answering.

"Say it anyway."

He crossed his arms, shaking his head, but then he finally said, "I'm going to get you."

I gave a short nod and went back to my mission, walking closer.

Whatever was brewing here, it seeped out toward me, greeting me, almost. Luring me with a warmth, a strange connection, like I was coming home, but to a home I'd never had. I moved closer, and not because I had to, not because this was my mission or duty, but because I wanted to. I was craving the contact.

I got to the place, and before I was taken over by whatever this was, I dropped the stone on the ground, so that maybe this thing's true colors would show through. Then I dropped to my knees, sinking my hands down into the snow until I could feel its warmth wrapping around me.

When I was yanked away this time, there was no relief pouring through me.

Hawk, who had just dumped me to the ground last

time, kept a hand wrapped around my arm, as if he'd sensed this place's draw on me.

I slowly sat up, trying to figure it out myself, and there was no explanation other than feeling like I'd fallen under the influence of something much stronger than myself.

"I don't know what's going on with that hill, but I'm not sure I should go near it again," I said.

He paused, not saying anything before he nodded. I didn't know how I'd appeared when I'd knelt in front of it, but he must have sensed something.

"What about the stone? What color did it flash?" I asked. I'd been so enthralled that I hadn't looked. Glancing over where I'd left it, I didn't even see a glimmer.

"There wasn't anything. Once you dropped it, it went clear."

Hawk's gaze shot up and over my shoulder. He straightened, and I jumped up to find Xazier standing not far from us. Why was he here? Had he followed us?

Xazier looked about the area. "Did someone call me?" he asked.

I got to my feet. "No one called."

"Oh," he said, smiling slightly. "My mistake. I'll just be..."

Lou appeared before Xazier had finished speaking. He scanned the area before he turned to Xazier.

"What's going on here? Did someone call me?" Lou asked.

"Nothing. I thought I heard my name called," Xazier responded.

Lou looked at us and then back to Xazier. "So you just happened upon them here?"

"Yes. That's exactly what happened. Same as you, I guess?" Xazier asked, as if leading Lou.

"Yes," Lou said, as he kept meeting Xazier's stare, like they were silently plotting with each other.

"Well, since no one called me, I'll be going," Xazier said, and then looked to Lou again.

"I will as well," Lou said.

Xazier's hand was by his leg, but I couldn't help but notice him put out three fingers, then two, then one.

They were both gone.

29

Hawk and I were in the upstairs sitting room, the one that sometimes opened to unknown destinations, sometimes his bedroom, and sometimes a random sitting room, as it was now.

I slumped on the couch. He was leaning beside a window that didn't exist if you looked at the outside of this building. Apparently the laws of physics didn't apply in Xest.

I'd lost track of how long we'd been in the room, both stuck in our own thoughts, trying to muddle through what had happened, why both Lou and Xazier had shown up. As usual, everything we found out led to more confusion, not answers.

I was the first to break the silence. "How do you think they knew we were there?"

He shook his head. "It wasn't the lame excuse of being called. Whatever is in that hill, they're somehow connected to it. We just don't know how or why."

"Why didn't they show up the first time?"

"Maybe because you connected to it a little stronger,

on a deeper level this time around. Or maybe not." He shrugged, still staring out the window.

I dropped my head back, shutting my eyes as I tried to shut out the world. If everything else went away, maybe the truth would show itself instead of overwhelming confusion.

"Did it feel anything like Dread? Any remnant or hint of the same magic?" Hawk asked.

"When I feel Dread, there's nothing but overwhelming rage and hate. Whatever lies in that hill feels like the complete opposite of that. It..." My voice faded as I recalled the warm feelings it had stirred in me.

He leaned his shoulder on the window frame, waiting for me to finish. "It what?"

"It wants me near it. Like it was calling to something in me, and it felt..." I shook my head. Hawk and I only talked half of the time I saw him. The other half were glares and stares of accusation. Discussing the overwhelming pull I felt from a mound of dirt with him was a huge leap.

He went back to staring out the window. "I don't think you should meet with Xazier anymore, or Lou for that matter. You said yourself that they want something from you. After they showed up today, I like the situation even less."

The fight coming could be seen from miles away. It was as if we were unable to be civil for more than ten minutes at a clip.

"I can't cut them off because they appeared in a field by a hill. I made an agreement," I said.

His eyes met mine. "You know there's something wrong. If you don't trust your instincts, you'll never survive here."

My spine straightened. "That subject is closed."

"I'm not suggesting you leave. After today, I'm convinced it's too late anyway. There are those that are hard to hide and others that are impossible. You fall into the latter at this point. This die has been cast. What I'm saying is stop being soft or you'll end up dead."

Soft? Did he think any part of me wanted to go to those meetings? It was the hardest thing I did. He didn't need any more ammunition to load the gun that would blow this whole deal sky high. *Soft* would've been agreeing with him and then letting him deal with the fall out. *Soft* was having someone walk me across the street every day.

"I'm on the hook with Xazier, and whether or not you want to admit it, I saved everyone's ass. I don't need to hear how I should toughen up. As to Lou, deal or no deal, if I stop speaking with him, it'll set off alarms. You can judge me all you want, but we would've already lost Xest if I hadn't done what I'd done."

"While you may believe that, it doesn't make it true."

He turned his attention, or at least his gaze, back to the window, like a man who wasn't used to having to compromise. According to the deference I saw around Xest, and Oscar's chat the other day, it was beyond obvious that he didn't get much pushback.

Oscar was crazy enough to think my unwillingness to bend to Hawk was why we'd be well suited? If he saw Hawk's locked jaw and bulging veins right now, or my clenched fists, he'd understand how foolish that notion was.

"Tell me one thing and I'll never give you grief about your need to sacrifice yourself again." Hawk locked eyes on me.

"What?" As much as I feared where this was going, I couldn't very well decline now.

"Why do you think you're worth so little?"

"I don't—"

"Either answer honestly or don't answer at all, but let's skip the bullshit." He shook his head and looked away.

"Let's not forget you wanted nothing more than to get rid of me, remember?" He was awfully quick to judge my actions. What about his own?

He pushed off the window and came to stand before me. "I was never trying to get rid of you. I was trying to shield you because I saw your worth. You're the only one who doesn't see it."

I huffed. "That's right. I forgot. I'm worth so much that you either try to get rid of me or act like I'm the only one who can save Xest.

"Seriously, you and the rest of this place think I can save something when I might end up being the thing you should get rid of. If I didn't think you weren't so confused about what I am, I probably wouldn't tell you. I'd be too afraid you'd kill me, but you're so intent on keeping your belief that it doesn't even matter." As soon as those words left my mouth, I wished there was a way to suck them back in. I didn't really want to die. Planting the idea that he was better off killing me was perhaps the stupidest thing I'd ever said, and I'd had quite a few stupid moments in my life.

He was still standing over me, silent. Should I run? Had my little speech made him see that light? When I finally looked up, there was definitely realization in his expression, but he didn't appear to be on the verge of attack.

"You think that's what's going on? I'm dug into a position and won't let go? I've already invested too much and have convinced myself, so I'm blind? Because I'll tell you right now, that's not the case." He shook his head and crossed his arms. "Is that why you offered yourself up as collateral? Why you're so determined to be angry with me? Easier to keep a buffer because one day I'll figure out that you're evil?"

I cleared my throat, letting out a forced laugh. "You're getting a little ahead of yourself with this psychoanalyzing crap. I'm trying to help you out, is all."

"I know exactly what I'm doing." Hawk sighed. "Don't go back to the hill alone."

"That I can agree with." It was the easiest agreement we'd ever made. I got up from the couch. We'd hit the witching hour, where all conversations would dissolve back into fighting if I stayed. I made my way out of the room before our high note finished with a low note.

Gillian was walking upstairs as I made my way down. She glanced up beyond me.

"Is Hawk up there?"

"Yes. He's all yours." I gestured back to direction I'd just come from.

"Oh. Another fight?" She could barely hide her smile.

"Isn't there always?" I smiled for her and softly laughed, giving her license as well. Then I walked away from her.

———

Hawk walked by me, but instead of ignoring me, he watched me. I wrote the wrong note for the third time in a row. I needed him to leave, or at least go back to ignoring me the way he had been. This constant feeling of awareness was doing me in.

It seemed like no matter where he was in the office, his

attention was on me. It was like a switch had been tripped yesterday. I wasn't certain where the switch was or how to turn it back off, but I was going to screw up work if he didn't cut it out.

Bibbi walked over and crouched beside my desk, resting her forearms on it as she leaned in. "What's going on?"

"What are you talking about?" I ignored the way she was watching Hawk watch me.

"Don't play stupid. I've been paying attention, and you know it. It's like some weird game is afoot, and I need to know the details. Something has changed in the dynamic here." The entire time she spoke, she never stopped staring about the room, watching where Hawk's attention went, which kept coming back to me.

"Can we talk about this later, when everyone else isn't watching? I don't want to turn this into a spectacle, if possible."

"So there *is* something. I knew it." Bibbi wasn't doing a great job of hiding her glee at being right.

There was a movement across the room, but I kept my eyes on my desk, refusing to meet Hawk's gaze again.

Bibbi whispered, "He just left. Now spill."

I stood. "Let's go get tea." I made my way to the back room before she could say anything else that might've been overheard. I couldn't say "let's go to the Sweet Shop" anymore because Bibbi hadn't set foot in that place in weeks because of her silent Gillian protest. I couldn't even say "let's have a cocoa in the back" because that was off the menu too. *Cocoa* had become a bad word around here. Even good-natured Bertha got an odd look when chocolate of any kind was mentioned these days, like someone had suggested sipping poison instead of sweets.

Bibbi followed so close that she caught my heel on the way to the tea kettle.

I'd barely tilted the kettle when Bibbi started in. "What happened in the last day or so that you two went from not looking at each other, to you still not looking at him but he looks like he wants to rip your clothes off? And I mean that in the best way possible." She was grinning and nodding, no shame in her game.

"I don't know what's wrong with him."

"You mean what's right with him?" Bibbi giggled.

I ignored that and the gleam in her eye. "He's acting weird for no reason."

"Did you kiss or something? There's got to be more to it." The grin was gone, replaced with a hard look, as if I'd ripped a good book out of her hands right when she was getting to the juicy parts.

"No. We had another one of our arguments, if you must know. We got into it as usual yesterday. Then I didn't see him again until he showed up in the office a little while ago with this weird attitude."

She tilted her head back, crinkling her nose. "What did you fight about?" she asked, as if that would make things clearer.

"Same old thing. He wants me to do one thing, and I'm going to do another."

"Very curious indeed. Are you sure there isn't something you're leaving out?" She sat down on the nearest chair, propping her chin on her palm, looking like the *Thinker* statue.

"Positive."

Oscar walked in the back door and came to an abrupt halt. His stare shifted between Bibbi and me.

"Hey, Oscar," I said, turning back to my tea.

Bibbi cleared her throat, got up out of her chair, and tilted her head back toward the door he'd walked in.

Oscar nodded.

"What are you two up to?" I asked, not liking the Kumbaya moment unfolding in front of me. These two in cahoots meant nothing but meddling and no good. They wouldn't just join forces, but multiply my troubles if they got on the same page.

"Nothing. Absolutely nothing," Bibbi said, chewing on her lower lip.

"Yeah, nothing," Oscar said, then looked at Bibbi and walked back out the door without another word.

Bibbi leaned against the table, suddenly having nothing to say.

I took a step toward the office. "You coming, or do you have something else you need to do?" I asked, as if she wasn't going to conspire with Oscar in the alley in two minutes.

She nodded. "I'll be there in a few."

Whatever they were plotting, I'd find out sooner or later whether I wanted to or not.

30

There was a strange vibe running through the back room at dinnertime. It started with the musical chairs as I went to grab a seat beside Musso.

Bibbi ran and sat in it first.

"I'm sorry, did you want to sit here?" she asked, as if I hadn't had my hand on it and been pulling it out.

"No, that's fine." I narrowed my eyes on her. Whatever she was plotting, it looked as if the first act was afoot.

Her eyes opened wider, as if she were as innocent as a day-old foal.

Unlikely.

I moved to a different seat, and Oscar settled in beside me. No sooner had he sat, his arm was resting along the back of my chair.

Musso and Bertha were looking askance but said nothing. Zab wasn't looking over at all, so whatever they were up to, he either knew or wanted to feign ignorance.

Whatever they were doing, at least I only had to deal with their weirdness and not Hawk's change of attitude on top of it. He'd decided not to show for dinner, which was usually hit or miss with him anyway.

"Do you like that seat for some reason, Bibbi?" Gillian reached for the large platter on the table, helping herself to a nice, big serving.

"I get cold. This spot is warmer," Bibbi said.

The spot she'd fought me for was closest to the back door and the draftiest in the room. No one, including me, bothered to call her out on that.

Hawk walked in the room, and Gillian beamed. I stared at my food. Everyone else acted like normal people would.

Hawk took the last chair available, which was nearest Gillian because no one sat next to her unless they had to.

"Here, Hawk. You should try some of this." She didn't wait for him to respond as she filled his plate for him.

He didn't seem to hear her, as he was staring at the back of my seat. Or, to be more accurate, the arm resting on the back of my seat.

"Bertha, these rolls are amazing," Gillian said, putting one on Hawk's plate. "You know, I have this chocolate spread that would bring them to the next level if you're interested?"

And *that* was why there was always an empty seat beside her. The closer the proximity, the harder it was to ignore those types of comments.

Bertha smiled. "I'm sure you do."

Oscar's chair shifted closer. "Talking about delicious, Tippi, you have to try this meat Bertha made." Oscar stabbed a piece on his plate and then held out his fork for me to eat off.

I went to push Oscar's fork away and tell him to get the

hell out of here with this hand-feeding act. I wasn't the type of woman who enjoyed being hand-fed, ever.

But Gillian's movement stilled my own. As she began to butter the roll on Hawk's plate, Oscar's offering looked better. I'd let Oscar feed me, whether I liked it or not.

I leaned in and groaned as the meat melted in my mouth. Oscar wasn't kidding.

"Wow, that is good. Bertha, you really outdid yourself. I'm not sure I've ever tasted anything more delicious in my life. You must've had a line around the block waiting to get your meals."

"Well, I was pretty busy," Bertha said. "I had a good half of Xest ordering from me. It got to be tiring after a while, all the hustle and bustle—"

"Oscar, I need to talk to you in the other room," Hawk said, his chair clanging as he got up.

The room went silent as we all watched the two of them leave.

Now what? If Hawk thought he was going to dictate who I was with, even if it was pretend, he had another thing coming. I went to stand, but Bertha grabbed my arm. My sweater blocked the tingle of magic-to-magic contact, but it was still not a done thing in Xest.

Her shaking head and serious face mirrored her actions. "They've been friends and allies for a long time. They can work it out. Oscar can handle himself."

I sat back down, and a glass of wine was placed in front of me. "Have a drink. It'll make you feel better," Musso said.

Someone should've poured Gillian one. She appeared to need it as she watched the door.

Raised voices carried into the back, but it was the kind

of yelling you did when you didn't want anyone to hear. The words were muffled.

Oscar must not have put up much of a fight, as they both walked back in shortly after they'd left. Hawk entered first, looking more determined. Oscar walked in right behind him. There was a flash of a smile right before he wiped it off his face, as if he weren't supposed to be happy about the outcome.

Hawk walked over to his spot and picked up his plate and glass. Maybe Oscar had won? Looked like Hawk didn't want to eat with us tonight after all. Then Hawk walked around the table, with Gillian watching his every move. Instead of leaving, he continued until he was standing in front of Oscar's seat.

Oscar walked over as well and picked up his plate before heading toward Hawk's abandoned seat.

Hawk settled in next to me.

"What's... What are you doing? Why are you switching seats?" How was I supposed to eat now? It was hard enough ignoring Hawk when he was at the same table. Now his elbow might brush mine.

I reached for my wine. There was going to be at least one refill in my future.

"What happened to my glass?" I scanned the table, wondering where it had disappeared. I glanced at everyone but Gillian. She was another one I'd have to ignore tonight.

No one said anything. If someone had taken my wine by accident, they weren't owning up to it.

"You can share mine," Hawk said, moving his glass in between us.

It seemed a bit intimate, but no worse than eating off Oscar's fork. Not a big enough issue to start one of our fights in front of everyone. This dinner was already too much of a struggle to make it through without at least another few sips of wine.

I took the glass and was a little greedier than I probably should've been. By the time I put the glass down, the entire table was staring at me in varying shades of shock.

"I was thirsty." They kept staring.

One would've thought I'd stolen the entire bottle and had an alcohol problem with the gaping mouths. Oscar was the only one who seemed quite pleased with my chugging ways.

I went back to eating, determined to ignore all the oddness of today. This meal couldn't be finished fast enough.

I was chewing huge chunks of meat, trying to get done, when the sniffling started. The sounds were coming from Gillian's side of the table. Had things gotten so bad that Hawk had to sit next to her or she had a meltdown? I glanced up, hoping she was getting sick instead. It would be much more respectable.

She was staring at me and Hawk, crying. No one was saying anything, as if this were normal. It was like the entire place had gone mad overnight.

"He's just sitting here instead of there. It's not a big deal. I'm sure he'll sit with you again tomorrow." The more I talked, the louder and uglier her crying got. By the time I was done, she was bawling.

Why was no one saying anything? She didn't like me. Shouldn't someone else step in?

"Hawk, can you go sit next to her so we can all eat in peace?" As much as it grated on my last nerve, no one was going to be able to eat if something didn't happen here. He'd either have to move or I'd have to go eat in my room.

"I can't," he replied crisply.

I turned to him. He was looking at Gillian. His face was solemn, but he wasn't getting up or saying anything.

The only thing that paused Gillian's sobbing was the occasional hiccup. She tossed her napkin down, scrambled up from her chair, and ran from the table.

Bertha was shaking her head and looking down. It was as if the entire table knew something I was oblivious to.

"I tried to tell her, but she wouldn't listen," Musso said.

"Tell her what?" I asked.

Bibbi looked like she could barely suppress her words. Her lips were pressed together so tight that I would've needed a pry bar to get her to speak.

I shook my head and stood. We might have our problems, but someone had to check on Gillian.

"You're not the one who should go," Bertha said, reaching out to me like she'd tackle me if I tried.

Zab shook his head.

Bibbi, lips still pressed together, had owl eyes as she slowly shook her head, warning me off.

"I have to handle this." Hawk got up and walked out of the room.

I hadn't wanted to go after Gillian, but that didn't stop the burning in my chest as I watched Hawk go instead. It was ridiculous, really. Hadn't I suggested he sit beside her?

Maybe the problem was that when she was upset, he felt the *need* to go to her. When I got attacked, battered and bruised, the only need he felt was to tell me how I'd failed. Who wouldn't want to hit him over the head?

The only upside was that I could eat in peace, because this dinner was the best I'd had in a month. I added another serving to my plate.

"What's going on with them? They having a lover's

spat or something?" I grabbed another roll to sop up the gravy.

No one said anything as they all looked at each other.

"If this is a secret, it's not a good one, since everybody appears to know but me." I took a huge bite, not really caring if they took half the night to come out with it, since I might be eating for that long. This meal was *that* good.

Bibbi looked at everyone else, waiting to see who would break first. It was clear she couldn't hold out much longer. I could see a little gap forming between her lips.

"What is it?" I asked.

That was all she needed, one last prod. Her lips burst open like she'd been holding back the entire Hoover Dam. "Hawk declared for you." Her eyes lit up as she bounced in her seat.

Oscar seemed quite pleased as well, in a more resigned fashion.

"What the hell are you talking about? Declared what?" Had Hawk gone back on his word to me and was going to try to kick me out of Xest again?

Bibbi flattened both palms on the table and said, "He declared his *intentions*." She watched me, waiting for a reaction.

"What intentions?" That son of a bitch. He had. He was going back on his words and intended to get rid of me.

"His interest. That he wants to be with you." Bibbi's voice rose.

I dropped my fork and leaned back, squinting in her direction.

She rolled her head. "You know, that you're the one? How many more ways can I say it?"

She watched and waited, staring at me as if a light bulb would turn on.

Bibbi had been waiting for this so long that she was losing her mind. "Are you sure you know what you're talking about?" I said. "I think you might've misconstrued something. Hawk and I aren't... It's not... Let's just keep it simple and say there's no way you've got that right." I went back to eating now that I didn't have to worry about packing my bags and finding a new place to live.

"Tippi, I know what I saw."

Bertha turned to Bibbi. "Maybe I should take a crack at this?"

Bibbi shrugged, relenting to Bertha, who would surely make more sense. Bibbi was so set on the way she wanted things to be that she was getting a little crazier than normal.

Bertha smiled at me and then said, "When Hawk shared his wine with you, it wasn't typical. He had you drink from his glass. That means he's declaring for you, and it's very significant. Like Bibbi said, it means he's interested and is declaring that interest. If someone else was interested, they'd have to say something to him, perhaps fight him. He's pretty much called dibs on you."

Bibbi was giving me the *now do you believe me?* look.

Zab occasionally glanced up and shared a look with Musso before the two of them went back to eating.

Oscar laughed softly to himself, nodding in Bibbi's direction as if they'd won a hard battle together.

"How can he declare for me if he's dating Gillian?" I dropped my fork and looked around the table.

"Oh, he's not dating her," Bertha said, shaking her head. "She wants him to, but he's not interested. We all know it. Musso tried to tell her that no good will come from it, but she wouldn't listen. Didn't want to hear the truth."

Musso shrugged as he continued to eat. That was as much involvement as he seemed willing to give.

I'd finally lost my appetite. "Don't I have a say in this? Shouldn't he have to get my permission to declare?"

"Why? It's not a contract with you," Oscar said.

"But you said someone would have to go to him if they were interested in me," I said to Oscar, daring him to deny what Bertha had said.

"Well, that's true." Oscar nodded.

"Nobody is going to fight him." I was the one raising my voice now.

There were nods around the table.

"Only people who don't want to challenge him," Bertha said, not seeming upset at all.

"Which is everyone."

"Well, yes, that's true," Bertha said.

Was she not understanding the situation? This was barbaric. Did none of them see this? As I again took the temperature of the people at the table, it didn't seem as if they did.

I got up and made the third grand exit of the night.

―――――

I paced in front of the door to the upstairs like I was driven by a steam engine with an inexhaustible heap of coal. Hawk was still upstairs. Everyone else had gone to sleep a long time ago, and he *still* hadn't come down. I would've stormed up there and barged in if I didn't want to be as far away from his conversation with Gillian as possible. Even being in the building didn't seem like a great idea, but there was a conversation that needed to be had tonight.

What was taking so long? Was he apologizing? *Sorry you were into me? Sorry I flirted with you in front of Tippi? Sorry I was nice to you?* Was that a thing you should say to someone?

I took another lap around the office before I made my way to the back room.

That was when the stairs creaked. I shot back into the office as Hawk walked in. He had barely got a second before I launched into the question that had been burning inside me for hours.

"What was that stunt you pulled at dinner?" I stood in front of him, arms crossed. He wouldn't be leaving here without answering.

"I'm not sure what you're talking about. You'll have to expand on what you mean." He walked past me into the back room.

I almost tripped on his heels. "You know what you did. What game are you playing now? You agree to stop pushing me out and now you figure you'll make it miserable for me to stay?"

"I'm not sure I understand how I'm making you miserable *this* time." He settled onto the couch, resting his arm on the back. He was looking at me as if he were completely in the dark.

"You know what you did, you know, with the wine and the declaration."

"You mean sharing my drink with you when you didn't have one?" He raised a brow, as if I were crazy.

Was I? It hadn't been my idea. Bibbi told... Okay, Bibbi could be a little crazy, but Bertha wasn't. And Gillian hadn't run out of the room crying for nothing.

"If that was nothing, then how come everyone else in the room saw it as something?"

"Because they like to believe in old wives' tales and weird rituals that are beyond antiquated. Think about this for a minute: I shared a drink with you. How many drinks have been shared in Xest? Does it make sense that would make it a declaration? What about Oscar sharing his food? Did he also declare?"

He had a point. Oscar had given me a bite of food. "What about how you moved chairs?"

Even as I pursued this line of questioning, I could feel the heat blooming in my cheeks. Was I really going to argue with him about how he'd declared for me when he was saying he hadn't? Next I'd be trying to bully him into confessing his love for me.

"Oscar's been playing his games for weeks, trying to instigate. I put an end to it in the easiest way possible."

I felt a frisson of anger.

It meant nothing. The fuel I'd been running on all night sputtered out. I took a few steps back, making my way over to the safer area by the tea kettle as Hawk watched. So he hadn't declared anything? I sank down onto a chair, the energy gone.

"Everything okay?" Hawk asked, his voice softer than usual, as he continued to watch me.

"Of course. I'm glad we got that cleared up is all." Yep, things were back to normal, just the way they should be.

"Glad I could help," he said, getting up.

I didn't watch him as he made his way out, even as he paused by the door for a few moments. Once he finally left, I waited another twenty minutes, long enough for Hawk to be long gone, before I grabbed my jacket and headed out the back door.

I'd walked from one end of Xest to the other, searching for grouslies, when a lone man happened upon me. His anger roiled off him in waves.

I turned, staring at him. The last fight I'd had, my odds had been much worse and my mood had started off much better.

"I wouldn't do what you're thinking, not tonight. It won't end well for you." The pent-up confusion and rage of my current situation must have seeped out into my voice, because he only paused a second before walking away.

I hadn't recognized him from the many faces of the last attack.

Actually, I hadn't seen any of the people who'd attacked me. Not a one. Not at the factory, and not in the streets. Hawk's words came back to me: "I don't feel like killing more people, and I'm sure they don't feel like getting killed."

31

"Now what happened? Why are you refusing to look at him? He declared for you. Doesn't that hit you anywhere warm and tingly inside? You can tell everyone else you're not into him, but I'm not buying it. I know. I can *see* it."

The second I walked into the back room for a cup of tea, Bibbi followed me, and it was clear what was coming.

"I'm not looking at him because I'm embarrassed. I accused him of declaring for me when he didn't." I'd barely looked up from my desk all day. I'd actually had to remind myself to look up occasionally so that I wouldn't seem odd.

"That doesn't make sense. What happened?" She glanced at the door to make sure we were still alone.

I took a sip of my tea, trying to find strength to rehash this. "I accused him of declaring for me and basically overstepping, and he said he did nothing of the sort."

My cheeks warmed just from uttering the words.

Bibbi's mouth dropped open. "He did too. I saw it."

"You saw an antiquated ritual."

"*Antiquated. Ritual?* That's what he said? I know what I know." She took a step toward the door, shaking her head.

I grabbed her arm, swinging her back to me. Bibbi had one purpose burning in her eyes, and she was not making this a debacle in front of everyone. As it was, I already couldn't look at Hawk. It was going to take days to undo the damage from last night.

"You are not saying anything. Promise me." I hardened my tone, letting her know just how serious I was. It was still iffy whether it would work. Bibbi didn't back down easy.

She looked at the door, as if it was taking every ounce of her control not to go walk in the office and lay all the dirty details out on the table.

"Bibbi?"

She clenched her fists. "Fine. I won't. But for the record, I don't care what he says. I know what he did. If he's telling you it wasn't a declaration, it's probably because you look ready to run at the first sign he's really into you."

"He didn't declare for me. Believe me, he's never made any declarations of any type of wanting anything but a couple of quick grabs." I tried to not sound disappointed or bitter. I wasn't sure I succeeded with either.

"That is so not true." Bibbi made it sound like she was defending Hawk's honor. "I'm not buying it. Look at it from my perspective. I nearly begged you to tell Gillian you and Hawk had something, but you wouldn't say a word. Just let her set herself up for a disaster." Bibbi crossed her arms.

"What disaster? I don't know what went down between them last night, but he was probably up there apologizing half the night." She was starting to light the fires to my anger.

"That's why she wasn't at breakfast?" Her incredulous disbelief was hard to ignore.

"She said she had an early order." Bibbi did have a point, but it was more likely they were still fighting. Gillian was the type to drag something out.

"You are so smart in some ways and so stupid in others that it nearly kills me sometimes." Bibbi threw up her hands, shaking her fist.

Gillian, the woman of the hour, walked in. We both fell silent. I scrambled to fill the dead air so we didn't look as guilty as we were.

"I really don't think we're getting a storm." I should've come up with a more believable topic, because I was the last person in Xest who could predict weather, and everyone knew it.

My efforts didn't have the effect I'd hoped for. Gillian walked over and took her cocoa off the counter. She smiled at Bibbi but barely tilted her head in my direction before heading back out of the room.

"Is she mad at me?" I kept staring at the door, wondering how I'd ended up on *her* bad side. "I think she is."

"Because I'm right and Hawk *did* declare for you. You weren't straight with her, and she figured it out last night." Bibbi hopped up on to the table and grabbed one of Bertha's pastries off the plate next to her.

Zab walked in, slumping into a chair. "Gillian is on the warpath. I had to get out of there quickly. You should've told her something was going on with you and Hawk."

"Nothing is going on with us, so there was nothing to tell." I was getting tired of no one believing me.

Zab huffed out a half laugh and shook his head.

"What's she doing?" I took a peek toward the door but wasn't close enough to see anything. From the glare I'd gotten a minute ago, I'd rather wait it out in the back room.

Zab sighed really loud. "You don't know the attitude she's dishing out. She walked in the office and started saying how she was leaving as soon as she got her things, that she'd been thinking about it all morning and we didn't deserve her, the whole time glaring at Hawk. And you know what's coming next, don't you?" He stared at the two of us.

I had a hunch, but I wasn't going to be the messenger. I'd quit the bad news delivery team. Bibbi seemed to have resigned as well.

"I'm going to get stuck walking her back to her place while she's in the middle of a fit."

Yep, that was what I figured. I sipped my tea, grateful it wasn't going to be me. I spared a look at Bibbi, who was trying not to grin.

"Zab," Hawk called from the other room.

Zab stood, cursing and kicking at the air before he walked out.

Hawk walked in a few moments later and made himself a tea. "Gillian moved out and there won't be cocoa for a while. She doesn't want any of us in the Sweet Shop."

"What makes you think that?" I asked.

"Because on her way out the door, she said, 'Keep all your assholes out of my store.'" He raised an eyebrow at us.

Hawk shrugged and walked back out to the main room.

A few minutes later, Zab strolled into the back room

again, shaking his head and looking even worse than he had before he left.

"That bad?" I was almost afraid to ask.

"Worse. We got halfway there, and I was so close to being rid of her when she decided she wasn't leaving after all. She's back." Zab groaned as if in real pain.

"She's back?" Bibbi said.

"Yes. Says her life is too valuable to be left unattended." He leaned forward, running a hand through his hair.

"So close," Bibbi said, and then groaned. I joined her.

"So very close," Zab agreed.

Gillian had gone back to her shop, so I was down to having to ignore two people. I still couldn't look Hawk in the eye, and Bibbi had been added to the list. Her *you're being so stupid* looks were a bit much.

At least I had an appointment this afternoon to take my mind off other things. That was a busy day, the way things were going.

When the door opened, I expected it to be Cassie, a low-level Middling and a fairly well-rounded witch who would still report for work. It was Mertie. Her coming here without a summons was strange enough. Her walking in with a bag thrown over her shoulder was the kind of thing that stole the air from your lungs. Or my lungs, anyway, because I was the only one who understood what was happening.

I hated knowing something was going to come back and bite you in the ass and yet there was no way to avoid it. All you could do was wait for the eventual problem, and then grin and bear it.

She scanned the office until she located me. The only

reason I was still sitting was because running out of the room would've been too obvious.

She walked over and dropped her bag on my desk. "I'm calling in my favor. Where's my room?"

With that sentence alone, all eyes swiveled from her to me.

Bibbi's jaw was hanging down. She'd had no problem believing Hawk declared for me, but this? This was clearly too much for her.

Musso groaned, which turned into a throat clearing. Zab shook his head behind her back.

I was afraid to look at Hawk.

"We had a deal," she said, getting impatient.

"And I'm going to honor it. I'm just surprised, is all. I didn't expect you yet." Or ever, at least when we'd first struck the deal.

"Yeah, well, that place was getting a little too weird for me." She took a cigarette out and lit it with her finger.

Bibbi stood. "You can't do—"

Zab pulled her back down to her seat and shook his head.

"Tippi, we need to speak," Hawk said.

"I'll be right back," I said. "He probably wants to talk about which room to give you. Why don't you go in the back room with Zab?" I ignored Zab's outraged look. "There's some good cocoa from Gillian back there."

Or had she taken it all away? Who could keep track anymore?

"Isn't that the woman who makes the good cocoa? That annoying Sweet Shop lady? I love her cocoa, but she gives me the creeps. I never go in there." Mertie let out a chimney's worth of smoke as she talked.

"Well, it's amazing, and there's a ton of it in the back."

"She's staying here too, right?" Mertie asked.

"She is. Is that a problem?" *Please let it be.*

"Nah. I'll get her in line quick enough. She looks like she scares easily. I'll take a cocoa as you two figure out which room." She went to turn but then paused. "By the way, I don't like too much sun. I have sensitive eyes. A shadier spot is better. And quiet. I'm used to a lot of privacy."

"Got it," I said.

Zab took a long few seconds to force his mouth into the shape of a smile. "Okay. Yes, I can take you to the cocoa." He wrung his hands as he walked toward the back, glancing over to keep an eye on Mertie's location.

Hawk's expression said it all so clearly before he uttered a word. "You invited her to stay here?"

The only good thing about this situation was that it totally eclipsed the awkwardness of last night. It was such a mess, in fact, that my accusations weren't a thing anymore.

"I didn't think she'd take me up on it. She doesn't like any of us, so why would she move in?"

"Well, apparently she thinks she is."

"We're already on top of each other anyway. What's one more body?" As reasons to let her move in, that one sucked. I'd come up with it, and even I could see the flaws.

"She's going to get on everyone's nerves," he said.

That had to be a joke of some sort. As if his Gillian didn't?

"Your invites haven't always been pleasant either." I pasted a fake smile on my face and held my fingers in the air, raising my voice high as I said, "*My cocoa is the best. I'm the best. I do everything better.*"

I dropped the act and nailed him with an accusatory glare that should've put him in his place.

Instead, he laughed. "She gets under your skin the most, doesn't she?"

How had this gotten turned back around on me? "She bugs everyone. Can you just make a room?"

I didn't wait for his answer. I had to go save Zab.

32

"Ugh. You're here. Some retreat this place is turning out to be," Mertie said. She was sitting at a chair pulled up to Zab's desk, her hooves on his paperwork.

I glanced around and saw Lou. The guy was creepy enough without sneaking in without a sound.

"Tippi, he's not moving in too, is he? I've got my limits of what I can stomach." She flicked her cigarette ashes into the pile formed on the ground near her seat.

"Yes, we all have our limits," Zab said, giving Mertie the side-eye.

"He's not moving in." I got up from my desk and made my way over to Lou, who was acting as if he hadn't heard a thing Mertie had said.

Before I got to him, Hawk's voice boomed out from behind me. "Can we help you?"

Lou looked over my shoulder before focusing his attention back on me. "I'm here to speak to you, but he can come along as well. Is there anywhere private in this place we can go?"

"Let's head to the back," I said, waving him to where

Hawk stood. It was as far into the building as I could stomach. If I took him upstairs, I doubt I'd be able to sleep there again.

Hawk waited for Lou to pass and then stepped in between us. The back room was empty, and a second after we were all inside, the place went quiet. It would stay that way as long as Hawk wanted it to.

Lou looked about the room as if he couldn't decide where it was safe to sit. He glanced at the couches before returning to the table, where he took a chair and settled down.

I took a seat opposite him and waited for him to speak. He'd come here, after all.

Hawk didn't bother sitting at all.

"I'm here to do you a favor." Lou bowed his head as if bestowing a benediction.

"Sorry if I don't jump for joy, but that's a bit hard to believe." I leaned back, folding my arms. I didn't need to see Hawk to know he was having the same reaction.

"Fine. I was trying to be pleasant, but it behooves me to help you." Lou smiled as if he were grinning through the pain as he plucked invisible lint from his white dress jacket.

"Why?" Hawk asked, the question sounding more like a demand.

"Because it does. So what will it be? Do you want my help, or would you prefer to let Xazier come and do things his way?" Lou tapped his fingers on the table and crossed his legs, while keeping his grin in place.

I leaned forward. "We'll hear you out, but let me make something clear before you go any further: we don't care what you do or how you help. We won't give you our allegiance. Xest is ours."

His smile grew a little tenser and more frigid, if that were possible. "I didn't think offering to help would be greeted with such hostility and resistance."

Hawk pulled out a chair, sitting beside me. "We're merely laying out our conditions, but we're listening."

"I'd heard you two weren't so simpatico, but I see that was faulty information." Lou sniffed in displeasure.

Neither of us replied as we sat shoulder to shoulder. We might fight constantly, but we did seem to unite at all the right times.

"I'm going to help, with no strings attached." Lou leaned forward, steepling his fingers in front of him. "I know how to put the monster back in its bottle. But if you don't care to know, send me away. It's your choice."

"And just how do we go about doing it?" Hawk asked.

"You don't." Lou made a swirling motion with his finger before he stopped and pointed it at me. "She does."

Just what I needed right now. Another delusional man —angel—telling me I could do things I couldn't. Why was it that every male in Xest seemed to believe I was more capable than I was? Under normal circumstances it might be flattering. Even in the beginning, it had been kind of interesting and cool to have people think I was special.

But the games were done. We needed hard facts and proven methods. I couldn't afford to get wrapped up in flattery. I needed a plan etched in concrete.

"If I've been able to, why haven't we found this special ability yet?"

"Because you haven't known what to do, and neither have your confidants. But I do." Lou placed a hand on his chest and graced us with a smug smile.

"What if it's a trap?" Oscar leaned forward in his seat.

Everyone had piled into the back room the moment Lou walked out, except for Gillian. It appeared she was planning on working later hours.

"It could be, but it's a chance I have to take," I said, my legs kicked up on the table in front of the couch as I tried to present a calm image.

"How are you supposed to get it there?" Bibbi asked, as if I hadn't left that part out on purpose.

"I can't say. It's a bit delicate." I *couldn't* say. If I did, everyone in this room would tell me I was crazy. I was still waiting for Hawk to say it.

"But Lou told you how to get it to come?" Musso asked. His forehead was wrinkled as he hung back over by the fireplace, as if he didn't want anything to do with what was to come.

"Yes," I said, having a hard time meeting his stare.

Hawk wasn't saying much. On the average day, knowing where Hawk stood on an issue wasn't a problem, but he was keeping his cards close to his vest. Reading him tonight was like reading Latin. I was committed to doing whatever I had to, and that meant trying out Lou's plan. But I couldn't stop myself from glancing at Hawk every few minutes, trying to get a read.

"Are you sure about this?" Bibbi lapped the room again.

"Yes," I said. "I have to give it a try. Lou said it wouldn't necessarily work forever. It'll just buy us time. It makes me believe he was telling the truth." He also said he couldn't guarantee it wouldn't hurt me, although he *thought* I'd make it out alive. They didn't need to know that much detail.

"There's no other options?" Bertha asked.

"No. We've been running around chasing our tails. We can't even pin it down. I'll think about it for a few days, but this might be the only way." I spoke a truth that no one else was willing to admit.

The room looked at me as if I'd announced the looming date of my funeral.

"You should do whatever you feel is right and I'll back you one hundred percent, body and mind." Bibbi squared her shoulders and her face firmed up, losing all softness.

"Thank you." The transformation Bibbi had made, from meek young girl to hard soldier, was nothing less than amazing. Or maybe it hadn't been a transformation at all but a shedding of an outer skin to reveal the truth beneath. Either way, I was proud to call her a friend.

"That goes for me too," Zab said.

"It goes for us all," Oscar said.

There was one voice that remained silent. I wouldn't look his way again, as if begging for approval. It had to be done, and I was the only one who could do it. No matter how much this show of support helped, other than lifting my spirits, it didn't affect the plan.

The time ticked by slowly as the room emptied until it was just me and him left.

"If you have a criticism, I'd prefer you say it. At least put it out there so I can tell you that you're wrong." It was unfortunate that I was only partially joking.

"No critique. I'm always on your side, whether you realize it or not." Hawk's calm statement helped settle something inside of me.

For the first time in hours, I met his gaze. He walked over and sat opposite me, resting his arm on the back of the couch, looking as tired as I felt.

"I'll back you up, whatever your decision," he said.

"Then why were you so silent?" I asked.

"It doesn't mean I like it. But very rarely am I happy with any of the plans you decide upon." His face softened.

"I want to do it tomorrow, early, before anyone knows we're gone." I toyed with the fringe on the throw blanket beside me. "Just us. That's it. If things go badly, I don't want to worry about anyone else getting caught in the crossfire."

"It's not going to be easy."

That sounded like the understatement of the decade. The way Lou had laid it out, I'd be lucky to make it through the first part of what was coming.

Hawk stood.

"You think it'll work?" I asked before he could leave, hating how desperate that had come out.

He took a step toward me. "You'll make it."

"How do you know?"

He leaned down, his lips crashing over mine, his presence swallowing me whole the way it always did when he touched me.

I was breathless when he broke off a few seconds later.

Hawk cupped my face with a firm grip. I couldn't break away from the intensity of his stare. "I can't stop you from doing this, but I'll be damned if I let you die."

He walked out of the room, leaving me stunned for different reasons.

———

It wasn't yet dawn when I made my way downstairs in what I considered my best combat gear of black boots with steel toes, leather pants, and a jacket that wasn't very warm but didn't have any bulk to slow me down.

Hawk was waiting for me, looking pretty kick-ass himself.

"You ready?" he asked as I walked into the room.

Sleep hadn't come to me until well into the night, but my tank was fueled with adrenaline. From the calmness that had settled over me, it seemed my engine ran cleaner on that stuff than sleep and good food. It was something to think about in the future. Or had I become adrenaline adapted? Either way, I was about as steady as you could get.

"Yeah. I am. Let's go catch some evil."

33

We walked to the spot, the place we'd always felt Dread the most. It wasn't there, but Lou had told us how to lure it out.

I held my palm out to Hawk, silently asking for his knife.

"You're sure?" he asked.

"As sure as anyone can be, given the circumstances."

He reached for the blade at his side and handed it to me then grabbed my hand. "You just need a little. Don't deplete yourself so much that you don't have enough to finish."

I nodded and steadied myself. He was right. I couldn't mess this part up. I was about to offer up a sacrifice to whatever the forces that ruled Xest were. I would say the words and then pierce my skin right above my heart. If I did it right, it would flow magic. If I did it wrong, it would flow blood. If it went really wrong, it would drain all the magic I had, and this wasn't the worst part of the plan.

Blade in hand, I said the verse I'd only learned yesterday.

"With this blade, I offer homage. I offer life; I offer payment. Do my will. Grant my wish; fulfill my destiny."

My chest grew warm, tingling.

I tugged my shirt down to right below my collarbone and dragged the point of the blade over my flesh. I cut just deep enough, but hopefully not too deep. Apparently slicing yourself open was a delicate thing.

I didn't stop until the line, which was red at the moment, was the approximate length of my fist, or heart. The red that seeped out, which I was sure meant I'd blundered, slowly lost its color, first turning clear, almost like I oozed aloe, until it began to shift. That was when things got really interesting. As I stared down at my chest, the clear jelly substance began to take on a tint of pink, then blue, silver, turquoise, until it resembled the rainbow of my magic. As it shifted, it lost its gel-like appearance, thinning into vapor and lifting away from me in a steady stream.

Hawk gave me a nod as I stood, waiting. Just as Lou had said, it didn't take long to get results. A trickle of unease settled over me. I could feel Dread nearing.

Hawk lifted his head, sensing it as well. Our gazes met. I tilted my head before I turned and started in the direction of the hill, the last place I thought I'd go back to.

Watching the stream of my magic floating on the air, I kept my pace slow and steady, leaving a lure for Dread to follow.

Every few moments, I'd glance back, checking the trail I was leaving behind.

I looked back to Hawk, who was also watching. He nodded again. He thought it looked good too, and we both better be right. This needed to work. It *had* to work. When Lou laid out the steps, the logic had appeared sound, but not without risk. I was bleeding magic in a world where that was the lifeblood that kept you alive in Xest. The risk was inherent and obvious from the start, and this was only the beginning.

We'd been walking for a good while when Hawk's attention shifted from the stream of magic bleeding out of my chest to my face.

He didn't need to say the words.

"I'm good," I said, even as I felt the drain. How much magic could I afford to lose before I wouldn't be capable of finishing the plan? I had enough for now, and it would have to hold.

Zab had once told me that I must be one of the lucky ones with infinite magic. I didn't have to live in fear like so many others, who needed to budget every day, knowing that each use might take minutes, hours, days, or even years off their life. I could use mine with abandon. But even Infinites needed time to recharge. What if I was completely drained before I could? But that was part of the point of this little endeavor. It would sense my weakness and finally make its move on me directly. That was when I'd get my chance, if I lived long enough.

I picked up my pace. I couldn't dwell on the negative, not now, when it might weigh me down. There could be no fear, no doubt. Only success. Weakness didn't win wars. And if I didn't win? I'd go out in one hell of a blaze of glory.

The hill came into sight before us; the presence of Dread had seemed to keep pace behind. As we got closer, Hawk distanced himself. In the end, this would be my battle alone.

The hill that had been nothing to climb before now made me slow my steps and breathe deeper. The doubts were trying to crowd my mind, but I forced my attention solely on my purpose.

I made my way to the spot that called to me and embraced its welcome, knowing somehow that whatever was beneath me, it was on my side. I knelt, knowing the next step was to close the cut on my chest, finish the offering. I placed one hand on the ground, and as I did, I felt a surge of power within me, the ground I knelt upon warming, and a connection that wiped away any weakness.

Hawk called out to me, "It's enough."

I shook my head. He didn't feel what I did. I could do this, and if the trail of my magic was what Dread wanted, it was going to get it.

"Tippi," Hawk said.

"You have to trust me." I placed my other hand on the ground, feeling more positive than ever that I was making the right choice.

Hawk was barely maintaining his distance, inching closer, not that it would stop Dread. As opposed to the rest of the witches and warlocks in Xest, which Hawk scared away without effort, when it came to Dread, I was the only thing it feared.

Both hands on the ground, I stopped fighting the feeling and connection.

Hawk wasn't moving, not a hair, fighting for control. I stopped looking at him, afraid a momentary slip on my part might trigger his undoing and ruin our progress, and there was some. I could feel Dread nearing, its evil swelling around me.

But as it came closer this time, it was if I were watching a winter storm ravage the land through a window. I felt shielded from the usual feelings of despair that would normally threaten to take me under. This time

I felt comforted, secure, as if I sat wrapped in a blanket in front of a roaring fire. Whatever magic was in this hill, it cocooned me.

Dread moved closer, its approach steady, and I wondered if the rest of the plan would go as Lou had predicted. Just as the doubts started to build, I felt a sensation where my hands were, as if I were on the other end of a force that was trying to pull at me. But the connection I felt to whatever was beneath the mound was stronger.

A howl erupted in the air and a vague form of a creature came in and out of existence, its outline never completely clear, bits of its form appearing on and off, as if it weren't quite from this plane. A large sinew of muscle would appear, before disappearing again, only to have jaws or claws come next.

I looked down, ignoring the sight of what was coming way too close, and focused on the tug of war that had begun.

My concentration was so fixed on holding my position that Lou's appearance didn't register until Hawk moved closer, planting himself in between us. He had one eye on me and one on Lou.

What was Lou doing here? When he'd laid out the steps, he'd made it clear this was all going to be on me. The intensity of his gaze sent a strange, creeping feeling down my spine, which settled into my gut, right around the spot where I got that stonelike feeling.

Dread tugged at my control, and I forced Lou out of my mind. Hawk would have to deal with him for now, because if I didn't put every ounce of what I had left into this battle, Lou wouldn't be an issue.

I kept my hands planted on the hill I'd never thought to touch again, feeling the immense power beneath it, letting it flow up and around and through me, feeling the tug it had on me and also Dread. It was as if we were in a three-way tug of war, and I wasn't a hundred percent sure where the lines were drawn. Would Dread end up in the hill somehow? Would I? Were we both connected by this source?

Bit by tiny bit, I could feel Dread getting pulled in closer. At the same time, I could feel myself linking deeper to it. Was this how it ended? Would Dread end up absorbed by whatever magic we were upon, and I along with it? Was this my end as well?

I shifted until my chest was resting on my knees, my hands still firmly on the ground in the exact same place they'd started as the battle I'd thought would take minutes stretched on. Minutes seemed to be dragging out as Dread fought the trap, making me fight for every tiny speck of progress. I dripped sweat in the frigid temperatures. My hands were so warm that they had melted through all the snow and then thawed the ground. They were lodged in mud that had begun to take on the same color of my magic, a rainbow sludge of sorts.

"Tippi..." Hawk took a hesitant step toward me.

"I'm good." I shot a hard look past him to Lou, who was waiting this out as well. With a last glance at Hawk, I said, "I've got this."

He nodded, letting me know he'd keep up his end, which meant he'd keep Lou from killing me, or whatever his plan might be. Lou was patient if nothing else, standing back and waiting.

Another hour or so rolled by, my body feeling battered as I stayed in the crumpled position, directing all my energy to the feeling of the hill. Mentally, I was no longer there. I was nowhere, nothing in focus but an internal battle to keep fighting.

When I did open my eyes again, we'd been joined by Bautere, and another ten of his kind. They'd joined Hawk, forming a circle around me and Dread as we battled, keeping Lou on the outskirts. The air around me was nearly glowing with my magic, lighting the entire hill as it continued to flow from my body.

Bautere nodded at me. I nodded back, hoping he could see the gratefulness in my gaze.

I didn't know if he could, but as I looked at the others of his kind, at Hawk, even at Lou, they all stared upon me with a mix of disbelief and awe in varying degrees.

I dropped my head to my knees again, concentrating all the energy I had on one sole purpose: Dread.

There was a gasp and my eyes shot open.

Dread, still not opaque but not transparent enough to let the sun filter through anymore, writhed forward, casting us all in shadow as it partially sank.

It got closer and closer to me as I struggled to not give an inch. I wanted to pull back from the approaching creature. The only thing keeping me going was sheer will.

The closer it got, the more I feared a trap, but not for *it*, as Lou had promised. It was nearly upon me when one last step set off a roar of agony that nearly shattered my eardrums and blew my hair back. The creature was slowly sucked into the hill, clawing at the air as it was.

I stayed in place, not sure if I could break contact with the hill or if I should, afraid it would rear up again.

Suddenly I was blasted from the spot and thrown several feet away.

Hawk was beside me within seconds, Bautere by him.

Hawk took my hand, laying it over my still-bleeding magic.

"Say the words. Say them," Hawk demanded, grabbing my shoulders and holding me up.

"My gift is finished."

My hand dropped to my lap and he moved his fingers to my wrist.

Hawk nodded to Bautere.

Bautere leaned his head back, raising his arms to the air. "I don't feel it anymore."

"Neither do I," Hawk said.

Neither did I.

There was nothing but silence as I looked around. Bautere's fighters had all closed ranks around us, protecting us as we regrouped.

"You did well," Bautere said, giving me a nod. As I looked past him, his people did the same. One by one, they all nodded to me, a heavy silence filling the air.

"Is there pain anywhere else?" Hawk asked, feeling the bones of my legs and then arms.

"No. I'm good." I tried to sit up on my own but didn't make it more than a few inches before leaning back into him.

"You did enough. Rest now. I'll take care of you." Hawk bent down and scooped me up into his arms. I didn't fight him. Couldn't if I wanted to, and at that moment, I didn't want to at all. I laid my head on his shoulder, knowing he'd get me home safe, no matter what.

A gap opened in the fighters' circle as Lou stepped forward. The fighters barely gave him more than an inch of buffer, making it clear whose side they were on.

He stepped forward, a smile forced upon his face.

"Impressive. I wasn't sure you would be up to it, but you've proven yourself quite capable."

"Thank you. It was a good plan."

Hawk said nothing, but his arms tensed around me.

Lou nodded. "I'm sure I'll be seeing you again," he said, before disappearing.

"You weren't supposed to survive this," Hawk said.

"No, I don't think I was."

34

"You're awake." Bibbi was sitting at the end of my bed, staring at me.

I nodded, wondering how long she'd been there as I stretched my stiff muscles.

"Hawk didn't want me to wake you, but I wanted to make sure you were okay. You were half out of it when you came back, and Hawk told us what happened. You should have told us what you were going to do. I would've come with you." She ran a hand back and forth on the quilted spread.

Which was the exact reason I hadn't told her. There was no way I was giving full disclosure so she could get herself killed.

Shit. Why did that have a familiar feel? Did that mean I was like Hawk?

No. Definitely not. Wasn't in the same stratosphere.

"I'm sorry. I woke up and knew I had to do it right then and there." It was all I had to offer, and I hoped it was enough.

She pointed to a tea on my nightstand. "I've been keeping it warm for you."

"Thank you. This is perfect," I said, wrapping my hands around the hot cup. A cold, invisible nose pressed against my arm, but I didn't dare pet Dusty while Bibbi watched. The last time she'd watched him, it had taken an hour to get the bow off his head and the shimmer powder off his fur. I'd woken to some dust bunnies for a few days after.

"As soon as you're ready, everyone is downstairs waiting for you," she said, her eyes narrowing on the indent in the cover where Dusty was sitting. He froze.

"Tell them I'll be down shortly," I said, knowing I owed Dusty. I got out of bed, throwing the blanket over where Dusty was.

"Great, see you in a couple." She only looked back at the bed a couple more times before she left.

A poof of dust exploded through a gap in the blanket.

"I already apologized five times. Was that really called for?"

There were a few chattering sounds, but no more dust.

The sound of talking, yelling, laughing, and just *being* met me as I made my way downstairs. How had I ever disliked this noise? It sounded like happiness and home. It was the best background music I'd ever heard.

As I headed for the back room, Helen began grinding her wheels until she made a whirring noise I'd never heard before.

I changed directions and walked across the workspace to lay a hand on her machinery, feeling a little buzz.

"I'm good. Just glad that day is over," I reassured her.

She made a humming noise that reminded me of a cat purring.

I walked into the back room and a roar went up. When Bibbi had said "they," I'd expected my roommates, not everyone who'd sweated out every moment of the last few months with us. The place had expanded to full capacity and they still barely fit.

Hawk walked over and put a glass of wine or something in my hand. Bibbi was right next to me a moment later, smiling and without fisted hands.

"Everyone is so excited about *Dread* being gone that they insisted on coming over. Nice, right?" She scanned the room as people began to notice my presence.

My stomach dropped.

Was that what they were being told? That it was totally over? I looked around, wondering how I was going to break it to them that it might not hold. We might have a week, or maybe a year, but I believed Lou when he'd said that it could only be temporary.

Oscar beat the crowd on their way over. "Why is the woman of the hour looking so glum?"

"She's afraid you're all going to be disappointed because we don't know how long it'll last," Hawk said, standing right beside me. He turned to me to me with a smile that shocked me almost more than what he said next: "They already know. They don't care. They're happy anyway."

Oscar waved a hand in the air. "Are you kidding? Anything is a relief. Plus, you did it once, you'll do it again." He shrugged and then topped off my glass with the bottle he was carrying.

"Yes, you will," Bertha said, walking over with a plate

of my favorite pastries heaped up high. "I made these just for you."

I grabbed one off the top. I mean, as long as they all knew, who was I to ruin the party?

"You got this," Zab said, squeezing in between Musso and Bertha and stealing a pastry off Bertha's plate.

"Heard you were pretty damned impressive," Musso said, and then was pushed out of the way for Zark and the burned beard guy as they all made their way over to thank me.

They all made a hole as Mertie walked over, her hooves clopping on the wood floor.

"Heard you didn't screw up? Good to hear." She grinned for a split second. It was the nicest expression she'd ever given me.

"Thanks, Mertie."

"Don't let it go to your head," she said, before walking away. "This place is too damned happy."

One by one, it seemed like half of Xest made their way over, either congratulating me or thanking me. Even Gillian nodded in my direction from across the room.

Several hours later, I dropped onto the couch, only the housemates left, except for Gillian, who'd left the party early to go check on her shop.

Oscar was playing a game with Zab, who kept losing. For which Hawk and Oscar teased him.

Bertha and Musso were sitting by the fireplace together, shoulder to shoulder, sipping tea and looking like they'd only been dating a week.

Bibbi came and sat down beside me.

"So it's over—for now, anyway. Are you relieved? Tired? How are you feeling?"

"At this very second?" I took a moment, letting the

setting marinate into my soul. It was hard to put a finger on the exact feeling. "I feel warm and gooey, like the center of an apple pie warmed up."

"You're happy," Bibbi said.

"Yeah, I am." No lies, vague answers, subterfuge—just the unadulterated truth. I *was* happy.

She smiled. "I'm glad. You deserve it."

"Only a couple things, or people, left to handle and then maybe we can get back to life for a while." Life? Here? I wasn't sure what that was like without something crazy going on, someone hunting me down, or trying to kick me out. What would living here be like when it was peaceful for a spell? Would I stay at the broker building, or should I get another place? The idea of leaving here felt alien to me, but there was no reason to remain. I'd have to wait and see what came. It would be foolish to make any hasty decisions.

"Do you think you'll stay for a while?" I asked, not wanting to pressure her either way, but I'd come to like the company. I wasn't sure what had happened to me, but the idea of this place empty made my heart feel like it was chilled. This place was changing me, and as much as I'd resisted it, maybe it was in a good way.

"I don't know. Maybe for a while, if I'm not in the way?"

"You're definitely not in the way. None of you are. Hawk made all these additions. It would be a shame to waste them."

"Do you think he'll mind?" she asked, her gaze shooting across the room to Hawk, before moving on to settle on Oscar and linger.

"Hawk? Not at all. Oscar might be staying on too, for a while." He would if I had anything to do with it. The two of them had meddled in my life enough. Only fitting I return the favor a bit if something was brewing.

I'd have to talk to Hawk about that. I glanced in his direction, and his gaze shot to mine, as if he knew the second my attention turned to him. And then it froze there as something warm fizzled in my chest.

Then a puff of smoke entered the room, breaking our connection as it made its way over to me. It shifted into ash next, and then, slowly, parchment, as everyone watched. We all knew what it was, having seen Xazier's messages before.

The parchment complete, it floated down and dropped onto my lap.

My gooey feeling was hardening. I didn't want to touch it or read it, but that wasn't an option.

It would be the last time. I'd meet him and tell him we'd fixed the problem. It would be over. It might ruin this evening, but by tomorrow, I'd wake up without this hanging over my head and be back to gooey pie feelings.

Hawk walked over, waiting for me to open it. "He wants a meeting, I assume."

I felt Bibbi shifting closer, everyone waiting for the inevitable.

I opened the parchment.

"Yes, he does."

35

"You don't need to come with me. I can handle it. You should be resting," Hawk said, stealing my lines.

"I rested all day and it's *my* meeting, remember? The invite was for me."

He was walking beside me toward the square, and for the first time in a long time, things felt like they were getting back to normal. I hadn't spotted a grouslie since we started out, and the ever-present feeling of Dread that had plagued Xest was gone. Lou had said that the hill we'd trapped it in might not hold, but I was beginning to feel like everyone else. I was going to enjoy the reprieve and revel in the success we did have.

"After what you did yesterday, most witches wouldn't be alive." There was a heavy pause before he added, "I've never seen anything like that."

He spoke in a tone I'd never heard him use, ever.

"Why, Hawk, you sound surprised. I didn't realize that was possible."

"I've known for a long time you were different, but that was an entirely different level."

There was that tone again, the one that made my spine feel an inch longer. As much as I wanted to thank him coolly, say something suave and sophisticated, I was afraid to speak. I felt like a dog that had just robbed a cupcake off the counter and gotten away with it. That the golden retriever inside of me would end up doing something goofy, like slobbering all over him for giving me praise.

Plus, the way he was looking at me was beyond words. I'd seen lust in his eyes before, but not this. This was something utterly different. No one had ever looked at me the way he did.

Had I been the idiot this whole time not believing Bibbi? Had Hawk declared for me? It wouldn't be my first blunder in judgment. Nor the second, or the hundredth, and definitely not the last.

My feet slowed as the shock to my system began sucking up all the available energy in order to process what I was sensing.

I kept slowing until I'd stopped completely.

"Are you okay?" he asked, stopping not far from me.

I stared at him for a few seconds, having a hard time believing I was going to rehash this conversation, and right now, of all times. "You did declare. You called it an old wives' tale, but it wasn't, was it?"

His eyes locked on mine. "I don't think the timing is quite right for this discussion," he said, before looking the other way.

Up ahead, Xazier stood, waiting. At that moment, I didn't care if Xazier waited. But what if Hawk was stalling so he didn't have to tell me how wrong I was right before this meeting? Did I really want to be rejected right now?

Hawk was right. This conversation was better off at a later time, or never. Maybe never?

All that gooeyness was getting to my head. I shoveled it away, focusing on Xazier. It might be an act, but he didn't look as angry or annoyed as I'd hoped. He had to know that we'd trapped Dread. He had his finger on the pulse of everything here, not to mention you could literally feel its absence.

"If things go bad, please, for the love of Xest, follow my lead for once in your life," Hawk said, hearing the same alarm bells I had.

I opened my mouth to say I would but then had to pause. "I'll try." It was the best I could offer. If he did something I disagreed with, I'd end up doing things my way no matter what I said. It was best to set realistic expectations.

He looked at me, shaking his head. "I gave you your way on the hill and I can't get this?"

"Let's be honest about that—you were touch and go at best. You were a hair away from stepping in and trying to call the shots," I said. He was going to play the hill card? That was hardly an earth-shattering compromise.

"But *I* didn't." He tilted his head, the way he did when he was convinced of his rightness.

"Is this really the time?" I asked, making a point of looking up ahead and smiling. If the hair on the back of my neck was accurate, it might be the only smiling that would happen for the rest of the night.

We walked the last bit in silence. It was better than yelling as we approached.

"Xazier," I said.

"Tippi," he replied, and then, with less enthusiasm, he added, "And Hawk."

"I'm guessing you'll realize there's no further need for meetings." *Please, realize.* I had no desire to fight with anyone tonight, least of all Xazier. All I wanted from him was his absence.

"Actually, no, I'm not quite clear on that at all."

Could he not feel the difference? How was that possible? He had to know. He had too many spies that would've told him something had changed. There wasn't a person in Xest who didn't feel something, either good or bad, with Dread's presence around, and now the lack of it.

"We handled the problem," I said. "It's over."

Xazier squinted and then began to shake his head slowly. "No, I don't think it is. There are a couple of issues with that interpretation of events. If you'll allow me to expand?"

I didn't answer. He was going to expand whether I wanted him to or not.

"Please do," Hawk answered, his words polite but his tone lethal.

"You agreed to eliminate a problem. Well, the first issue with that is you didn't actually do all of the eliminating, did you? It wasn't your plan. That had all the hallmarks of Lou. He's the only one who would've known how to utilize that hill."

"She did it all, and there's no changing that," Hawk said.

Xazier put his hands up. "I'll give you that point if you insist, but there is another problem that is still lingering. That is most likely only a temporary fix."

"You don't know that," I said. No one did. Not even Lou.

"Oh. But I do, or Dread wouldn't have happened in the first place."

That was not good news, and not because he'd broken out of it once already. Dread had originated from the hill.

It hadn't only been a cage. It had been its birthplace. If our magic was so similar, what did that mean for me?

"You're not taking over Xest, and you're not taking her." Hawk was bristling in a way I'd never experienced before. There was a strange feel to his energy, as if I were standing beside a bomb about to blow.

"I've decided to allow some leeway for partial progress."

My heart was thumping. I wasn't sure which was going to be worse: Xazier trying to take Xest or me, and then what would come next.

"I'll just take you," Xazier said, smiling.

"She offered up collateral that isn't hers to give," Hawk said. "She had a previous binding contract with me. You can't have her. To be honest, I'm surprised you didn't already sense it. Must be off your game."

"You gave me a false pledge?" Xazier was darkening by the second. His eyes filled with awareness as the truth hit him.

"You're never getting her," Hawk said. He wanted the fight. Him holding back was the most surprising part. Was this sort of like Rest rules, where he wanted Xazier to swing first so he could kill him?

"He's not getting her or Xest," Lou said, appearing out of nowhere.

Great, the gang was all here. The only surprise was that I hadn't expected it. Maybe we could have a little tea party next.

Lou closed the distance, looking unhappy with everyone but landing his primary focus on Xazier.

"You've overstepped, Xazier. Did you think you could do this under my nose? That I don't have as many eyes and ears in this place as you do? Maybe more? You wouldn't even exist if it weren't for me. Xest is neutral territory. You can't do anything without informing us. Those are the rules."

Maybe the additional company wasn't so bad. If Xazier was too busy fighting off Lou, there wouldn't be much fight left for us.

"I know exactly who I am," Xazier replied. "I think you holier-than-thou people might have overestimated *your* place." He took a few steps toward me. Lou matched him step for step.

Hawk moved closer until his arm brushed mine, the violence vibrating in the air around him.

"What's going on? What do you both want with me? Let's cut the bull and put it all out there," I said, fed up with all the games these people played. It was worse than recess at grammar school.

"Yes," Hawk said. "Why don't we all lay our cards on the table."

Xazier looked at Lou. Lou looked back. I crossed my arms, biting the inside of my cheek so as not to rush them. This might be my only shot at getting some answers. I wouldn't force it to an early conclusion that might end badly for me.

Hawk was still beside me. He tended to be more patient than I was, but my gut said this was killing him too.

Finally, Xazier shrugged, still looking at Lou. "I'll tell if you do. Not sure there's much harm after what happened yesterday anyway. Only a matter of time."

The hill. Were we going to find out what the hill was? It might be bad news, and my breath faltered as I waited for Lou to respond. Good or bad, at least we'd know, and the answers seemed so close.

Lou took another second, playing hard to get. Being the angel of the two, it was a bit shocking that he seemed to be the bigger jerk. Nah, that wasn't really fair. They both sucked equally.

Lou took a step away, crushing any hopes.

Then he stopped, back still to us. "Fine. Might as well."

It was something. I'd be getting some kind of answers. One of the many knots I was tied up in came undone.

Lou turned and waved at Xazier. "Go ahead. Tell them."

"You do it," Xazier said.

Lou looked Xazier up and down, sighed, and shook his head. "Are there no depths to the levels I'm supposed to sink to in the name of good?"

"Oh, please. Like you're good. We both know you aren't. That's why you have the job you have. If they didn't need a necessary evil, you'd be rolling around in the muck with me every single day and *lo-ving* it." Xazier leaned forward with a big smile on his face, as if he knew Lou better than he knew himself.

"Not true." Lou looked away.

Not exactly a convincing argument.

When they both stopped talking, Hawk said, "Can we keep this meeting moving?"

"I always have to do the dirty work," Xazier said.

Lou laughed. "Yes. And that's fitting, don't you think? Why break with what's working?"

If these two started fighting, no one was ever going to tell us what was going on.

Xazier shook his head before looking at me and Hawk. Was he going to talk?

"This could take a while. I'd prefer somewhere warm

and comfortable." Xazier looked around at the harsh landscape I'd come to love.

Why did he even want this place—or did he?

"We can go back to the broker building," Hawk said.

Xazier nodded, and then all four of us were in the back room. I wasn't sure who had moved us here, but my coin was on Xazier.

The place was eerily quiet, but that would be Hawk's doing. This was not a situation that needed any more company.

Xazier took a seat on one couch. I took a seat on the opposite one. Hawk remained standing beside my couch. Lou looked at Xazier's couch and rolled his eyes, as if there were no way he'd sit anywhere near him. Lou took a step toward mine. Hawk shook his head.

"Fine," Lou said, taking a seat in a chair.

Xazier finally began. "A couple of hundred thousand years ago, give or take fifty, right around the time of..." He looked at me and shook his head. "Doesn't matter. You weren't around to know any of this. Point is, when you people, humans, started showing up and then talking, there became an increase in workload.

"All you people did was pray for things. Ask for things, barter, promise, blah, blah, blah. In the beginning, we tried to accommodate some of your wishes here and there, if it fit our purposes. But the load became tedious. That's when Xest was formed. In essence, we needed to contract out some of the work. It was just too much—"

"And too tiring," Lou said. "We had no time for fun anymore. You people just got needier and needier."

Xazier nodded as the two found common ground on how irritating people were. "It was ridiculous, wasn't it? And they wouldn't stop breeding, either. How many do they really need to have? Take a breather." He rolled his eyes. "We couldn't take it anymore. We weren't in the business of worrying about your everyday wishes and desires. You live your life, and after it's done, we judge you for it. That's the way we wanted it."

Lou cleared his throat, turning to Xazier. "By the way, have you noticed how underrated judging is these days? Everyone wants to have their cake and eat it too. Are we supposed to let just anyone in?"

Xazier tilted his head back. "You don't like that part? I find that the most entertaining. I love watching as I play back their greatest hits of sin. Best part of my day. I have specific orders that I'm to be alerted when someone really good, or bad if you want to look at it like that, is about to cross over."

"I'm sure it's wonderful. Can you get back on track?" I asked. Did witches have the same afterlife? Was I going to end up with one of these two ruling my ever after? Please let me have a different end, even if that was a hole buried in the ground. It might be preferable.

Xazier glanced back at me. "Oh, yes, sure. So we were getting killed by the workload, but neither of our bosses cared. After all, like most businesses, we ran most of the show and carried most of the weight. We decided to call a little meeting, where we agreed that some outsourcing needed to be done to dump some of the work, you know, all the *I need* and *I want* and *I have to have*. We agreed quickly, too, which nearly never happens, that something had to be done or our quality of life would continue to tank."

Lou kicked his heels up on the coffee table and a brandy appeared in his hand. "We didn't want it anymore. We'd put our dues in. It was time to relax a bit."

Xazier pointed to Lou's glass. "Is that the twenty-four?"

"Yes. Would you care for one?" Lou swirled his glass.

"Of course," Xazier said.

"Anyone else?" Lou asked.

"No," Hawk said.

"No, thanks." Bibbi would kill me if I drank that. That might rank almost as bad as drinking Gillian's cocoa.

A glass appeared in Xazier's hand. He took a sip before he continued. "We had one issue. If you think of Xest like a business, it required some startup cash, so to speak. You needed some resources to get it going, which both sides were supposed to invest *equally*." Xazier shot a look at Lou, and the apparent truce seemed on shaky ground again.

"I didn't do more than I was supposed to. You did less than *you* were supposed to," Lou said.

"We set an amount agreed upon. I did the right amount," Xazier said.

"You can say that all you want, but why did our contribution seem heavier?" Lou argued.

"If you were so mad that mine was light, why did you care when I fixed it?" Xazier said.

Lou dropped his feet to the ground so he could lean toward Xazier, pointing. I wasn't overly concerned. He wasn't bothering to put his drink down, so he couldn't be that mad.

"Because I had to add more after you did. You didn't fix it. You weighted it, which made me have to add on, and you know that's a problem." Lou leaned back in his chair again with a huff.

"You wanted it that way so Xest always leaned a little bit to your side," Xazier said, but the tension had already eased a bit.

It was hard to decide whether I wanted to keep letting the information flow as it was or ask for some explanations. I was getting the gist, but being sure would help out a lot, especially in wondering how I'd ended up with the same magic that was in that hill.

"Can you get back to the story?" Hawk asked, not having the same internal debate.

"I'd love to, but he just never lets it go. Centuries and I'm still hearing about this," Xazier said.

"Gentleman, please," I said, wishing I hadn't declined the drink.

Hawk, who'd been on high alert, took a seat beside me on the couch, as this story was beginning to look like it would drag out.

"We both put in startup magic to get things going," Xazier said.

"Were your bosses aware of what you were doing?" I asked.

"Of course they were. They know everything," Lou said.

"But like we said, they don't want to get involved in the nitty-gritty, everyday stuff so we might've glossed over a detail here and there." Xazier shrugged and then took a large sip of his drink.

"Like how much startup we'd need," Lou said, a little softer-spoken this time.

"And a couple other little details here and there. Nothing major, you see," Xazier said.

"How did Dread happen?" I asked.

"On occasion, we both might've had to add a little more magic here and there, trying to fix the original imbalance that kept manifesting," Lou said. "We think the imbalance created it, but we aren't sure. Just as we aren't sure how you came to be or how you have so much of the magic we used to start Xest."

They stared at me, and the room went utterly silent. Was Hawk shocked too? I was afraid to look.

"I didn't take magic out of that hill," I said, finally finding my voice.

"But it happened, and we don't know how to get it back there," Xazier said.

That was why I was on that hill. It was all so clear now.

"You thought that the hill was going to suck me in too, like it did with Dread, or at least all my magic, didn't you? That's why you gave me that plan?"

"I take offense at that. I didn't know what it would do." Lou's chin went up an inch.

Xazier snorted. "For an angel, you lie better than some of my coworkers. Just tell her. That's exactly what you were trying to do. You figured you'd suck Dread back in the hill and it would take her with it, and the problem would go away." He looked at me. "I have to say, it would've been the easiest solution, but it didn't work. That in itself is very odd."

"Very," Lou added.

They were both staring at me.

"You're not touching her," Hawk growled.

"You mean kill her? I'm not sure we can," Lou admitted.

"So now what?" I might have been holding my breath as I asked the million-dollar question.

"You have too much of our magic, and it doesn't seem to want to go back where it belongs," Lou said, shrugging. "We've got a problem."

"A very big problem," Xazier said.

Hawk stood. "And what exactly do you think you're going to do about this problem?"

Xazier stood too. "That remains to be seen." He looked at Lou.

Lou also stood. "We'll be in touch."

Lou and Xazier looked at each other before disappearing at the same time.

The room went quiet as I let it all settle in. I stood, wiped my hands on my pants, and walked to the counter. My hands were steady, my breathing even.

"Tippi?" Hawk called after me.

"Yes?"

"What are you doing?"

"Tea." With the kettle in my hand, I'd thought it was pretty obvious.

"Are you all right?" he asked, walking over slowly as if a fast movement might startle me.

I poured a cup and took a couple of sips, trying to figure out the nicest way to explain it.

"I've had Marvin abduct me, immigration try to run me out, Raydam, Dread, and a horde of other witches try to kill me, and I'm still here. Let Lou and Xazier do their worst. I'm done running and I'm done being scared."

Hawk got a gleam in his eye as he leaned closer. "You sure about that?" he asked, smiling.

"I think so," I said, putting my tea down with a slight shake in my hand. "I've got some paperwork to do."

I could hear him laughing from the back room.

The Witch of all Witches available now!

Use this QR code to sign up for new release notices from Donna Augustine. Don't worry! I won't flood your email box. You're more likely to wonder if you signed up correctly. Two emails in one month is my record.

Or, follow me on one of these platforms:
https://www.facebook.com/groups/223180598486878/
http://www.donnaaugustine.com
https://www.bookbub.com/authors/donna-augustine
https://twitter.com/DonnAugustine

ACKNOWLEDGMENTS

Each book has its own set of hurdles that are unique. Without this group, I'd never make it over the finish line!Donna Z., Lisa A, Camilla J., Lori H. and Ashleigh M., thank you for helping me overcome all the bumps, valleys and hills of this story.

ALSO BY DONNA AUGUSTINE

Ollie Wit

A Step into the Dark

Walking in the Dark

Kissed by the Dark

The Keepers

The Keepers

Keepers and Killers

Shattered

Redemption

Karma

Karma

Jinxed

Fated

Dead Ink

The Wilds

The Wilds

The Hunt

The Dead

The Magic

Born Wild (Wilds Spinoff)

Wild One

Savage One

Wyrd Blood

Wyrd Blood

Full Blood

Blood Binds

www.ingramcontent.com/pod-product-compliance
Lightning Source LLC
Chambersburg PA
CBHW061542170626
46811CB00001B/52